D1470518

One
Is One

One is one and all alone and
evermore shall be so.

Green Grow the Rushes O

The Nautilus Series

One
Is One

BARBARA LEONIE PICARD

Paul Dry Books

Philadelphia 2006

First Paul Dry Books Edition, 2006

Paul Dry Books, Inc.
Philadelphia, Pennsylvania
www.pauldrybooks.com

Text type: Berthold Walbaum Book
Display type: Historical Fell Type Roman, Quadraat Sans Bold
Composed by P. M. Gordon Associates
Designed by studio ormus

1 3 5 7 9 8 6 4 2
Printed in the United States of America

Library of Congress Cataloging-in-Publication Data

Picard, Barbara Leonie.
    One is one / Barbara Leonie Picard. – 1st Paul Dry Books ed.
        p. cm. – (Nautilus series ; 1)
    Summary: A contemplative and sensitive young boy, seen by his
family to be unfit for the life of a fourteenth century nobleman, is sent
to a monastery but he is determined to prove himself worthy of nobility
and capable of being a knight.
    ISBN-13: 978-1-58988-027-6 (alk. paper)
    ISBN-10: 1-58988-027-7 (alk. paper)
  [1. Knights and knighthood – Fiction. 2. Great Britain – History – 14th
century – Fiction.] I. Title. II. Series: Nautilus series (Paul Dry Books) ; 1.
    PZ7.P55208One 2006
    [Fic] – dc22

                                                            2006001446

ISBN-13: 978-1-58988-027-6
ISBN-10: 1-58988-027-7

For Charles

with my love and thanks

ACKNOWLEDGMENTS

I should like to offer my grateful thanks to Miss Muriel H. Simpson, A.L.A., Librarian of Berwick-upon-Tweed Public Library, and to Mr. L. F. Salzman, C.B.E., for their kind help in supplying and tracing information required for Part Three; and to my friend Charles Stewart for so much help and advice throughout. Without the support of his artistic knowledge and experience I should never have managed to write this book.

B.L.P.

CONTENTS

AMILE

Part One

ONE

There was a rowan-tree growing in the inner bailey of the castle, planted there, maybe, by someone as a protection against witchcraft; or perhaps a seed dropped by a bird had taken root between the paving slabs and been allowed to grow and flourish for the sake of its virtues. The June sunlight trickled through its branches making a chequered pattern of light and shade on the flagstones around the base of its grey bole. Being near midday, the dappling formed a neat circle directly below the spreading crown. The little boy who stood beneath the tree studied the pattern on the ground. He had seen it often enough before, but somehow, in none of the other summers of his life had he ever consciously examined it: how dark the shade was and how bright the light; how many of the shadows – particularly near the edge of the design – were themselves perfect rowan-leaves, pinnate, elegant: dark likenesses of some individual green leaf far above.

There was a breeze in the topmost branches, so that the shadows flickered and wavered and changed continually. The boy frowned: he wanted the shadows to stay still so that he might study them the better; it was hard to follow the pattern when it kept altering. Besides, where the rowan-leaves showed plain and clear, he would have liked, in some way, their portraits to remain, a record of themselves, forever; even after autumn had come and they were fallen.

Facing the trunk, he looked upwards into the boughs, narrowing his eyes against the dazzling sunlight flashing and moving above him. Stay still, he thought. Stay still. The leaves and the dangling bunches of immature, unripe berries, outlined against the sun and seen from below, were no longer green as he knew they really were, but as black as their shadows on the flags beneath them; and this in itself was a puzzle to him.

Something fell with a brittle crack behind him, brushing his back lightly as it fell. He turned and saw a dead branch lying at his feet. It must have dropped from the tree, he thought; and wondered that he had not seen it fall.

"After it, now! After it! Fetch it!" The restraining hands gone from its collar, pushed forward from behind, the shaggy black cross-bred dog belonging to Wat the farrier bounded forward eagerly, barking after the stick that had been thrown.

Under the rowan-tree, the boy's head jerked up at the sound, his mouth opened wordlessly, his eyes widened with terror. Taken by surprise, he turned in a blind panic to run and heard, immediately afterwards, the whoops and shouts of delight from the children who had been hidden with the dog, just out of sight around one corner of the square tower of the keep, behind a concealing buttress. He trod upon the stick, lost his balance and fell sprawling – an added diversion which his tormentors had not anticipated. By the time he had picked himself up, they were all about him, laughing, jeering, leaping and clapping their hands in glee at the success of their trick.

The first shock over – and the dog's collar held, he noticed thankfully, by his cousin Edmund – he was able to stand and face them. They were, as usual, his own two sisters, the younger among his half-brothers and half-sisters, several cousins and the children of his father's knights, together with a few smaller children, sons and daughters of the upper servants of the castle. Their gleeful shouts and leapings had calmed now to a monotonous singsong and an encircling walk, as they moved around him, their fingers pointing at him, chanting, "Stephen is afraid of dogs. Stephen is afraid of dogs," occasionally varying this by asking, "Who is afraid of dogs?" and answering themselves in one triumphant howl, "Stephen is afraid of dogs!"

Nine-year-old Stephen de Beauville was quite still now, his eyes very dark in the white, expressionless mask of his face. Inside, his heart still hammered wildly, but the seeming indifference which, already at his age, he had learnt to be the only defence against mockery, was serving him as well as ever. His eyes glanced warily from side to side, under his dark lashes, as he kept in sight as many of his tormentors as he could, while trying, at the same time, to give an appearance of not regarding them at all.

The most vehement of them, he saw, was, as usual, his sister Joanna, sixteen months older than himself. Her pointed face, sharp with malice, was oftener near him than the faces of the others; and her pointing finger, stabbing at the air, was oftener in his sight.

Very slowly he edged towards the grey wall of the keep, knowing from experience that it was best to have one's back against a wall at times like this; and they all moved with him, circling about him, chanting rhythmically; and they seemed to him – as they always did – like a multitude: a multitude of mocking, terrifying faces; though, in truth, there were only sixteen or seventeen of them. His youngest half-sister, Margaret, only five years old, was with them this time, he noticed; tripping along after her brother John, with a pointing finger held stiffly out, chanting loudly with the others, concentrating resolutely on doing as they were doing, her plump, baby's face solemn with determination to keep up with her elders.

Still looking at none of them directly, but still hoping to be ready for any other move they made, Stephen continued to try to give the impression of ignoring them. Only once, when one of the pointing fingers came too close, did he strike it down and away from him ineffectually. The important thing was not to let them see he cared. His white face might seem calm, but inwardly he was praying for deliverance. Let someone come, so that they go away and leave me. Holy Father in heaven, let someone come. Prayers, he had found, were usually left unanswered; but just occasionally one was given what one asked for.

Then suddenly, while he was still several feet from the protecting wall, as if at a given signal, like a flock of birds obeying some instinct to act as one, they fell upon him, all at the same moment, pushing, pinching, punching and scratching, and bore him to the ground, shouting and yelling with triumph and jubilation. Stephen crouched down, his hands over his face, and hoped agonizedly that it would not be too long before they tired of their sport. And then, quite unexpectedly, and when it had almost seemed too late, his prayer was answered. Lady Elinor, the Countess's waiting-woman, came down the covered outside steps from the big doorway of the great hall, calling out reprovingly in her precise and careful manner, and bidding them make less noise.

"Go away. Go away at once. My lady has the headache and we can hear you right up in the solar. Go and play some-where else and be quiet, or you will all be whipped." She shook her plum-coloured skirts fussily at them, as though she had been a hen-wife, shooing chickens. "Away with you all. Away with you."

She was closely followed by one of the Countess's squires, carrying a switch, in case her authority should need the support of force; but the children did not wait for force. The group around Stephen broke up and scattered, giggling, Joanna and another of the girls dragging little Margaret between them; and in a matter of seconds they were out of sight. Stephen alone made only a half-hearted attempt to escape – he knew himself for the moment to be safer where he was – so that he was the only one to be caught. Lady Elinor cuffed him hard and gave him a sharp scolding on the impropriety of noisy games, before returning with the squire to the solar, the private apartment of the Earl and his family, on the third floor of the keep.

The injustice of the penalty made no impression on Stephen. He was too used to injustice to care. Grown-ups were always arbitrary and unjust and unpredictable; one moment surprisingly lenient, another time punishing one for nothing at all, or blaming one for someone else's misdeeds. But for all that, they were infinitely to be preferred to children, who were always unkind if they were given the chance. God, Stephen often thought, must be a sort of superior grown-up; much larger, much more arbitrary, far more unpredictable and no more just – with the added advantage of being invisible and everywhere. But even so, God sometimes took one's side against one's enemies: as on this very occasion.

Stephen rubbed his smarting cheek where Lady Elinor had struck him, looked cautiously around him at the now quiet inner bailey and, with thankfulness, saw no one but a few servants going about their business. He pushed back from his grey-blue eyes his dark, untidy hair, and made his way once more to the rowan-tree, noticing how the light-and-shadow pattern had moved along the flagstones a little to the east, so that the perfect circle about the base of the trunk had been in some small degree elongated and spoilt.

TWO

He had been born on the twenty-sixth of December, 1309, St. Stephen's Day; and they had called him after the Jewish deacon who had died beneath a shower of stones. It was a not inappropriate name for a boy who was to have so many hard words flung at him in the years that were to follow. He was the son of the second wife of Robert de Beauville, Earl of Greavesby, in Yorkshire, and he had two sisters of his own, one older and one younger, as well as four half-brothers and two half-sisters by the Earl's first countess. At the time of his birth his eldest half-brother was already fifteen and serving as a page at the court of the royal Earl of Lancaster. Stephen's mother had died soon after the birth of her third child; and because it was not customary for a fourteenth-century nobleman to remain a widower for long, Stephen soon had a stepmother. His stepmother took a kindly interest in him at first, until she had a son of her own to claim her attention; but after the birth of her second child she became a querulous, fretful invalid, who rarely left her bed save to sit huddled in a chair before the fire in the solar, her face as white as the miniver which lined the mantle she clutched about her. Yet through all his childhood Stephen had a vague though comforting memory of a pretty young woman with a golden chaplet around her blue veil, whose voice and hands were warm and gentle; but he never knew whether she had been his own mother or his stepmother – or perhaps even the Holy Mother of God, stepped down from heaven for a moment out of pity for him.

There was another thing from those very early years which he had forgotten. As long as he had known anything at all about himself, he had known that he was afraid of dogs – all dogs, from his stepmother's little white Italian greyhounds and those favoured hounds, belonging to individual members of the family, which lurked beneath the trestles in the great hall at mealtimes and gnawed the bones flung down to them, to the huge, fierce, short-muzzled bandogs and the deep-flewed, bell-voiced slot-hounds in the kennels. But he had no recollection of the day on which it had begun: Stephen, some fifteen months old, staggering unaided across the floor after a rolling ball of stuffed leather, stumbling and falling in the rushes every now and then, only to rise and continue the pursuit with a crow of triumph, reaching the ball to give it a mighty push that carried it forward another foot or two – and the half-grown hound pup, strayed in where it was not wanted, lolloping across the room to join in the game. At the onrush of the animal, Stephen had fallen and then looked up to see above him the huge-jawed, panting monster with hanging tongue. Afraid, he had tried to scramble to his feet, tried to thrust the menace away, tried to hurl the ball at it. Delighted, the young creature had leapt about him, barking ecstatically. Its grinning jaws had come closer and he had felt its hot breath upon his face. Wildly he had struck out at it, one arm finishing between the gaping jaws and the other hand catching the startled beast a blow on its eye. Involuntarily its jaws had closed on Stephen's arm and he had begun to scream. At the outcry, his nurse, who had been neglecting her charge to gossip with another of the servants, had come running, kicked away the yelping hound and snatched up Stephen. When she saw the tooth marks and the blood upon his arm, she had relieved her guilty conscience by slapping Stephen soundly and blaming him for not having remained where she had put him.

The episode had been thrust down deep into Stephen's mind, far below the level of remembrance; the bite scars on his arm had faded, but the scar on his spirit had remained and he was terrified of dogs. Until he was four, the sight of a dog or a hound had set him screaming with fear. After that, his terror was quieter, but no less strong. Until he was about seven, a dog within three yards of him had been enough to send him scurrying to a safe distance; but after that, goaded by the jeers and taunts of the other children and the disapproval and contempt of the grown-ups, he had learnt to overcome his terror to the extent of not running away; though he would remain rigid with fear, watching warily the animal's every move, so long as it was near him. Taken by surprise, however, he was still liable to lose his self-control and run away; a fact which resulted in frequent amusing tricks being played upon him by the other children.

By nature a quiet, reserved and sensitive child, the teasing and mockery which fell to Stephen's lot hurt him far more than they would have hurt most children, and he tended, from a very early age, to withdraw farther into himself after every fresh attack. Had he retaliated with taunts on the failings of his playmates and joined with them in the pranks they played upon each other, he might still, in spite of his temperament, have been accepted by them. But he made no attempt to conform; instead, he used all his energies in trying to fashion for himself an impregnable armour of apparent indifference behind which to hide and nurse in secret his wounded pride and sensibility; so that, in time, his fellows ceased to be his playmates and instead became in turn his tormentors who baited him mercilessly for their own amusement, and his contemptuous superiors who disregarded him as being of no account. But such is the contrariness of a sensitive nature, that Stephen – relieved though he always might be when he was ignored instead of teased – never failed to feel a sense of injury and loss when he was not invited to join in games and escapades in which he had not the slightest inclination to participate.

From Stephen's very real fear of dogs, and from his quiet, unassertive temperament, grew up the idea of his cowardice. Because the others believed he was a coward, Stephen, too, believed it, and, as they did, assented to it without question, never stopping to consider, any more than did those others, whether it was true or not. Born in an age when strength and physical courage were all important, and brought up in surroundings where only the knightly qualities of valour and fighting skill were esteemed, Stephen's position was not enviable. But no one cared enough about him to help him. He had been accepted as a coward and a weakling, and he had accepted himself as such; and however much he might have longed to prove himself to the members of his family to be as good as they in the respects that mattered to them, repressed by their indifference and by their open acknowledgement of his disabilities, and discouraged by their attitude towards him, he made no effort to do so.

As for his father: Earl Robert had enough stouthearted, promising sons to be able to suffer with equanimity one failure – one boy who would never make a knight. He shrugged his broad shoulders without rancour, and said, "Stephen shall be a monk." Besides, it was to the advantage of every family to have one of its members who would spend his time in praying for the good of the rest of them. So: "Stephen shall be a monk."

THREE

Earl Robert and his two eldest sons, Godfrey and Henry – both eager fighting men – spent most of their time, when at home, on the tilting-ground; they would ride many miles to take part in a tournament, and they never missed an opportunity for war against the Scots – not from hatred of the Scots, but from love of war.

In the June of 1314, when Stephen had been four, they had gone with King Edward the Second on his ill-fated campaign against Scotland; and after the disaster at Bannockburn where they had lost a number of their horses and several men-at-arms, they had returned home to Greavesby, grumbling and discontented and blaming, not the Scots, but the King, for the English defeat. Earl Robert had never had much good to say of Edward of Caernarvon, but he had always retained the hope that he might yet prove himself the warrior and battle-leader that his father had been; but after the defeat at Bannockburn, the Earl had abandoned this faint hope and no longer said anything but ill of the King; and in this he was supported by his sons.

It was not surprising. Indolent, careless and easy-going, preferring to watch a cock-fight to fighting himself; and able to find more to talk about to his grooms and his kennelmen than to his earls and barons, King Edward was hardly likely to be admired by the warlike and haughty de Beauvilles.

FOUR

Stephen had been six years old when he first saw the sun. He had been aware, as anyone is, of the flaming, fiery ball that rose in the morning, passed across the sky and sank down in a blaze of pink and golden clouds; but he had never seen the sun, because he had found that it is impossible to look at it, save through a blinding veil of tears. And then, one winter morning, all had been changed for him.

On the floor above the solar, in the room where the younger children slept with their nurses, he had been sitting quietly on a bench near the fire-place, watching a maidservant blow up the embers to a blaze. His breakfast of bread and a cup of buttermilk was finished; the other children were chattering together, while the nurses scolded or fussed about. Stephen swung his legs and watched the sparks go up the wide chimney as the red-faced girl plied her bellows.

One of Stephen's elder half-brothers came into the room, hawk on wrist, hound at his heels, and called to one of the women. She hurried to him and they stood talking for a few minutes. At the sound of his brother's voice, Stephen turned, and seeing the hound which accompanied the young man, he stiffened and kept his eyes on it. It began to move about the room, snuffing amongst the rushes on the floor for anything eatable; and as it came nearer to the fire-place, Stephen slipped off the bench, and keeping close to the wall and never taking his eyes from the hound, he moved round to the other side of the room. When he saw the hound, muzzle to the floor, cross slowly over to his side of the room, he moved quickly along the wall to the doorway and through it. Outside the room he hesitated.

On this fourth floor of the keep there were two large rooms, one leading into the other. In the inner room slept the ladies-in-waiting and upper serving-women of the castle, and in the other the younger children of the Earl's family who would have been a nuisance to their elders in the solar. This fourth floor was reached, as were all the others, by the spiral staircase which wound its way from the depths of the storerooms to the battlements and the open air. To Stephen's right the narrow stairway twisted upwards to the battlements, and to his left it twisted downwards towards the solar, and below the solar to the great hall, and below that to the men-at-arms' quarters over the storerooms. If he went downwards, he thought, it was likely that someone would meet him and send him back; if he remained where he was, his brother would come out with the hound; if he went up, he could wait on the battlements until the hound had gone – or until someone came to fetch him.

He went up. Scrambling from one steep step to another, round and round up the narrow stairway, ill-lit only by its window-slits, he at last arrived at the top, breathless, to find the wooden door ajar. He pushed it open and went through into the sudden light of the morning. Never a very adventurous child, he had not before been up on the battlements alone, and he now stepped cautiously forward, half expecting someone to shout at him and send him down again. But there were only two guards, chatting by the parapet near the foot of the watch-tower, with their backs to him.

It was cold, so high up in the frosty air; much colder than it had been close to the leaping flames; colder even than it had been on the draughty stairway. He shivered and almost turned to go down again, thinking to wait instead, hidden by a twist of the stairway, and watch from there for the departure of his brother and the hound. But then, over a crenel, in between two upspringing merlons, he saw the sun. Not now that golden glare which dazzled one and made one weep, but a blood-red, perfect sphere set in a cloudless sky as dull as unpolished silver. It was the colour which first caught his eye, and then the roundness of it. He stared at it, overawed, but at the same time, overjoyed; then he ran towards the guards. "Hold me up," he demanded. "I want to look at the sun."

The men turned and saw him. One of them picked him up and stood him on the parapet, holding an arm about his legs. "Have yon never seen the sun before?" he asked, laughing.

"I've never been able to look at it before." Stephen stared entranced.

Immediately below lay the castle spread out in his sight: the inner bailey and the outer bailey with its score of buildings; and then, beyond the wall and the moat which was fed by a hill-side spring diverted from its course, down the hill to the south, the village; beyond that again, the barren, sleeping fields and bare trees, and the swollen river swirling over its rocks; and south-east beyond the bleak winter landscape, across the dale, the glory of the new-risen sun. Watching it, Stephen was moved by a half-felt longing that the moment might last for ever; that he might, in some way, keep the sun always as it was then, to look at and enjoy. But, young though he might be, there was in him the knowledge that – for all one's desires – one cannot stretch a single minute into an eternity. So, while he could, he looked: and looked that he might remember.

Grinning, the other man said, "Now that you've seen the sun at last, little master, what do you think of it?"

Stephen, not tearing his eyes away for a second, said slowly, "It's good. Very good."

Both guards laughed, but not unkindly; and Stephen, standing there, high above the world, oblivious of the biting cold, was filled with exultation.

Then his nurse came fussing and puffing up the stairs and out on to the battlements, saw him, and came grumbling towards them. The guard lifted him down, she shook him and boxed his ears and, still grumbling, dragged him off down the stairs away from enchantment, threatening punishments should he dare to do such a thing again. But to Stephen none of that mattered, for she could not take from him the inexpressible coloured glory of what he had seen.

FIVE

In the chapel which stood beside the keep, there was a painting of the Annunciation on the wall. Against a pale-green background it showed the Blessed Virgin in a blue gown trimmed with red, a chaplet of golden daisies about her brow, standing with her hands raised in stiff surprise at the appearance of Gabriel, who stood before and above her, balanced on the air, his flowing robe white and his tremendous wings flaring blue and gold. And all about them both, from top to toe, and across the whole of that wall of the chapel, their green background was spotted with tiny golden stars.

Stephen admired this painting very much, and would slip alone into the chapel and watch it for long minutes at a time. It was seen to most advantage when the candles by the altar were alight; though Stephen liked it best when the sun was shining through the narrow window opposite and he could watch the pillar of sunlight creeping slowly across it, picking out the colours one after another; first, a few stars on the green; then, inch by inch, the blue and red of Mary's gown; then stars and green again; then the white of Gabriel's robe and his long, solemn face; and then, bit by bit, as Gabriel's face was lost in the shade that was so dark by contrast, the sunlight reached the final, blazing splendour of his wings.

Stephen would have liked pictures to have been painted all around the chapel walls, instead of only on one side. He wondered how a picture got on to a wall, who put it there, and why, what sort of person he was, and how he did it. And then, one day, sitting quietly on a corner of the floor-rug by the fire-place in the solar, still as a mouse, and as much unnoticed, he picked up a half-burnt stick, fallen from the blaze. Idly playing with it, trying to break off the blackened end from the unburnt part, he found that with it he could make a dark line on the grey stone of the hearth. He made another black line and one more crossing the second; then, fascinated, he improved upon his cross by crossing it again, so that it looked a little like a daisy. He blackened the middle of his daisy, to represent its yellow centre; and then

16

thought that his daisy looked more like a sunflower, or even the sun itself. Beside the sun he drew a man: round head, straight body, two legs and two arms. One of the arms was too long, and he found that it was possible – at the price of getting one's fingers dirty – to shorten an overlong line by rubbing it out with one's hand. He sat back to admire his drawings, then slid along the floor a little way to a clean flag-stone and began ambitiously and with much concentration, his lower lip caught between his teeth, to draw a horse. It needed a good deal of rubbing out to gain the effect he desired, and both his hands and his face were streaked with charcoal before he had finished; but at last, satisfied, he contemplated his horse with pleasure.

He was so intent that he did not hear his sister Joanna as she crept up behind him, and he only realized she was there when she gave a delighted squeal and then clapped her hand over her mouth and looked to see if any of the grown-ups had heard her and were going to scold. But no one had. At the sound Stephen looked up over his shoulder at once, his peace shattered.

"You have made a picture of a dog, Stephen," giggled Joanna.

"It's not a dog. It's a horse."

"It's not, silly! Of course it's a dog." She turned and beckoned, whispering with exaggeratedly open mouth, as if that would carry her words farther. "John, Elizabeth, Alison, come here." They came. "look, is it not funny? Stephen has made a picture of a dog. A dog, of all things!"

His younger sister, Alison, said pertly, "Are you not afraid that it might bite you, Stephen?"

"It's a horse," protested Stephen, "not a dog."

Elizabeth, his half-sister, who was three years older than he was, said scornfully, "Of course it's not a horse. No horse looks like that."

"But it is a horse," said Stephen.

Six-year-old John, first-born of the third Countess, who was nearly three years younger than Stephen, said, "It has no saddle or stirrups. No one could ride it. It's a dog."

Stephen said no more – what was the use of it? They jeered at him and teased him in whispers for a few moments longer, and then, growing bored, left him and went away giggling together.

By himself again, Stephen relaxed and once more considered his horse. But it had been spoilt for him by the others. Looking at it now, he saw that it was indeed not much like a horse. It could very easily be mistaken for a dog. Suddenly dissatisfied, he abruptly rubbed it out with both hands, then, sighing, flung his piece of charcoal into the fire.

SIX

Stephen had a more than ordinary awareness of the shapes and colours of things around him, and, left so much alone, he had time to study them. He noticed how the shapes of similar things differed subtly from each other: the wings of a hawk against the sky from the wings of a pigeon; the shape of a leafless oak from the shape of a leafless ash; the leaves of ivy, according to from where on the branch one picked them; the head of an ox from the head of a cow. And colours he noticed: how the colour of clothes changed according to whether one saw them by sunlight or torchlight; and the way the flames of the fire made flowers blossom on the plain stuff of a gown; the sheen of certain beetles, like metal, yet like no metal that he had ever seen; the colour of people's eyes – no one's eyes were quite the same shade as anyone else's; and how the river in the dale changed with each change of the weather. And then there other things he noticed, too: the fluid rippling of – what was it? bones? flesh? – beneath the shining hide of a well-groomed horse when it moved; the way one could actually see the invisible wind when it blew over a field of corn; the riddle of why a person standing in the great hall looked shorter if one saw him from the gallery, and even shorter if he were in the gallery and one were standing almost directly below him; and where exactly lay the difference between a girl's face and a woman's. All these things intrigued him and puzzled him, and he would have liked to ask questions about them, but he had no one of whom he could ask questions.

They had laughed at him one day, the other children, when they had come upon him watching a butterfly that was sunning itself on the warm stones of the wall of the inner bailey. He had been standing there a long time, thinking to himself how beautiful it was with its bright, clean colours and the round blue eyes on its reddish wings, when several of them had come along and stopped to jeer. One of them had made a grab at the butterfly and it had flown away; and his cousin Edmund, a sturdy, freckle-faced boy, who was half a year or so his elder, had been amongst those who had laughed at him the longest.

A few days later Edmund and two or three other boys approached him, Edmund holding something in his cupped hands. "Here, Stephen," he called. "I have something for you."

Stephen stood still and waited for them to come to him. "Have you?" he asked, suspecting them.

Edmund held out his hands to Stephen. Stephen made no move. "Well, do you not want it?" Edmund asked, grinning.

"What is it?"

"A butterfly. I thought you liked them." He parted his fingers a little and Stephen bent forward cautiously and looked. It was indeed a butterfly, he could see its wings throbbing within the prison of Edmund's hands, and he hated to see it there. "Well, do you want it? Are you going to take it?" demanded Edmund.

Stephen held out his hand.

"Where are your manners, Stephen?" said Edmund in a mocking parody of Lady Elinor's mincing voice. "Ask for it prettily."

Despising himself, Stephen said, "Please."

"That's better." Edmund opened his fingers and then, in one quick movement, plucked off one of the butterfly's wings and put it on Stephen's outstretched hand.

Stephen, who had too often had his hair pulled or his arms wrenched not to feel for a tortured insect, winced when the wing was torn off; but before Edmund could pluck off another, the butterfly freed itself from his clutch and fell to the ground where it fluttered desperately with three wings. One of the other boys, laughing, with his left foot held up behind him, gave an accurate one-legged jump and landed with his right foot squarely on the butterfly.

They all laughed then, Edmund loudest of all, at the bewildered and pained expression on Stephen's face.

"Why did you have to do that? It was beautiful and you spoilt it." He looked at the wing on his hand, its delicate scales smeared by Edmund's fingers, its colours already faded and dulled in dissolution. Suddenly he was angry, so angry that he forgot caution. "It was beautiful, and you killed it!" he shouted; then, without warning, he flung himself on Edmund, hitting out wildly at him. Far slighter and quite inexperienced, he was no match for Edmund, and in a very short time he was on the ground, gasping and winded, his nose bleeding and one eye turning black. After a few parting jibes, the other boys left him, escorting the victorious Edmund and laughing over their shoulders at Stephen, huddled on the flagstones. Stephen, humiliated, miserable and hurt, made no attempt to rise and face the world again, but lay where he had been left, his head pillowed on one arm, fighting back his tears and swamped in self-pity.

One of Earl Robert's squires, who had been watching the boys, came over, wondering if Stephen might perhaps be more hurt than had appeared. He hauled Stephen to his feet by the neck of his tunic, saw that there was not too much damage done and said, not unkindly, "That's no way to fight, flinging your arms about in that useless fashion. They will always beat you if you make no better effort than that. You should do it like this. See?" He balled up his fist and punched sharply upwards at Stephen's chin, pulling back the blow before it landed. In spite of himself, Stephen, raw from his recent disaster, flinched a little, and the young man noticed. He shrugged his shoulders and laughed gently. "You'll never make a knight, Stephen," he said. He turned and strolled away; and Stephen, looking after him and wiping the blood from his nose with one hand, clenched his teeth and said under his breath, "But I will, I will, I will. One day I shall be a knight as good as any of the others."

SEVEN

At that time Stephen was ten years old and no one had made any effort to teach him how to handle arms or to equip himself in any way for the life of an earl's son. He had, it is true, learnt to wait upon his father and his eldest half-brothers at the high table in the great hall, to pour their wine and hold the silver laver of water and the linen towel, that they might wash their hands before a meal; and he had on occasions accompanied them hunting and hawking. But he knew how to use neither a sword nor a lance, and he would have been hard put to it to hold a dagger correctly. He was going to be a monk and it had therefore not occurred to his family that it would be other than a waste of time to teach timid Stephen to do these things – and that in spite of the fact that in such lawless days when robbers and footpads abounded on the roads and even abbeys were not exempt from attack, it was wise that a monk, as much as any man, should know how to protect himself.

But his father had remembered Stephen's future enough to reflect that a monk needed to know how to read and write; and to this end, Stephen, from the age of eight, had been ordered to spend three hours every day with Earl Robert's chaplain learning his letters and the Latin which he would find necessary in the religious life.

To Stephen this meant no hardship. The humiliation of being the only one of his family who was expected to know more than how to spell his name and to read an occasional word – for reading and writing were for clerks and monks; knights and noblemen had far better and more important ways of occupying themselves, and in any noble household there would be clerks and scribes enough to deal with documents, accounts and correspondence – the humiliation was, for Stephen, tempered by the advantage of three hours' daily freedom from the persecution of the other children in the peaceable company of Sir Gilbert the chaplain. Sir Gilbert was a quiet, melancholy man with an air of almost perpetual abstraction. Everything about him drooped: his shoulders beneath their sober black, the deep lines that ran from nose to mouth, his mouth itself – even his large, dark eyes seemed to droop at the corners. Summer and winter alike he felt the cold and would sit with his hands tucked into his sleeves and his shawl about his shoulders. He always collected Stephen's mistakes with a weary resignation; and it seemed to Stephen surprising that he noticed them at all, with his permanent air of preoccupation.

Despite the many hours they passed together over the years, he had no feeling whatsoever for Stephen, and Ste-

phen had none for him. Sir Gilbert was not an approach-
able person; intimacy with him would have been impossible; all personal feeling offered to him would have been
chilled and frozen long before it penetrated the calm isola-
tion of his gaze and reached through to his consciousness.
But he was never unkind – he never came close enough to
Stephen for that – and in all their lessons together, Stephen
never once knew him to raise against him either hand or
voice; and though he felt no affection for Sir Gilbert, Stephen
was always to remember with a faint gratitude the hours he
had spent in the chaplain's company in his little room, built
in the thickness of the wall of the great hall, its entrance
honoured by a real wooden door which let in the draughts
and creaked on its hinges, instead of the leather curtain
which hung before the little rooms of lesser persons. Here
in his room Sir Gilbert kept his four books and his writing
materials. In summer the dust motes danced in the shaft of
sunlight that made its long way down through the small
window, to strike at last on the faded red coverlet on the
priest's narrow bed; and in winter the room was ankle-deep
in straw, in a vain attempt to keep the cold from Sir Gilbert's
chilly feet.

Just as in Latin Stephen progressed from declining
mensa and reciting the present tense of *esse* to translating,
swiftly and correctly, long passages from St. Jerome's Bible,
so in writing he progressed from forming pot-hooks and
hangers on a slate – through all the intermediate stages
of learning to hold and cut a pen, to use ink without making blots and to copy chapter after chapter from the Bible –
to being able to write, in either French or Latin, anything
dictated to him by Sir Gilbert in his clear, distant-seeming
voice.

Stephen liked writing. He took a pride in being neat and
in keeping all his letters the same height; and though he

was not allowed to use red ink for his capitals, as time went on he made them increasingly decorative and ornate, after the fashion of the rubrics in Sir Gilbert's missal.

Three of Sir Gilbert's books were plain and unadorned, but his missal had not only red capitals but its every page was embellished by a border of twisting stems and coloured leaves and flowers, with stiff, formal little animals and birds among the trails and tendrils. After the morning's lessons were over, Stephen would often ask if he might stay on in Sir Gilbert's room and look at his missal; and Sir Gilbert always let him. And so, for half an hour or longer, while Sir Gilbert read to himself from one of his other books, Stephen would sit quietly turning the pages of the missal, enjoying over and over again the decorations of which he never grew tired. Sometimes he would copy a favourite one on to his slate; and sometimes, greatly aspiring, he would even draw with pen and black ink a sombre border of flowers and fruit and animals of his own around that day's dictation, at which he would be mildly rebuked by Sir Gilbert for wasting time which could have been better spent in study – that was, when Sir Gilbert noticed what Stephen had been doing, which was by no means always.

But, so far from being a waste of time, drawing was for Stephen an entry into an unreal – yet, to him, in some way, strangely true – world where his daily life could be forgotten; and each sojourn there renewed a little the strength he needed to face the real world about him.

As for the thought of his future as a monk: little as Stephen cared for this thought, it was still dim, and the idea was not entirely credible, that he should ever be a monk – he, whose family was lords and knights. He had once questioned Sir Gilbert and learnt from him that most youths were entered as novices in monasteries at the age of seventeen or eighteen; and at eight, or even at eleven, seventeen is a lifetime away, and in such a span any miracle may happen; one may even acquire courage, impress one's family by some unsurpassed bold deed, be approved of and praised by it and, eventually, be accounted worthy of knighthood.

There was time, Stephen thought – even while time was passing with all the swiftness of boyhood's days – there was time; and meanwhile he was grateful enough at being able to escape from persecution in reality for three hours every morning, and to escape from persecution in imagination for all those other, countless, hours during which he indulged his fancy in endless daydreams where he made good in the eyes of his family and won its respect.

EIGHT

It started as a summer's day like any other, and at first there was nothing about it to show that it was to be of great importance to Stephen. The June sun of Stephen's eleventh year had shone that morning as it had shone on many previous days that month; there had been a short, sharp shower to lay the dust on the flagstones of the inner bailey and make the leaves of the rowan-tree shine, yet it had not lasted long enough to do more than dampen the surface of the hard-stamped earth of the outer bailey, and it had certainly not raised the summer level of the water in the moat which encircled the castle walls. It was about half-way through the morning, Stephen's lessons were over and he and several of the younger members of the family were in the great hall, occupying themselves in one way or another. As usual, Stephen sat alone. Today he was trying to carve a horse's head from a block of wood, but the knife was blunt and the wood was hard and his first enthusiasm was waning, as the wood stubbornly refused to take on the shape he had envisaged with such hopeful fancy.

Joanna came in up the covered stairway from the inner bailey, shaking a few raindrops like diamonds from her hair and her skirt. She called to Edmund and Alison, "I've just seen William and he told me that Princess whelped yesterday. He says he'll show us the pups now, if we wish."

Edmund jumped up excitedly. "My lord uncle will be pleased when he gets back from York. I wonder how many there are this time."

Princess was Earl Robert's most prized boarhound bitch, and there was always at least one hound of outstanding qualities in each of her litters, so that her whelping was ever something of an event.

John and Margaret, as well as Edmund and Alison, joined Joanna, and with them went two other young cousins, brothers. As they made their way to the doorway of the great hall, they passed by Stephen, ignoring him – having forgotten that he was there, as they usually did when they were not engaged in teasing him. Joanna, hurrying eagerly ahead, turned back to urge the others to make haste and caught sight of Stephen. Her eyes instantly lighted up with malice. "What about you, Stephen? Are you not coming with us?"

Stephen shook his head and murmured something about wanting to finish what he was doing and bent lower over his whittling. But Joanna ran back and stood by him, and the others stopped on their way to the door and watched her.

"Are you afraid that a day-old pup might bite you, Stephen?" Joanna asked in her clear, high voice that could be plainly heard right across the hall.

Edmund and one of the other cousins laughed, and Margaret gave a shrill little giggle.

Stephen flushed and looked up at his sister. "Of course I'm not."

"Then come on!" When he did not immediately rise, she leant forward and knocked the block of wood and the knife out of his grasp. "Come on, you're keeping us all waiting."

Stephen bent to pick up the wood and the knife from the rushes on the floor, saying nothing.

Edmund called out scornfully, "Leave him, Joanna, if he is afraid to come."

Young John started to chant vigorously, "Stephen is afraid of dogs. Stephen is afraid of dogs."

"Hold your tongue, brat, you'll deafen us." Edmund, grinning, aimed a mock cuff at John's head, and John, grinning back, skipped out of his reach.

Joanna leant forward and hissed in Stephen's ear, "Coward! Coward, coward, coward."

Stephen put the block and the knife down on the bench beside him and stood up. "Very well, I'll go with you."

Alison, one hand over her heart, the other outflung, staggered dramatically. "Hold me up, someone. Quickly! I think I'm going to swoon. Stephen is coming to the kennels with us. What courage!"

Everyone except Stephen laughed uproariously, as though Alison had made a very good joke; and hand in hand, or with arms about each other's shoulders, wasting not another glance on Stephen, they went on their way, leaving him to follow.

Reluctantly he trailed after them down the steps past the doorways to the two lower floors, the guards' quarters and the storehouse; across the inner bailey past the rowan-tree, and through the small gatehouse into the outer bailey where the stables and kennels, the smithy and all the other many outbuildings of the castle craftsmen stood all around the inside of the high outer wall.

The kennels, where, as well as hounds for hunting stags and hares and boar, the Earl kept – as did the King – a small pack of shaggy-coated little otterhounds, were noisy with barking and they stank of dogs and rotten offal. Stephen, tense and whitefaced, went after the others, trying to look as though he did not mind. Princess, as befitted her importance, was in William Huntsman's own quarters. A quick glance around showed Stephen that there were no other dogs there, and he relaxed a little. Princess lay on her side on a heap of straw, her eyes moist with ecstasy, her whole being radiating pride. Six blind, brindle pups, lying in a row, fed greedily. A seventh, smaller, and with a white throat and muzzle, scrambled sightlessly on the edge of the group, trying feebly and unsuccessfully to clamber over the others and reach food and warmth.

"There they are, seven of them. Four dogs and three bitches," said William, proud and pleased as he always was over a successful whelping. Three fine dogs and three fine bitches. One of the dogs is weakly, but it hardly matters, with the other six so sturdy. You'll not miss one of them, will you, old lady?" He bent and scratched Princess behind the ear and then picked up the weakly pup and made room for it amongst the others. For a short time it drank ravenously; but before long it was thrust away anew by its stronger litter-brothers and sisters, and was soon feebly striving to regain its place. William made room for it once more.

Stephen, standing as far away as he might without its appearing noticeable, looked without enthusiasm at the puppies, wondering how soon he could escape from the kennels. Edmund, listened to enviously by the other two cousins, was discussing dog-breeding in what he imagined was a knowledgeable manner with William, who was politely humouring him. The girls and John were kneeling down, admiring the puppies with shrill delight.

Still politely agreeing with what Edmund was saying, William cast an eye on the litter and once again stooped to replace the weakling at the bitch's side. "Come on, you little fool," he said. "I cannot forever be doing this for you. I've

28

other work to do." To the children he said, "I doubt if this one will be worth the trouble of rearing. I'll give him a couple of days to see if he picks up, then, if not, I'll drown him. It takes time to raise the sickly ones, and then they rarely turn out to have been worth the pains. Princess has enough healthy pups in this litter, there'll be no need to waste time on saving this one."

Stephen thought to himself that, so far as he was concerned, William might drown the whole lot and it would be no loss to him. No one seemed to be taking any notice of him, so he began to edge towards the doorway; and a few minutes later he was outside. Leaving the kennels with relief, he made his way across the outer bailey, thankful that the morning's ordeal had not been worse. Why, oh why, did the others always have to torment him? Why could they not be content with their superiority and let him be? They were like those six sturdy, guzzling puppies, he thought disgustedly; while he, he was the weakling whom no one wanted. Had he been a pup, he reflected bitterly, they would have considered him not worth rearing and drowned him at birth.

At the gateway to the inner bailey he stopped, seeing again in his mind Princess and her litter, and was suddenly filled with an overwhelming pity for the poor, wretched, hungry little creature which was going to be denied a chance to live, only because it was weaker than the others. It was cruel and unjust. Before he realized what he was doing, he had turned and was running back to the kennels. He burst into William's quarters, interrupting something which Joanna was saying, and blurted out, without even knowing that he was going to say it, "You are not to drown the weak one, William. You must rear it."

They all stared at him, speechless for once; and then William said slowly, "But why, Master Stephen?"

Stephen, beginning to be conscious of what he had done, and beginning, too, to wonder what had possessed him, tried to bluster. "Because I say so."

"But why, Master Stephen? Why should you say so?" With that half-veiled contempt beneath his courtesy, which Stephen was only too used to receiving from the upper servants, William said very gently and half-smiling, "Is it because you want the pup for yourself, perhaps?"

Alison gave a quickly suppressed giggle – choked back not through tact, but because she, like the others, did not want to miss one single word of Stephen's embarrassed answer.

With everyone watching him, waiting for his reply, Stephen, already blushing, went an even deeper crimson, utterly at a loss as to how to extricate himself from the situation he had brought upon himself. The silence lengthened and became yet more unbearable. Stephen looked at no one but William – waiting with quiet courtesy for his reply, yet with a mocking challenge in his eyes – but he knew how the others were regarding him: he had seen their contempt too often not to know each separate expression on their individual faces; and he heard Alison stifle another delighted giggle.

"Well, Master Stephen?"

It was the final challenge. Stephen, sick with shame and misery, held up his head, staring back at William. "Yes, that's it. I want that one for myself."

"Very well, Master Stephen, I'll rear the weakly one for you." William's courtesy was the extreme of mockery. He flung his last stone. "As soon as he is weaned, I'll let you know, and you can have him."

Stephen did not wait a moment longer; he turned and fled, and after him came their laughter, peal upon peal; and he could hear that now William Huntsman was laughing too.

NINE

Many, many times during the next few weeks Stephen was to recall with shame and in an agony of apprehension his impetuous folly. It was too much to hope that William would forget; too much to hope that, out of pity, he would intentionally not remember. But for all that, Stephen assiduously kept out of William's way, so that no possible sight of him might remind the chief huntsman of his promise.

But though he knew that William would not forget – would not put aside for any reason of compassion the opportunity of baiting him – there was always the chance that the weakly pup might not live and so spare Stephen further humiliation. In his prayers every day Stephen fervently implored that the wretched creature might die; and though it often seemed to him that such good fortune was never likely to be his, at other times he allowed himself to think that surely so heartfelt a plea, so often reiterated and with such intensity, would stand a chance of being heard. But even this poor hope was to vanish.

After some three weeks had passed, in the great hall after supper one evening, William deliberately sought out Stephen to say to him, with apparent respect and a feigned assumption that his words would be welcome to the hearer, "You'll be wondering about your pup, Master Stephen. You've not been along to the kennels to ask, so I thought I'd better let you know how he is. I'm taking good care of him for you, and he's doing well enough now. He's still weakly, and smaller than the others, but he'll live all right, and he's getting stronger every day." He watched Stephen steadily as he spoke, to see how he would receive the news.

It was fully twenty seconds before Stephen found any voice to answer with. "Is he?" he then said in a tone quite without expression. Try as he would, he could not manage to force the smile that might have been expected from anyone else for the occasion. But neither did he betray himself by showing his despair at this shattering of his only hope.

"I thought that you'd be pleased to know." William smiled a little.

"Yes. Of course." Stephen was still finding it difficult to speak. "Thank you, William."

"I'll let you know the moment you can have him, Master Stephen. Meanwhile, you can trust me to do my best for him. I'd not want you to be disappointed, for all the world."

"I know I can trust you, William." Stephen turned away in dismissal, thinking bitterly: Oh yes, I know I can trust you. You'll not let it die. You would not miss the fun – would you? – for all the world.

As soon as it was plain to him that he was not going to be able to avoid being given the puppy, Stephen set himself to think up some means of disposing of it immediately it was in his possession; for it was unthinkable that it should remain a perpetual reminder of his weakness, a daily witness to his cowardice, and a living humiliation for him from which there could be no escape. He would have liked to have been able to give it to someone who would have been glad to own it; and this was, indeed, the first solution which presented itself to him. But to whom could he give it? Almost any of his younger brothers or cousins would have been glad to have one of Princess's pups – even if it were the weakling of the litter – but, under the circumstances, no one would be willing to take it from him and thereby miss the pleasure of seeing him suffer. If, at the best, someone did accept it, then it would only have been got rid of at the price of constant mockery from that person for many months – no, years – to come. He could, of course, take it down to the cottages of the villagers which clustered around the foot of the hill upon which the castle was built, and give it to one of the villeins or tenants for a watchdog and say to William Huntsman and the others that he had lost it; but sooner or later – probably sooner – word would get back to the castle that Master Stephen had given a hound pup to someone or other, and then there would be accusations and jeers and laughter enough to last his family for weeks.

No, he could not face that, he decided. He would have to kill it and pretend that it had disappeared. If he were to feign a search for it and ask people whether they had seen it, they would surely believe that it was lost. And even if they did not believe him, no one could prove he was lying. Yet he balked at the idea of killing it with his own hands. He could always, he thought, throw it into the moat after dark – but at this time of year, at the height of summer, the moat was almost dry. He could take it down to the village pond, and while the peasants were working in the fields and there was no one about, he could drown it there. But somehow he shrank from the idea of drowning it. He had saved it from drowning once already. Had he prevented William from drowning it, only to drown it himself? He could instead, he thought, drop it down from the battlements; that would be a quick and certain death.

For days his mind considered, rejected and reconsidered; not only in his waking hours, but during sleep as well; so that several times he awoke from nightmares in which he had frantically been trying to find an answer to his problem. But little by little, he reached the conclusion that, since it was he who had insisted that the pup should have a chance to live, it must have that chance. He finally made up his mind to take it, at the first opportunity after it was given to him, to some distance beyond the castle and there deliberately to lose it. That way it would have its chance of life: there was always the possibility that someone would come along and find it before the foxes and the crows got to it. And that way, too, he would not be lying when he said that he had lost it.

TEN

In September, some ten weeks after the birth of Princess's pups, the dreaded day arrived for Stephen. Once again, after supper in the great hall, William looked for him. This time he was smiling broadly, as though he bore excellent news.

"You can have your pup any day you want now, Master Stephen."

Stephen, who had seen him approaching across the hall with the inevitability of the day of doom and known what he was going to say, had himself in hand, his face a wooden mask, his head held high – only his over-sensitive mouth betraying him, and his eyes, watchful and pained. He had, however, no reply ready, for he was still feverishly considering how he might postpone the unavoidable and gain a few more days' grace. His delay undid him.

"No doubt you'll want him as soon as possible. Perhaps you'd come to the kennels tomorrow and fetch him? Or would you rather I brought him up here for you?"

Stephen had a sudden vision of himself in the great hall, being handed the creature by William, while everyone looked on. "No, no. I'll fetch him," he said quickly.

"Very good, Master Stephen. What time shall I expect you?"

Stephen thought rapidly. The later he left it, the more likely it would be that the others learnt of it and went with him. The earlier he got it over, the less likely that there would be anyone other than William to see him in the agonizing moment when he had to take the pup. "I'll come first thing in the morning," he said.

"Holy saints!" laughed William. "You are eager, Master Stephen. There's no doubt about it."

Stephen passed a miserable night, during which he slept very little, but tossed and turned in his bed in one of the small rooms built off the gallery above the great hall, that big bed which he shared with the other boys of the family: whichever of the younger of his elder half-brothers might be at home, eight-year-old John, and his three cousins. His restlessness at last woke Edmund, who punched him and told him to lie still unless he wanted to be pushed off the bed on to the floor. After that Stephen lay rigid and unhappy, waiting for the dawn.

He ate his breakfast bread standing in a window embrasure in the great hall, looking out across a narrow strip of the awakening countryside, wishing desperately that the terrible moment might be put off, feeling every mouthful of bread choke him – and being glad of it, because that meant it took so much the longer to eat.

But what must be done has to be done, and at last he forced himself to go down to the kennels and made his way to William's quarters. William was waiting outside the door for him. He bade Stephen good morning, adding, "You're good and early, as you said," and stood aside for him to enter.

After only a second's holding back, Stephen stepped through the doorway and then stopped stock-still. They were all there before him, waiting silently. As soon as he entered, the silence was broken.

"Good morning, Stephen," chorused the girls, their voices high with spite. The boys said nothing – as yet.

Stephen recoiled involuntarily and found William behind him blocking the doorway. With an effort he moved forward into the middle of the room. Fool that he had been, he thought bitterly, ever to suppose that he might be allowed to endure this moment unobserved.

"Everyone seems to be about early this morning," re-marked William.

"I wonder why?" said Alison, and giggled.

Stephen said nothing, but looked from one to another of them and then looked away, hating them.

William bent and picked up something from a corner of the room and held it up high, level with his shoulder. "Well, here you are, Master Stephen. Here's what you've come for." It was the white-throated, brindled pup dangling from William's hand by the scruff of its neck. Had the rest of the litter been there for Stephen to compare it, he would have seen that it had still not caught up with the others, though it looked healthy enough and fairly plump. Stephen stared at it with distaste, hanging there, whimpering slightly, its tail between its legs, its round, brown eyes starting from its head, its four legs making feeble little movements in the air.

"He's still not of a size with the others," William was say-ing, "and he has not the spirit that they have. He never seems to stand up for himself, not ever." Then he added, "But I dare say you'll not mind that, Master Stephen."

The very faint emphasis on the pronoun made Stephen flush; and Edmund laughed. Then there was silence, bro-ken only by the whimpering of the pup.

"Well, are you not going to take him, Master Stephen?"

Stephen, still looking at the pup, never moved.

"There's no need to be afraid, Stephen. I should think he is probably too small to hurt you," said Joanna with mock solicitude.

"Stephen is afraid of dogs," chanted Edmund very, very softly.

"Well, Master Stephen, do you not want him after all? Have you changed your mind?"

As before, the final challenge had come from William, and he had to meet it. He said abruptly, "No!" set his teeth, took a pace forward and held out both hands, palms flatly upwards.

So slowly that it seemed to Stephen that minutes were passing, William lowered the pup on to his hands. At the touch of the soft, warm body, Stephen almost drew back. But he overcame the spasm of revulsion which for a moment shook him, and kept his hands before him, rigid, with the pup on them. As William let go of it, it began to move, and Stephen, thinking that it might fall, was obliged to bring his hands nearer to his chest. The little creature was still whimpering and, at the unaccustomed touch of his cold hands, it began to tremble. Forcing himself to stand there holding it, knowing that everyone else in the room was waiting in expectant silence for him to reject it, to fling it on the floor and run from the place, Stephen was suddenly aware of the fact that the pup was as much afraid of him as he was of it. For a moment this knowledge enabled him to forget his own fear in pity for it. He held it closer to him, to warm its trembling little body. "What's the matter?" he said gently. "Stop shivering. No one is going to hurt you. Come on, now." He turned, and carrying the pup carefully as well as cautiously, he went out, leaving behind him a surprised and disappointed silence.

Only Margaret, too young, still, to feel she had been fooled, ran after him, and skipping along beside him, asked, "Are you not afraid of him, Stephen? Are you not afraid of him?"

Unexpectedly, Stephen turned on her and said, "Oh, go away, Margaret. Go and play with your doll," so that she was startled into speechless indignation, and stood in the middle of the outer bailey, watching him walk away from her, carrying his pup.

ELEVEN

Soon after the midday meal, Stephen, with the pup hidden under his cloak, left the castle by the postern gate in the west wall. The castle had been built at the very end of a narrow spur of high ground running out into the dale from the fells on the west to overlook the river which curved about it. The main gates on the south opened on to the road which led down to the village, the field strips and the grazing grounds at the foot of the spur; but this postern led to a rough sheep-track at the very top, used mainly by shepherds and hunters. The hill was covered by coarse grass from which sprang boulders, large and small; save here and there, where the grass gave way to patches of bare limestone, like scars upon the hill-side. There was one such stretch of rock at the top of the spur, where the castle stood, so that, in places, its outer wall seemed but a continuation of the ridge upon which it had been built.

Stephen walked quickly westwards along the track until he was well away from the gate, then he put down the pup and took off his cloak, flinging it, folded, over one shoulder, for the mild September day made the going warm and there was little breeze, even up here on top of the ridge. The pup looked about it at the strange surroundings and then began to explore cautiously. Now that it appeared no longer afraid of him, Stephen's aversion to it had returned in full. He picked it up in a fold of his cloak – so as not to have to touch it more than he needed – and carrying it under his arm, wrapped in the end of the cloak with only its head showing, he went on, hating himself for what he was going to do; his nagging conscience reminding him, every moment or so – and being resolutely ignored – of himself, not seven hours before, assuring the trembling creature that no one was going to hurt it.

Along the spur, about two miles from the castle, there rose a sudden outcrop of steep rock, and here the track dropped down from the top of the ridge – where the going would have been hard – to run along its northern face on a level shelf of rock for a short distance. For a hundred yards or so there was a sloping wall of limestone to the south of the path and a straight drop of about a hundred feet over a cliff to the north. It was a place where two horsemen did not ride abreast, and where one was well advised to take care and not risk a slip. Beyond the outcrop the path turned sharply up to the south and broadened, and one was once again on top of the ridge with the ground sloping more gradually north and south on either hand.

About a quarter of a mile on from here, Stephen put down the pup and looked about him. It did not seem to him a very kindly place in which to be abandoned if one were a young dog; but no doubt, he tried to reassure himself, some herdsman or hunter would come that way before nightfall. On an impulse he bent and patted the pup which was sniffing at the ground near his feet. It was the first time he had touched it unnecessarily. "Good-bye, and good luck," he said to it aloud, and turning, began to walk quickly back along the track. Twenty paces on, the pup bounded after him. He stopped. He had not anticipated this. He ordered it back to where he had left it: but naturally it did not obey. He tried to chase it back, but it would not go. At last he pulled up a grass plant by the roots and threw it from him as far as he could; and while the pup ran after it, Stephen ran in the other direction. A minute later the pup was with him again, panting but happy. Stephen threw another uprooted clump of grass and once again was free of the pup for long enough to run for a short distance before it followed him. This happened several times more. Stephen had made very little progress on his return journey and his nerves were beginning to feel the strain. The pup was growing tired now and less inclined to play games and more disposed to reserve its strength for following Stephen. He tried again to order it back, to threaten it, to frighten it away with waving arms and shouts. But the pup, though hesitant and puzzled, still pursued him.

"The devil take you!" said Stephen, very near to tears, and flung a small piece of rock at it, taking care to aim at the ground a few feet in front of it. After the fourth stone, the pup, bewildered, sat down on its haunches on the track, its tongue lolling and its sides heaving, and stared uncomprehendingly at Stephen.

Stephen took advantage of this respite to turn and run. A little way farther on was the point at which the track curved sharply down to narrow above the cliff. Once down there, the rock wall on the south hid him from the pup. He dropped his pace to a safe walk and then, just before the track rose again steeply and broadened out, he turned and looked back. The pup was not in sight. He quickly mounted to the top of the ridge and began to run once more. At last it was done and finished with; but where there should have been a sensation of relief, there was only a feeling of guilt.

Suddenly, from some distance behind him, the pup screamed. Stephen stopped abruptly to listen. There was another scream of fear and pain, and Stephen turned and ran wildly back the way he had come. This time, as he approached the curve down to the cliff, he did not even slow his pace but ran downwards and round precipitously and rashly.

He looked along the narrow path. The pup was not there. He had not expected it to be. He guessed only too well what had happened. He walked on slowly, calling to it and looking down over the cliff. Half-way along he could hear it whining; and at the farther end he saw it, some thirty feet below, held in the tangles of the bramble bush which had broken its fall. It was struggling frantically to free itself, with every terrified movement becoming more deeply enmeshed in the strong, barbed strands.

Calling encouragingly to the pup, Stephen knelt on the edge of the cliff and peered over. Nowhere did it look particularly easy to climb down; but to his right, about ten yards from where the pup was caught, a series of jutting rocks and a few small bushes offered some sort of foothold and handgrip downwards in an uneven line, ending about – as far as Stephen could judge from overhead – six feet above a narrow ledge which continued across the cliff face to lose itself in a large outspringing buttress immediately beside the brambles where the pup struggled. If he could walk along that ledge and climb over the buttress – whose top seemed about four feet above the level of the ledge – he could then reach the pup, he thought. But it would be far from easy.

He stood up and took off his cloak which was still hanging loosely from one shoulder, folded it so that it made a long, narrow strip, and slung it over his left shoulder, passing it firmly through his belt at both back and front. That way, he believed, it would impede him least in his descent: for he had to take it with him, as he could think of no other means than his cloak of carrying the pup while leaving himself two hands free with which to climb back. With a last shout of encouragement to the pup, he walked to his chosen spot and let himself cautiously down the cliff.

It was slow going; and some of the footholds, when he came to them, proved less secure than had appeared from above; and once a small bush at which he had grasped to steady himself between one protruding edge of rock and another, came away in his hand with a shower of small stones, and he only saved himself from falling by clutching with his nails and finger-tips at the uneven surface of the rock. He clung there, unnerved with the sudden shock of it, and trying not to imagine what it would have been like had he fallen. After five minutes or so, he went on again, but now suspecting every rock and every plant of being about to dislodge itself at his touch; yet at last he reached the place from where he had to drop on to the ledge. Holding tightly to a jutting rock beside him, he looked down to the foot-wide ledge below him. Seen from the top of the cliff, it had appeared less distant than it really was. Now that he was closer to it, he found that it looked to be nearer ten than six feet below him. This gave him pause for a while; but he could think of no other way of reaching the pup from where he was than by the ledge, so, finding himself two firm handgrips, he slowly eased himself down until he was hanging from his hands, his toes dangling some two feet above the ledge. Though, for all that he could tell with his face pressed against a wall of grey limestone, it might have been fifty feet – or he might have been dangling over empty space.

He hung, hesitating, until his arms began to ache and his grip to give; then, when there was nothing else for it, he let himself drop, his stomach lurching sickeningly. He landed on both feet, squarely on the ledge, just saving himself from overbalancing backwards by scrabbling at the rock. Comforted to find himself still alive, and encouraged by his success, he began to edge his way along the ledge towards the pup. At one place the rock face bulged out slightly above the ledge, so that he had to lean a little backwards for a yard or two, clinging to the bulging rock while his feet dragged their way, inch by inch, below him. Half-way, when he was at the widest point of the projection, he stopped dead, convinced that he could go no farther and that one more halting step sideways would be his last. Then he heard the pup's continual whimpers change to a howl of pain, as some fresh calamity came to it.

"Wait!" he gasped. "Wait for me! Not much longer and I'll be with you." With a tremendous effort he moved his right foot a fraction to the right, and then another fraction, and then his left foot after it; and so on, inch after inch.

Once past the bulge, the rest was not too hard, and he found himself beside the upper portion of the buttress which separated him from the pup in its bramble bush. He clambered on to the top of the buttress and over it to the other side, and discovered that he could reach the pup easily. After a few tries, he found a way to brace himself with his back against the cliff, one leg beside the bramble bush and one foot out-thrust sideways against the buttress over which he had just climbed, so leaving him both hands free to disentangle the pup. This proved slow work, since he did not want to hurt the dog more than it was hurt already, and it was caught fast in the very middle of the brambles and would not stay still, but wriggled frenziedly at his approach, undoing much of his work as he did it.

About a quarter of an hour later the pup was in his arms. Half sitting, half leaning against the buttress at which the ledge had terminated, he held the whimpering animal close to him, speaking soothingly to it, picking out from the loose, velvet-soft skin the curved thorns and wiping away the blood with his sleeve. His own hands were bleeding, too, so that it was a little difficult to see whether it was his blood or the pup's that stained the brindled coat.

Poor, unloved, wretched little creature, he thought. No one wants you, just as no one wants me. Even I, who should have known better, did not want you and tried to throw you away. After a while he was aware of the sobs that were shaking him and of the tears that were streaming down his cheeks; but he was not sure whether he was weeping for the pup or out of self-pity.

The pup, grown less afraid, and comforted by the warmth of Stephen's arms and the gentleness of his voice, had stopped its trembling, and it now raised its head to lick at Stephen's tear-stained face with a warm little tongue that tickled him. Weakly, at the tail-end of a sob, Stephen found himself smiling and almost laughing; and then suddenly, with such a shock that he went stiff with surprise and his tears stopped flowing instantly, he was conscious that for – how long? the last half-hour? – he had been handling and holding a dog without either repugnance or fear. It was quite unbelievable, yet it was happening.

A little while later he shivered, and looking up at the sky, saw that the September afternoon had advanced, and knew that here, on the north face of the spur, it would soon be cold. Holding the now calm pup, he stood up carefully and surveyed the cliff above him. Carrying the pup, it would be impossible for him to return the way he had come; that was obvious. He looked downwards. He was about a third of the way down. For about sixty feet below him, the cliff, though it dropped sharply enough, was less sheer than that part down which he had already climbed, and there were many more jutting ledges and bushy growths to make a descent less precarious; after those sixty feet the cliff ended and the remainder of the descent into the dale would be on easily sloping ground. Once in the valley, he could follow the hill eastwards and turn southwards around the end of the spur and make his way to the village on the southern foothills and up to the main gates of the castle. It would be several miles longer than his outward journey, and so Stephen decided he had better not delay if he wished to reach the castle before dark.

"Time to go home," he said to the pup, and tucked it securely between his tunic and the cloak, tightening his belt a little to make sure that the ends of the cloak would not slip free with the weight of the pup. Then he started down the cliff.

It was, as he had anticipated, a good deal less hard and hazardous than the first part of his descent had been; but it took him long enough. Yet at last he stood at the very foot of the spur, tired but triumphant.

It had never occurred to him, at any time during his climb down the cliff, that had any members of his family seen him that afternoon, they might have changed their minds about his cowardice; and it certainly did nothing to change his own mind over what was to him an accepted fact.

He sat to rest for a few moments with his back against a boulder, and then, finding that it was by now chilly, he set the pup on the ground and pulled the ends of his cloak from his belt. He shook it loose and wrapped it around him, then, taking up the pup and keeping it pressed warmly to his side, he set off along the base of the hill.

When he trudged through the village, the pup fast asleep in his arms, the sun had set down there at the hill's foot, though he could see its fading light reddening the castle walls above him; and by the time he came round the last bend of the road up to the gatehouse the drawbridge was being raised for the night, so that he had to run the last fifty yards and shout to the guards to wait for him.

TWELVE

It would not be true to say that Stephen overcame and lost his fear of dogs in the course of one September afternoon, for it was a long-drawn-out proceeding lasting several months, going from stage to stage and having its setbacks as well as its advances. But the cure which Stephen unknowingly had begun on that occasion, he was able, with determination, to continue; going slowly from a small beginning to a triumphant conclusion, using the confidence he had gained from his experience with his own small pup to serve him with, eventually, all other dogs. It was of necessity slow, for however he might feel regarding a dog which was his own, he was bound at first to feel differently towards all others. And once young dogs seemed no longer objects of fear but playful, trusting, rather helpless creatures, then there were fully grown dogs to be encountered; and amongst those there were some which were friendly and therefore emboldening, and some which were fierce and so of their nature offered a serious check to his progress.

Even with his own pup there was at first the occasional reverse; as when, worrying at his hand in play, the sharp little milk-teeth had pierced through the skin, causing Stephen a few moments of blind, unreasoning panic which he fought down with all his will.

Yet though it took months, there was at last a time when the customary jibe of "Stephen is afraid of dogs" was so manifestly untrue that there was no longer any point in making it; and by that time Stephen's family and the whole castle had grown used to the fact that he did, indeed, no longer fear them, and he was thereby saved a certain amount of persecution. Even the Earl's jester had had to concede this circumstance. He no longer baited Stephen for the family's amusement with sly or spiteful words regarding hounds; nor did he any longer suddenly drop on hands and knees and hurry on all fours over the rushes to crouch beside Stephen, aping a dog, panting with open mouth and lolling tongue, and barking – a trick which had never failed to win a laugh from his master and delight everyone else.

Yet the legend of Stephen's cowardice, which had had root in his fear of dogs, still persisted, and very largely because Stephen himself still accepted and believed in it, while at the same time he longed for it not to be true.

From the moment that he had brought it back to the castle with him on that September evening, Stephen had kept his pup with him all the time. When it did not follow him of its own accord, he carried it around; encouraged by surreptitious titbits of food, it stayed beneath his stool at the high table on the dais in the great hall during meals; and at night it slept in his arms until it grew too large, and then Stephen made it a nest beside the bed out of two old cushions, some straw and a moth-eaten cloak.

The first evening when he had taken it with him to the bedchamber off the gallery above the great hall, the other boys had objected – for no better reason than because it was something which Stephen wanted to do, then it was up to them to prevent it. However, he had quietly but stubbornly insisted on his right to have his pet with him; and finally their never very wholehearted protests had died at the unaccustomed sight of Stephen clutching a puppy in his arms, and in the malicious hope that he might suddenly recollect himself and take fright, or wake up in the night in terror at finding a dog in the bed. So Stephen's pup had joined the other pets in the room: Edmund's sparrow-hawk on its perch at the head of the bed; the raven, belonging to one of the other cousins, which would sidle in and out of the narrow window, croaking dismally; and young John's two squirrels in their wooden cage.

After the first few days of being in Stephen's possession, as the strangeness of its new way of life wore off, the pup became more self-reliant and less dependent upon Stephen. In the same way, as he became used to the strangeness of the companionship of a dog and the still almost unbelievable fact that he was not afraid of it and had, indeed, advanced from pitying to liking it, Stephen, who had always avoided dogs and had therefore known little about them, found that he was learning something new about the pup each day. Together, through the weeks, they grew in understanding of each other. Stephen was always patient and gentle, and the pup soon felt an affection for its master which it did not hesitate to show. To Stephen, who had never known affection from anyone, this was amazing and filled him with delight. That any living creature should offer him trust and devotion and truly enjoy his company, seemed to him a miracle.

It was on the day when he first realized that he had at last found what he had for eleven years lacked and thought he never would possess – a friend – that Stephen knew what he was going to name the pup. He had for some time been divided in his mind between Bran and Cerberus – both fine-sounding and the names of famous hounds, he knew – but now, all at once it did not seem important any longer that the pup should grow to a hound which would emulate the feats of legendary forerunners; what alone seemed important was the fact that Stephen had found himself a friend. Even if the pup never battled with monsters and won, never saved its master from a pack of hungry wolves, never ran more swiftly than the wind, it had something to offer Stephen of more value than all those things. On the day Stephen realized that, Bran and Cerberus were rejected, and Stephen named his pup Amile, after one of the two heroes in his favourite story: Amile the young knight of French romance who had been willing to sacrifice all he held most precious in order to save his dearest friend.

By his eleventh birthday, at the end of 1320, when Amile, now six months old, was discovering each day some new and absorbing fact about the world of sights and sounds and

48

smells around him, Stephen had begun, for the first time, to find life a thing which could, quite often, be enjoyable.

THIRTEEN

Stephen was determined to train his pup himself, yet having very little idea of how to set about it, knew that he would have to seek advice; but he was equally determined to ask help neither from any of his elder brothers nor from William Huntsman. He had almost decided to speak to one of William's assistants, a quiet, knowledgeable young man named Diccon, when William himself said to him one day, "If you want any help with training your pup, Master Stephen, just let me know and I'll be glad to help," with an air which appeared to assume that sooner or later Stephen would be bound to need his help. Stephen made some equivocal answer; but after this, he knew, it would be impossible for him to insult and antagonize William by consulting one of his underlings.

Trying to think, unsuccessfully, of anyone in the castle whom he would not be reluctant to approach, Stephen remembered Goderic, one of the tenant farmers who tilled a medium-sized holding a short way from the village. A few years before, when he had been eight or nine, Stephen's pony, startled by a plover which arose from the ground almost beneath its hooves, had shied and thrown him as he was riding by Goderic's farm, and Goderic, working in the fields with his wife Edith, had come running. Stephen, in spite of a burning pain in his ankle, had been ready to remount and ride on; but Goderic and Edith had insisted on his resting. Goderic had carried him into their two-roomed farmhouse and set him down upon a straw-stuffed mattress with a cup of goat's milk to drink, while Edith had laid cloths, ice-cold with water from their well, on his rapidly swelling ankle. They had been kind and respectful; and, unlike his groom, had made no covert suggestions that the fall might have been Stephen's fault. Ever since that day, whenever he passed their farm, Stephen had made a point of looking out for Goderic or Edith and greeting them; waving his hand to them if they were at a distance and stopping to speak a word or two if either of them was near enough. Goderic was a man of slow speech, with an honest, open face and a steady gaze; while his wife was round-cheeked and cheerful; and Stephen came as near to trusting them as he came to trusting anyone. For their part, they were grateful for such unusual courtesy from one of the Earl's family and, childless themselves to their sorrow, considered Stephen as lovely as an angel and every inch fit to be a prince – though naturally Stephen, with his poor opinion of himself, would have been astounded to learn of this.

Goderic had two watchdogs to protect his farm, fierce-looking creatures which, in accordance with the harsh forest laws that forbade a peasant to hunt the game on his master's land, had been lawed – rendered unfit for the chase by the removal of the three middle claws of their feet. These ban-dogs barked and growled at any stranger, but obeyed their master instantly and meekly, and were ready to fawn on anyone whom he welcomed. It was, in fact, on these two dogs before any of those at the castle, that Stephen had first tested himself when, not long before, he had felt sufficiently bold to approach any fully grown dog deliberately. This was not because the dogs themselves had inspired him with any great confidence, but because he had not been afraid of mockery from either Goderic or Edith, should his first attempt at facing a grown dog have proved a failure.

It was therefore to Goderic that Stephen now went for advice on the training of Amile. Goderic, surprised at being thus singled out, was both pleased and honoured and gave

Stephen whatever help he asked, without being either offi-
cious or interfering.

FOURTEEN

Besides eventually releasing him from his fear of all dogs,
there was another respect in which Amile changed Stephen's way of life. Stephen had always found it the wisest
policy to suffer slights and violence without attempting
reprisals; for thus, he had discovered, one gets hurt the less.
It had been only rarely in his life that in his dealings with
the other children he had forgotten himself and retaliated –
and then he had always regretted it soon enough. But he
now found that this expedient did not serve when one had
some other creature than oneself to defend. One could not
stand by and wait for the storm to blow over when it was
not oneself, but one's pet, that was likely to be struck by
the lightning.

The other boys, particularly Edmund, on more than one
occasion took it upon themselves to tease Amile, mainly in
order to distress Stephen. Usually Stephen managed to
snatch up Amile and remove him from them without much
harm being done; but one wet afternoon Edmund, bored
and spoiling for a fight with someone, whilst keeping one
eye on Stephen, deliberately kicked Amile, who was quietly
lying on the floor, chewing at a large bone, trying out his
new adult teeth.

Amile, with a yelp, was lifted a foot or so into the air and
landed a yard away in a flurry of disturbed strewing-rushes,
right at Stephen's feet. As Stephen hastily made sure that
Amile was not badly hurt, Edmund laughed. Stephen let go
of Amile and straightened up. "How dare you kick my dog?"

"I'll do what I wish to your dog. You'd not be able to stop
me, anyway," jeered Edmund.

"I can at least try," said Stephen. He clenched his right hand into a fist and smashed it at Edmund's grinning mouth. Edmund sidestepped from the blow, hit Stephen neatly on the jaw and knocked him down. Stephen got up and flung himself at Edmund, who promptly hit him again. Stephen went on fighting as long as he could still manage to struggle to his feet after each blow that sent him to the floor; and he succeeded in the course of their fight – more by luck than by any good judgement on his part – in hitting Edmund twice. But in the end, winded by a blow to the stomach, he crouched doubled up on the floor, quite unable to rise again. Edmund stood over him. "Now tell me that I can kick your dog whenever I want. Come on, say it." He jabbed his foot into Stephen's ribs. "Say it, Stephen."

Stephen managed to gasp, "No, never!" as he began to regain his breath.

Edmund twisted his hand in Stephen's hair and pulled. "Say it. Come on, say it."

"No."

Edmund gave a sharp tug. "Hurry up, Stephen, say it."

"If you kick my dog again," said Stephen, "I'll . . . I'll kill your sparrow-hawk!"

Edmund kicked him again. "If you do that, I'll kill you!" he said furiously.

"You could kill me if you liked," said Stephen, "but, remember, you'd have lost your hawk."

For a few moments Edmund considered this rising spiral of revenge and how profitless to anyone it was likely in the end to prove. He let go of Stephen's hair and said, "Very well, let's call a truce as far as Silver and your pup are concerned. You keep away from Silver and I'll not touch Amile. Agreed?"

Stephen looked up at him suspiciously; but Edmund, standing arms akimbo, looking down on him, seemed to mean what he had said. He became impatient at Stephen's hesitation. "Oh, come on, Stephen! Do you agree to a truce, or not?"

"Yes, I agree."

"That's that, then." Edmund, having worked off his spleen, strolled away to see if it had stopped raining; and Stephen, having never before gained so much by endurance and fortitude, got painfully to his feet and called to Amile, who was peeping out nervously from beneath a bench.

FIFTEEN

Amile was to repay Stephen in full for those occasions when he had defended him. It was a few days before Stephen's twelfth birthday, when Amile was some eighteen months old: there had been a heavy fall of snow the night before, and all that morning the younger folk of the castle had been snowballing each other in the inner bailey with much noise and enthusiasm. Stephen, as usual, had tried to avoid the others' games; yet though he had thrown no snowballs at anyone except little Margaret, who had demanded that he should, he had had a number thrown at him. And somehow the snowballs that were aimed at Stephen always seemed to contain a stone or a sharp piece of wood, or some other object which could bruise or hurt.

He had evaded the others after the midday meal and spent the afternoon racing round the outer bailey with Amile, both of them keeping warm and enjoying themselves thoroughly. As dusk began to fall, it became noticeably colder, and the surface of the snow, trampled by many feet and softened by the sun, began to harden, shining whitely in the frosty, darkening air. Stephen, with Amile at his heels, made for the great hall where the torches were already lit and the trestles were being set up for the evening meal.

As he neared the covered outside stairway which ran up beside the three lowest floors of the keep, not Edmund, but his two other cousins, one six months younger and the other a year older than himself, leapt out at him from behind a buttress, knocked him down and began to roll him over and over in the snow, rubbing crisp, icy handfuls into his smarting eyes and mouth.

Stephen put his hands over his face, but made no other attempt to defend himself beyond trying to wriggle out of their clutches. Then suddenly there was a furious growl, one cousin was sent sprawling over Stephen, and the other, bitten sharply in the leg, yelled out in surprise and pain.

By the time that Stephen had managed to drag himself out from under the confusion of bodies, seize Amile by the collar and pull him off his victims, both the cousins had been bitten. One of them was sitting up in the snow, nursing a bleeding hand, and the other was standing watching with some surprise the blood that was staining his torn hose and beginning to trickle down his leg into the snow.

"It was your fault," said Stephen. "You started it, both of you, not I."

Neither of the other boys said anything; and after a moment Stephen turned, still holding tightly to Amile's collar, and walked up the stairway into the keep, his heart singing within him because his friend had rushed to his defence. For the first time in his life, he had not been left to endure alone.

After that, far fewer practical jokes were played on Stephen. Even if Stephen himself were considered undeserving of regard, Amile's teeth had won respect; and for almost all of the time now, instead of only for part of the time, Stephen was ignored – which suited him. He rode out with Amile running by his horse's side, or went on long, exploring walks with him. Together they hunted on fell and in dale;

flushed rabbits and hares and gave chase – and even when they caught nothing, they enjoyed themselves. Stephen's little weakling pup had grown into a fine hound which the critical William Huntsman was ready to praise; and even Stephen's second eldest half-brother, hot-tempered Henry, who was twenty-five and had been a knight for the past six years, and who hardly spoke ten times to Stephen in the course of a whole twelvemonth, stopped one day to look at Amile appraisingly and say, "You have a pretty good hound there, Stephen, I'd not be sorry if he were mine."

SIXTEEN

At the end of 1321 the old antagonism between King Edward the Second and certain of his lords under the leadership of his cousin, grasping Earl Thomas of Lancaster, the most powerful magnate in the kingdom, had flared up at last into open war. The King, for once acting decisively, had raised a large army, and by the January of 1322 he was making for the north, where the Earl of Lancaster and his supporters were conspiring with the Scots and completing an alliance with them.

In his own home, as did so many of the lords of England, Earl Robert was never tired of criticizing the easy-going, feckless King and his unpopular favourites, the Despensers, father and son; and his sympathies were wholly with the Earl of Lancaster, whom he would have been pleased to see wearing his cousin's crown. He had fully intended, in the event of civil strife, to put himself, his elder sons and his men at the service of Earl Thomas; and he now spent the first half of the month of February making ready to join Lancaster at his castle in Pontefract.

And then, at the last moment, he changed his mind. Afterwards he spoke of it as brilliant foresight, while the

Countess called it a merciful warning from heaven: yet it was probably neither, but merely a sudden excess of ignoble caution. Whatever the cause, Earl Robert found himself, just at that moment when he should have been marching out from Greavesby, stricken with a mortal illness which necessitated not only the attendance of his sons at his deathbed, but also the presence in the castle of all his men-at-arms – though how they were essential to either the settling of his worldly affairs or the salvation of his eternal soul, he never troubled to explain. His illness lasted unabated until the end of February, and even then he went on dying well into March.

Meanwhile, on March the twelfth, the King at Tutbury in Staffordshire proclaimed his cousin a rebel, and midway through that month their armies met at Boroughbridge on the River Ure. Lancaster was defeated. With his captains he surrendered to the King and was taken as a prisoner to his own castle at Pontefract, where, it was rumoured, he had built a strong tower to serve as a prison for the conquered, captive King. Here, in his own castle he was judged and condemned, and from Pontefract he was taken to be beheaded; and so at last the King had his revenge for the murder of his friend, Piers Gaveston, ten years before, and vengeance for the long years of humiliation he had suffered at his ambitious cousin's hands. Lancaster's death was soon followed by the executions of several of his adherents, as the King seized the opportunity of ridding himself of a number of his old enemies.

When, after a tedious month's dying – spent sitting up in his bed propped against his tasselled pillows, playing chess with one or another of his elder sons and grumbling continually at his enforced inaction – Earl Robert received the news from Pontefract, he sprang out of bed, called for his clothes and ordered the chapel to be made ready for a solemn service of thanksgiving for his deliverance. Sir Gilbert the chaplain, who normally spoke clearly in his somewhat thin, dry voice, was forced on this occasion to mumble the prayers almost inaudibly, since he was unsure of whether he was supposed to be giving thanks for the Earl's recovery from illness or for his escape from defeat and execution.

On Stephen, absorbed in Amile, neither the important happenings in the world beyond the castle walls, nor the open secret of his father's counterfeit illness, which dominated his own world in Greavesby, made much impression; save that each in its own way demolished a day-dream which had grown up in his imagination as the preparations for his father's military support of Lancaster had been going on, a daydream of himself – his father and his brothers and their men all having ridden away to war – defending the Countess and those remaining in the castle and saving them, single-handed, from the King's forces, and winning for this deed a lifetime of adulation from his grateful and admiring family. But, because of Amile, a day-dream destroyed and lost mattered so much less than it would have mattered eighteen months before.

And so, for over two years, Stephen was less unhappy than he had been at any time in all the years before. He had a friend, unexacting, devoted, loyal; and he was alone and lonely no longer.

SEVENTEEN

It all came to a sudden end for Stephen in the January of 1323, when he was just thirteen. One morning, quite without previous warning, the Earl sent for him and informed him that he had made arrangements for him to enter the Benedictine monastery at Richley in Bedfordshire that spring, and that Abbot Waldo was expecting him in three months' time. As Earl Robert's own affairs would take him to his Bedfordshire manor, which was not far from Richley Abbey, before May, he himself proposed to escort Stephen southwards and hand him over to the abbot.

Stephen was at first speechless at this blow, and could only think: So soon? So soon? But at last he was able to stammer that he had thought a novice was not accepted until he was seventeen.

"No doubt, in most cases," said the Earl easily. "But as far as you are concerned, where is the point in waiting longer? It will be the right life for you, and the sooner you start it the better. You'll not be professed yet, of course, but Abbot Waldo has been very co-operative in agreeing to take you so young."

If Stephen had been appalled by this news, it was nothing to what he felt when he learnt, immediately afterwards, that he would not be allowed to take Amile with him. He pleaded desperately for a delay – if not for the four years which he had expected, then for just one year, for six months, even.

But Earl Robert was firm. "All the arrangements are made and I am not altering them to suit any childish whim of yours. You'll be happy enough when you get to Richley. The life of a monk – heaven preserve me from it! – is the only life for which you are fitted. Let me hear no more objections to my wishes."

When Stephen dared to protest further, he was summarily dismissed from his father's presence and threatened with a beating if he said another word. The Earl added, "Nothing – I repeat, nothing – is going to alter my arrangements for your future, so you might as well make your last weeks here comfortable ones. For I warn you, if I have to beat you myself every day for the next three months and then hand you over to Abbot Waldo tied hand and foot, you'll go to Richley when I say, and not a week later."

For all that he meant them, the Earl was, in fact, smiling good-humouredly when he said those last words; but Stephen, white and shaken, with his whole life shattered about him, was not aware of this.

He spent the rest of that day with his mind in a painful turmoil. It was unthinkable that he should be parted from Amile. Yet, if he had to leave Amile behind, to whom could he entrust him? Goderic was the only possible person. But then, as the dog of a peasant, Amile would have to be lawed, and the thought of Amile's paws mutilated was unbearable to Stephen. It was at that point that he made up his mind to run away. The next morning he went. He went impulsively and recklessly, without considering the best way to set about it, intent only upon getting himself and Amile away from Greavesby as soon as he might.

From the start matters were mismanaged. Stephen was not a fool, and had he planned ahead and used a little common sense, the escape would probably have been successful. As it was, he made no plans at all as to where he would go and what he would do when he got there; and he did not even consider how best to evade pursuers. Such incaution was due, at least in part, to a mistaken assumption that, since no one had ever cared for him, no one would now be likely to trouble to fetch him back – but he had discounted Earl Robert's dislike of being thwarted and of having his plans overset.

With three full months in which to plan his going, Stephen went the very day after his talk with his father; so that the moment his absence was discovered, the reason for it was instantly apparent to the Earl. Stephen chose and saddled a horse for himself, giving no explanation to the grooms, believing that the less he said to anyone, the less would be remembered later; but he took no care to avoid being seen strapping the bundle containing his clothes and other belongings to his saddlebow. And, thinking to make an early and unnoticed start, he succeeded only in drawing attention to his absence hours before it need have been found out.

There was just one person in the castle to whom it was important that, at a given hour each day, Stephen should be in a given place. Stephen should have thought of making his excuses to Sir Gilbert, or he should have ridden away after his morning's lesson. As it was, Sir Gilbert sat in his little room, musing, until, glancing at the hour-glass upon his desk, he realized that half of lesson time had passed and Stephen was still not with him. He rose, opened the door and looked out across the great hall. The youngest of Stephen's elder half-brothers, seventeen-year-old Thomas, happened to be standing near and Sir Gilbert asked him if he knew where Stephen was.

Thomas, who had for the moment nothing better to do, said with enthusiasm, "He's playing truant, is he? I'll find him and send him to you. And I'll give him a good thrashing first, the lazy young cub." He organized a search for Stephen, sending scurrying in various directions a number of pages whom he had found idle. One of these, inquiring in the stables, heard from a groom about the bundle which Stephen had been seen to take with him when he had ridden out two hours or so before. Thomas drew his own conclusions from the bundle and went at once to his father.

"Stupid little fool," grumbled the Earl. "I might have known that he, of all my sons, would do something witless and absurd."

Within three hours of Stephen's departure four separate bands of men-at-arms, each led by one of the Earl's knights, had set out from Greavesby in different directions to look for him.

Stephen was certainly at fault for his lack of planning; and for taking with him no food but, instead, stopping twice during the first day to buy bread and meat from two villages through which he rode, and so leaving a trail leading eastwards behind him; and then for passing that first night in a farm still on his father's lands, where he was recognized by the farmer, who had been to the castle with produce on more than one occasion. But though he might be blamed for careless mismanagement and lack of foresight, he could not be blamed for the fact that his horse went lame on the second day, so that, reduced to a walking pace, he lost valuable hours of flight.

He was overtaken by one of the parties sent out after him on the morning of the third day, in a small town on the road to York, while trying at a tavern to exchange his lame but valuable horse for an old hack whose only recommendation was that it had four sound legs, and finding it hard to persuade anyone that his own temporarily useless mount had not been stolen. One of the men-at-arms was left in the town to take charge of the lame horse, Stephen was remounted on this man's horse and escorted ignominiously home.

On his return to Greavesby, at the orders of the Earl, he was confined in one of the small prison-rooms built half underground in the thickness of the storeroom walls. He was given one blanket, a pitcher of water and a loaf of bread, and the heavy oaken door was bolted on him. During the three days that he was there, Amile lay outside the door, waiting for him, going without either food or drink so long as his vigil lasted.

On the fourth morning one of Earl Robert's squires came and unbolted the door and Stephen was told that if he gave his word not to run away again, he would be released. In reply, he asked that Amile might be allowed to share his prison with him. Only when this had been firmly refused by the Earl, did Stephen give his word, and he was immediately freed, to be reunited with Amile in the storeroom, among the bins of grain and the tubs of salted meat.

An hour later his father sent for him to tell him that his eldest half-brother Godfrey would be escorting him to Richley, not in three months, but in four days' time. "What Abbot Waldo will say to this change in our arrangement, I have no idea, but the sooner you are off my hands the better I'll be pleased. That is all. You may go."

Had Stephen still had the three months which he had expected, he might well have broken his word and run away again, and on that occasion been successful; but four days is not time enough for a solemn promise to grow frail and a given word to be stretched to the breaking.

EIGHTEEN

The next morning Henry came to Stephen and said, in an offhand manner and as though he were conferring a favour, "I'll take over your hound from you when you go. I've always had a fancy for him since he turned out so well."

Stephen was utterly dismayed at this unexpected offer. Henry always rode his horses too hard and Stephen had often seen him beat his hounds mercilessly for little or no fault at all. Whatever happened to Amile, he was determined that Henry should not have him. As soon as the first shock was over, he said quickly, "I'm sorry, you're too late. I've promised him to Goderic." This was untrue, as Stephen had not even mentioned to the farmer, whom he had not seen for days, the possibility of his having Amile.

"Goderic? Who is Goderic?"

"Goderic the farmer."

"That man! Why ever do you want to give him a good hound? There's surely no need to be more of a fool than God made you, Stephen. You'll give the dog to me."

"No. I have promised Goderic." And in spite of the fact that Henry soon lost his temper and clouted him several times, Stephen still held doggedly to his falsehood; and Henry finally strode off furiously to tell the Earl of Stephen's latest folly.

Earl Robert sent for Stephen. "What is all this nonsense I hear about your refusing to give your hound to your brother?" he demanded as soon as Stephen appeared in the solar.

"I promised Amile to Goderic the farmer," lied Stephen desperately. "I must keep my promise."

"Of course you must not! I've never heard such foolishness," said the Earl, who had himself very precise convictions on the matter of a man's word of honour – but only if it had been given to a noble or a gentleman. "Henry wants the hound and he must have it. After all," he added reasonably enough, "you cannot take the animal with you, so you might as well leave it here in its own home instead of uprooting it and banishing it to a peasant's hovel."

"I gave my word," protested Stephen.

The Earl, already annoyed, became downright angry. Punctuating his words with fist blows on the arms of his chair, he said, "You will do as I say, boy! I forbid you to give your hound to Goderic." More calmly, but no less firmly, he continued, "Henry wants it, so Henry must have it. This is my last word in the matter: either you give the hound to your brother, or you have it put down. Do you understand?"

White-faced, Stephen whispered, "Yes, sir."

"Very well. Now, for the love of heaven, take yourself off out of my sight and let me hear no more of you for the next three days."

Stephen left the solar shaking and feeling physically sick. There was now no other way: the decision had been made for him. He could not give Amile to Goderic and he would not give him to Henry – at all costs Henry must not have him. So there was only the one alternative.

In an agony of mind, with Amile by him at every moment, Stephen considered this alternative and came to the conclusion, in the end, that, as well as the only permitted fate that he himself could bear to contemplate for Amile, it would, also, be the least cruel destiny for Amile who – even had he shown it by nothing else before – had proved by his three-day watch in the storeroom his single-hearted devotion to his master. But it must be done, thought Stephen, in the quickest and the cleanest way; so quickly that Amile would never even suspect what was going to happen to him before it was over and done. Anguished, Stephen considered ways and methods.

NINETEEN

On the afternoon of the day before he was due to leave for Richley, Stephen, followed by Amile, went to find Randle, who was the castle butcher. He found him in the slaughterhouse neatly hacking into large joints for the castle kitchens a skinned ox which was laid on his huge chopping board. Randle was a big man, his muscles bulged on his thick arms and on his broad, naked chest, and his greasy leather apron was stained and stiff with the blood of years-dead cattle.

When Stephen had told him what he wanted, Randle stared first at Amile, who was snuffing hopefully at the smell of the fresh meat which was all around him, and then he stared at Stephen. "Surely you cannot want me to do that?" he asked.

Stephen said, "Tomorrow I go away to be a monk. I cannot take him with me." He clenched his fists at his sides. "I do not wish to leave him for anyone else. He would pine for me."

"Aye, that's true enough, I suppose." Later, over brimming mugs of the good ale from the castle brewery, Randle was to tell the tale to his cronies with amusement at the oddness of Master Stephen; but for the moment, looking at Stephen's face, it was impossible not to be moved. "All right, Master Stephen, I'll do it for you." Randle patted Amile and began to unfasten his collar.

"You'll be quick and not hurt or frighten him?" Stephen's hands were still clenched convulsively.

"He'll not know anything about it, I promise you. And it'll be over in a moment, never fret yourself. I've not been my lord's butcher for twenty years without being as skilled in my trade as any man in England." He handed the collar to Stephen. "Off you go now, Master Stephen, and I'll see to it right away for you."

Stephen shook his head dumbly. He gulped and at last managed to say, "I cannot leave him to die alone. I'm staying with him until it's over."

Randle looked at Stephen, wondering whether to try and argue him out of his decision. Then he shrugged his shoulders. "If you insist, Master Stephen." He turned away, and taking up a knife, cut a few collops of meat from the carcase on the chopping bench. He offered them to Stephen. "Here, give him these. It would be a shame to bring him among all this good meat and then not let him have a bite."

Stephen took the meat and, for the last time, fed Amile.

TWENTY

Late that evening, stumbling like someone only half awake, Stephen, who had missed the evening meal, came into the solar. Once in, he stopped and looked about him with a puzzled air, as though wondering how he had got there and, being there, for what he had come.

Henry, put out at having searched in vain for Stephen earlier in the evening, said irritably, "Where have you been, Stephen? I've been looking for you. You'd better let me have your hound now, as you'll be making an early start with Godfrey tomorrow, and I've no mind to be up before dawn to cope with either you or the dog."

Stephen looked at his half-brother blankly, hearing his voice as if from a long way off.

"Oh, for heaven's sake, Stephen, wake up and stop looking like a lackwit! Where's the hound?"

Stephen, his white face expressionless and his voice flat, said slowly, "Amile is dead."

"Dead! What are you talking about? What has happened to him?"

"He is dead." Stephen tried to twist his cold hands together and found that he was holding something in one of them. He stared uncomprehendingly at it for several seconds before he saw that it was Amile's collar. He looked up again. "I had Randle kill him," he said, his voice still without emotion.

"How dared you do that when you knew I wanted the hound?" Henry stepped forward, his face flushed with anger. "You did it to spite me because you were not allowed to have your own way." He raised his hand to strike Stephen, but unexpectedly the Earl broke in.

"No, Henry. Let the boy be. He's not entirely to blame. I gave him the choice between letting you have the hound and having it destroyed. He may have made the worse choice and the one I never thought he'd make, but I did give him that choice." He added, "And the hound was his."

"But, sir, it is preposterous that he should be allowed to flout me in this manner!" exclaimed Henry.

"I told you, Henry, let him be." The Earl looked at Stephen's face. "I should imagine he's been punished enough already to satisfy even you," he remarked. To Stephen he said, "You'd better go and find yourself some supper and then get some sleep. As Henry said, you have to make an early start tomorrow."

Stephen stared at his father until the Earl almost lost patience with him, then he turned, and dragging his feet, made his way from the solar, the empty collar dangling from one hand.

PAGAN

Part Two

ONE

The novice master's voice droned on and on, explaining the passage of Holy Writ which Arnold had just read out to them. A bluebottle buzzed restlessly from side to side of the cloister and finally shot triumphantly through one of the unglazed windows into the open air. Outside, in the square cloister garth, the late spring sun was bright, but here, where the novices were taught in the north-facing southern walk, opposite the monastery church, the afternoon sunshine never came. The warm northern walk, under the south wall of the church, where it was pleasantly sunny even in the winter-time, was reserved for the brethren and was partitioned, on the garden side, into little carrels where the monks sat to study or to read, with their huge books resting on the reading-desk with which each carrel was furnished.

The novice master talked on; the bluebottle reappeared. Arnold listened intently to all that was being said; John and Raimond sat up straightbacked, their hands folded on their knees, their attitude of rapt attention no more than a sham, for their two separate minds were miles away in the outside world from which they had been exiled.

Stephen sat on the end of the hard bench, watching out of the corner of his eye to make sure he was not observed, half of his mind on what the novice master was saying – to be ready when he began to question them on the lesson – the other half given to the slate on his lap upon which he was drawing the sun shining through two clouds on to a tree. It was an oak-tree, thought Stephen, as he made it sturdy and broad, with a slightly flattened top. Outside, pigeons cooed and a starling suddenly whistled, gay, impudent and vulgar. Stephen began to draw a starling beside the oak: thin beak, short tail. For a moment he gave it too much of his attention and failed to take the necessary care, so that his slate pencil squeaked against the slate.

The novice master paused in his discourse. "Are you writing down what I am saying, Stephen?"

Thinking: You know perfectly well what I am doing – just the same as I am always doing when you catch me; Stephen said, "No, sir."

The novice master held out his hand. He now no longer troubled to say, "Bring me your slate," each time.

Stephen rose and handed it to him. Brother Hilary looked at the sun and the clouds and the oak-tree and the unfinished starling and rubbed them out with the duster that was always tucked into his wide black sleeve. He handed the slate back to Stephen and reached for the birch beside his chair.

John and Raimond, who had returned each from his own distant wandering when Stephen rose, were grateful for even this small and not unusual diversion and the break it made in the lesson.

"Stephen, I have lost count of how many times a week I have to correct you for inattention. I am growing tired of it. 'Idleness is the enemy of the soul,' as our great Founder said . . ."

Stephen, standing before the novice master, his eyes cast down, listened to the long rebuke that always preceded the inevitable beating and thought: I am going to be a knight. I will not let them make a monk of me. I am going to be a knight like my brothers. I am going to be a knight – but I wish they would not always stop me from drawing pictures on my slate.

TWO

It was now May and Stephen had been at Richley Abbey for three months. He had arrived with his half-brother Godfrey on a wild, wet February afternoon, and they had been received by the abbot in his parlour. Abbot Waldo, who now – as ruler of the convent lands and the owner of many serfs, with power of life and death over wrongdoers in the district – was the equal in rank of a secular lord, was the son of a London vintner and had never quite outgrown the respect which his father had impressed on him for the old noble families which had come to England with Duke William. He had greeted Godfrey and heard his explanation of Stephen's unexpectedly early arrival with equanimity; and he had received with real gratitude the Earl's gift of a purse of gold pieces – a donation towards the cost of the new organ and the pair of candlesticks which, at the time Earl Robert had last been at Richley, the abbot had mentioned as being needed for the church. He had then asked at great length after the Earl and inquired about the health of the Countess.

"When Earl Robert was last here, making arrangements for us to receive your brother, I promised him a special draught which Brother Infirmarer was to prepare from certain herbs and berries, and which he is certain will be beneficial to her condition. You are here earlier than we expected, but I know that Brother Infirmarer has the cordial all ready and bottled, so before you leave on your return journey tomorrow, I will have him give it to you and explain to you how often your lady stepmother is to take it." There had been much more in this vein, to which Godfrey had replied with formal courtesy, curbing his impatience, and Stephen had stood by, seemingly quite forgotten.

But finally the abbot had turned to him, smiled kindly and spoken graciously, "We are very pleased to welcome you and to know that once again we shall have a de Beauville amongst us. It is fifty years, you know – before my time here, I fear! – since we last had one of your illustrious family in our community. So you are doubly welcome – for your family's sake as well as for your own."

Fifty years, Stephen had thought. Why could they not have waited another fifty years? And why did it have to be me? Dear Lord in heaven, help me to get away from here and to be a knight.

"You are young to join us, but from all that your good father told me of you when I saw him in the autumn, I am sure that you will be very fitted to life amongst us. I only trust," the abbot had ended sincerely, "that you will not miss too much the companionship of those of your own age. Our other novices are all older and will soon be ready to take their vows." He had hastened to reassure himself as much as Stephen. "But I remember the Earl saying that you were quiet and fond of study, so I have few real doubts." His round face had beamed benevolently at Stephen.

At last, Godfrey had taken a brief and temporary leave of the abbot, before retiring to the abbot's guest house, where noble and important guests were lodged, to make ready for supper, which he was to take at the abbot's table. He had then turned to Stephen and said shortly, "Well, good-bye, Stephen. Behave yourself. You'll never be a credit to the family anywhere else, so mind you do not disgrace our name in here." And without waiting for Stephen's reply, with a courteous gesture to the abbot, he had gone from the parlour; and Stephen had wanted to run after him, to catch hold of his hands, to kneel to him and implore him to take him away and give him a chance to prove himself a worthy member of his family. But he had known it would be useless, and his knowledge had given him the strength to spare himself the humiliation of certain rejection.

Three months had passed since that day on which Stephen, still numbed with grief for Amile's death, utterly alone again that his only friend was gone, had been abandoned to his new life. When he had been able to think again of anything but the loss of Amile, it had been only of his determination to be a knight. And during those three months, whenever he had knelt to pray, he had not failed to implore for his desire: Holy Father in heaven, let me be a knight. Blessed Mother of God, pray for me, that I do not have to be a monk.

But gradually, through the weeks, as the sharpness of his grief for Amile had been blunted, and as his homesickness for the home where he had too rarely been anything but unhappy was lessened, and as he was caught up into the calm and ordered daily round of the convent, something of its years-old tranquillity reached through to him and he became – not reconciled, for he believed he never could be that – but less despairing, and he even began to find that life at Richley, when compared with life at Greavesby, had its compensations.

THREE

The abbot lived in his own apartments in the monastery, and he was often away on the business of the convent or at the King's court; so Stephen was, after the first day, to see little of him. He had his own personal servants as well as his own chaplain and two pages of the same age as Stephen, who had looked Stephen up and down with scornful pity on his arrival, because, unlike them, he would never rise to be a squire and a knight.

As the convent was not a large one, it had only three novices at one time, instead of the six that were usual in the larger houses. Stephen – accepted amongst them in spite of his youth, only to oblige a family from which had come for many generations the most open-handed of the convent's patrons – being as yet only a boy and unlikely to take his vows for another four or five years, was extra to this number and made a fourth.

Of the three, Arnold was a man of twenty-seven, who had after due deliberation, chosen for himself that way of life for which he was most fitted. He was an earnest, thoughtful man and spoke little to the others, but he seemed to have an inner contentment as he waited quietly yet eagerly for the day of his profession. The other two, John and Raimond, had, like Stephen, had their futures decided for them by their families. They were of an age, both being eighteen, and were inclined, from the superior position of their five years' advantage, to consider Stephen a mere child and of no account. Stephen was too used to a similar attitude on the part of his family to be distressed by this, and he was, indeed, glad to be left to himself and undisturbed during his hours of leisure.

The four novices, under the watchful eye of the novice master, slept at one end of the dorter, the monks' dormitory, each on his own truckle-bed. To Stephen, who had suffered much from the high spirits of his brothers and his cousins, who too often regarded bedtime and the moment of waking as occasions for practical jokes and horseplay, a bed all to himself – however narrow and however hard it might be – seemed like luxury. Even the loss of the warmth of one's bedfellows on a chilly night, was compensated for by the fact that in the dorter one was expected to sleep in all one's clothes.

The monks' beds, which stood with their heads against the walls along both the long sides of the dorter, were separated from each other by wooden screens which gave each bed's occupant a measure of privacy. Stephen, with his reserve and his liking for being by himself, considered this an excellent idea, and quite often thought that his own tiny, private bedchamber with its oaken bedstead would be something to look forward to, when he had taken his vows. And then he would remember that, of course, he never was going to take his vows, because, in spite of his family, he was going to be a knight. Somehow, it would be achieved.

Beyond the dorter lay the long, narrow necessary-room with its row of seats along the wall, each divided by partitions and having its own small window, Stephen found this an improvement on the privies at Greavesby, built in the thickness of the walls, no more than two or three to each floor, so that one usually found them occupied and was obliged to wait one's turn.

Below the dorter was the frater, the monks' refectory, in the charge of Brother Fraterer, who took his duties very seriously and always looked a little worried, being responsible not only for the buttery and the meals, but also for the handsome carved stone laver which stood in the cloister outside the frater door. Here, at a circular basin set about a central pillar up which the water came to gush through spouts, each monk might wash his hands and face before meals and dry them with the clean towels which were kept in two cupboards, one on either side of the frater door. Sometimes, during a dry summer, the water did not flow too freely from the taps, and in the autumn, the leaden pipes which carried the waste water to the primitive monastery sewer would become choked with fallen leaves; while in damp and

sunless weather it was not always possible to have an adequate supply of dry, clean towels. All these little things
helped to keep the fraterer anxious, and increased the –
largely imaginary – difficulties of his life.

In the frater the four novices usually served the monks
as they sat eating in silence, listening to one of the younger
brothers who stood in the frater pulpit and read to them during the meal. The food was passed in dishes or in bread-
baskets from the kitchen through a hatch at one end of the
frater to Stephen or the other three as they waited to receive
it from the kitchen servants.

Meat was never eaten in the frater, but only fish – salted
or from the monastery fish-ponds – and vegetables grown
in the monastery garden; yet meat was permitted to any
monk who was ill and in the infirmary, while the other
brethren were allowed to dine twice a week in the misericorde adjoining the infirmary, where meat was served. Abbot Waldo, partly out of consideration for Stephen's youth
and partly because he wished to indulge the first de Beauville novice for fifty years, had given Stephen leave to eat in
the misericorde on any day of the week save Friday, and on
Wednesdays, which were also fast-days.

The infirmarer, a cheerful, kindly man, always chaffed
Stephen good-humouredly about this privilege, prophesy-
ing that by the time he was professed, Stephen would be so
fat and round that he would be hardly able to waddle about,
and his brethren would have to carry him in the Sunday pro-
cession each week, when, with cross and lighted candles,
starting from the church, the whole convent, singing, walked
two by two right round the cloisters and so back into the
church; and he would slyly suggest that Stephen might like
to sweat off a little of his extra weight by weeding the infirmary garden for him, or picking herbs to be dried.

"For I will not have the servants in my garden," he would say. "They are all dunderheads and do not know chives from rushes. Let them near my herbs and they would pull up all my pennywort which I have been at such pains to grow for the healing of burns and scalds. Or they would pick hemlock along with the parsley to season the fish, and then not even seeds of rue steeped in wine could save us."

And Stephen, slim and slight, and in no danger at all of growing fat, would find himself plucking sage leaves and spreading them out to dry in the sun, or pulling up chickenweed from amongst the parsley. And, kneeling on the stone paths that ran between the herb beds, the spring sun shining warmly on his back, grubbing in the damp earth with his fingers, Stephen would wonder why he, who was – in spite of them all – going to be a knight, should not mind doing work more fitted to a serf.

Perhaps, he thought, it was because some of the plants were so beautiful with their aromatic leaves all in subtly differing shades of green, from almost blue to almost yellow, and of every shape, from the broad, flat orbs of the coltsfoot – so good for coughs – which came after the flowers were gone, to the feathery foliage of the fever-relieving yarrow, which, in spite of its many good properties, was, so Brother Infirmarer said, dedicated to the Devil. There were flowers, too, in the infirmary garden: purple self-heal for the curing of all wounds, periwinkle for cramps, a few late celandines like little golden suns, the first of the yellow irises – so beneficial for sore eyes, an early ox-eye daisy or two – a sure cure for the toothache, and a stiff-leaved shrub with a strong, clean scent and little mauve flowers where the bees gathered, which, so Brother Infirmarer told him, was called rosemary and was probably the only rosemary tree growing in England. So that Stephen felt that even if his heart ached and he was all alone and friendless once again, in a world where lilies of the valley grew and smelt so sweetly, surely somewhere – somewhere – there might be happiness for him?

FOUR

After a particularly warm and fine week, there came a day towards the end of May which was more like March: fitful sunshine, an occasional short, sharp shower, and a surprisingly cool wind blowing from the west.

The lesson was Latin, at which Stephen, thanks to his hours with Sir Gilbert, was far more proficient than either John or Raimond; so that, along with Arnold, he was usually given a passage from the Bible, or from one of the old Fathers of the Church, to study by himself during the time that the other two were reading and translating their passages with the novice master.

Arnold, at one desk, was reading avidly, his finger moving rapidly below each line and his lips soundlessly mouthing the words his eyes were seeing. Though he was always welcome to discuss what he read with Brother Hilary, during many of the novices' lessons he was left to his own devices and he managed, Stephen considered, to read an unbelievable amount.

Stephen, on the other hand, was expected, at the end of the lesson, after John and Raimond had finished their translations, to answer questions on the passage which he had been reading. Today Brother Hilary seemed to have set him a particularly dull piece. He sat at another desk, trying to concentrate on one of St. Augustine's letters, but without much success.

Raimond was reading aloud from the story of the crossing of the Red Sea, previous to translating it; and Stephen, his attention drifting from Augustine's exhortatory sentences, half listened to him.

"*Persequentesque Ægyptii ingressi sunt post eos, et omnis equitatus Pharaonis, currus eius et equites, per medium maris . . .*"

It was colourful and far more interesting than old Augustine. *Omnis equitatus Pharaonis, currus eius et equites:* all Pharaoh's horses, his chariots and his horsemen. It brought a vivid image before his mind's eye. Stephen reached for his slate with its pencil tied to it by a cord and drew it softly towards him. He took up the pencil and began to draw one of Pharaoh's chariots. He made it like his stepmother's travelling carriage, which she used on those rare occasions when she could not – though she usually managed to do so – avoid a journey. Long and brightly painted, with a curved roof and little flaps which one could raise in order to look out and see where one was going, it was a very uncomfortable conveyance but far more impressive than a mere horse-litter. Stephen was not sure what Pharaoh's chariots would really have looked like, but he was certain that they would have been grander than a baggage wagon, therefore he drew the carriage. He nearly put the de Beauville coat of arms on its side – a sanglier, a wild boar, passant, a sword held in its raised dexter forefoot – and then remembered that it would be unsuitable for the Egyptians. When he had finished the carriage, he drew Pharaoh's horsemen. The slate was not wide enough for more than one horseman to ride after the carriage; the others, he thought, would have to follow it in a spiral up the slate, as though they were climbing a hill by a curving track, like the road which went up the hill to Greavesby Castle. The horsemen of Pharaoh were fine knights on their chargers – just as he would be one day, please God – and Stephen had drawn three of them and was so intent upon the fourth that Brother Hilary had to call his name twice before he heard him.

"Stephen, are you making notes on St. Augustine?"

"No, sir."

Brother Hilary held out his hand and Stephen walked across to him and handed him the slate. Brother Hilary considered the carriage and the knights for quite a long moment before rubbing them out with his duster. Then he looked at Stephen.

"Stephen, this is the first and the last interruption which I am going to permit you to make in today's Latin lesson. Nor am I going to waste my time beating you today, as it seems to do you no good. Instead, let us see if a different punishment may not be more efficacious. You will go now and find Brother Ernulf in the scriptorium and spend the rest of the afternoon with him. Give him my compliments and ask him to find a use for you until vespers. Perhaps he will be able to cure you of your bad habit. Now be off with you, but close the *Epistolae* and mark your place before you go."

Stephen did not notice the twinkle in the novice master's wise old eyes, and knowing the scriptorium as the place where the monks wrote the convent's letters, copied out manuscripts and made the books needed for their study and for the church services, and presuming that Brother Ernulf – whoever he was – would set him to copying or to scraping old correspondence off parchment so that it might be re-used, he did not see how so mild a punishment was likely to cure him of anything. But as he went to close the book on his desk as he had been bidden, he caught the glance of amusement which passed between John and Raimond before they both looked at him with quick grimaces of mock sympathy.

When he went by Brother Hilary again on his way to the east cloister, the novice master handed him his slate with its pencil. "You had better take this with you. You may need it."

Stephen went along to the end of the south cloister, turned into the eastern walk and met a gust of wind. The scriptorium lay between the chapter-house and the south wall of the church. As Stephen came abreast of the chapter-house he paused and looked about him. There were very few of the monks in sight, and all who were near him seemed occupied with their own pursuits. As a novice, Stephen was not admitted to the daily meetings of the chapter, when the affairs of the house were discussed and wrongdoers were punished; but he was present every evening at the collatio, the evening reading from the lives of the Fathers, so he knew that there were some fine paintings on the walls of the chapter-house, and he had long wanted to examine them more closely than he had so far been able. Now, he thought, he might snatch a quick look at them. The door was ajar; he put his head around it, saw no one and slipped through.

Richley Abbey had a handsome chapter-house; its vaulted roof was supported by two rows of pillars and there were coloured tiles in a pattern on the floor. But it was the wall-paintings which interested Stephen most. There was no time now to examine closely more than one wall, that to the left of the door, but he stood and gazed with joy and with a strange lightening of his spirits at a representation of the Palm Sunday scene: Christ on the donkey, followed by the disciples and a large crowd of men and women – looking like any street crowd one might see on market day – holding leafy branches and casting them before the Saviour.

It would be good to be able to see such beauty every morning when he was a monk, Stephen thought. Surely the sight could never grow stale for him? But of course, he was not going to be a monk. His family cared nothing for monks, so he was going to be a knight. Yet, for all that, the painting was beautiful and he almost felt a stirring of regret that, as a knight, he would have to miss its daily inspiration.

But he had already taken too long. He tore himself away, slipped cautiously out into the cloister and hastened to the scriptorium, the wind flapping his novice's habit about his legs as he went.

The scriptorium was a long line of little rooms, all opening on to the south and having each its own window facing to the north to catch the best light for writing by. There were ten of these little rooms and every one had its door shut on this breezy day. Stephen had no idea in which of them he would find Brother Ernulf. He knocked reluctantly on the first door and opened it a foot or so. A monk was perched on a stool at a desk below the window opposite, writing in a large book. He turned his head inquiringly as Stephen came in hesitantly. He was quite young, and when he saw Stephen, he smiled.

Stephen lost a little of his diffidence. "Brother Ernulf?" he asked hopefully. There was supposed to be complete silence at all times in the scriptorium and one was meant to ask for things one wanted by signs alone; but since Stephen had never been there before, he was not aware of this.

The young monk, realizing Stephen's ignorance, broke the rule to answer him. He seemed to find Stephen's question amusing, because his smile deepened as he shook his head. "No, not Brother Ernulf. I am Gerard."

"Where will I find Brother Ernulf?"

In the room at the very end." He added, "But are you obliged to see him now? He hates to be disturbed at his work."

"Brother Hilary has sent me to him."

The young monk shrugged his shoulders slightly. "Ah well, in that case . . . In the last room." Then, because he was still very young, before turning back to his copying, he grinned boyishly at Stephen and said, "Good luck."

Stephen walked rather slowly along the covered passageway to the end room and stood outside the closed door for a moment before knocking, wondering why Brother Gerard should have thought he would need good luck. At his knock a voice from inside growled, "What is it?"

Stephen opened the door. This little room was crowded and untidy, unlike the other into which he had seen. As well as the desk under the window, there were two small tables cluttered with all manner of things: jars and boxes, a pestle and mortar, rags, little platters for mixing paints; even a crock half full of eggs and a very stale-looking loaf from which pieces had been broken. Above one of the tables was a shelf holding two rows of jars and, standing on their ends and propped against each other, pairs of wooden boards tied together with coloured cords; while, from a peg fixed to the edge of the shelf, was hanging a bladder, filled with some substance and blotched with green stains. Beneath the other table was a basket containing scraps and trimmings of parchment.

Stephen stood on the threshold, waiting awkwardly. After a full two minutes the figure hunched over the desk half turned to see him and said irritably, "Who is it?" Brother Ernulf, a law unto himself in many ways, as Stephen was to find, paid no respect to the rule of silence in the scriptorium.

"Stephen de Beauville."

The monk turned right around on his stool. "I asked you what you were, not your name," he snapped.

"I'm the new novice."

"Then what in the world are you doing in here?" He never stopped for an answer, but went on, "Either go away and shut the door or come in and shut it. You are letting in the devil's own draught as well as interrupting me."

Stephen shut the door and stood just inside the room. This provoked another burst of irritation.

"And come over here if you want to be seen. How do you think I can see who you are when you stand over there?"

Since the little room was very light and the monk not twelve feet away and staring straight at him, Stephen could not understand why he could not be seen. For himself, he could see the monk perfectly well. He had, thought Stephen, a most unexpected face; though he was not, in those first agitated moments, sure why this should be so. Brother Ernulf's nose was straight and faultless and belonged to a face of flawless beauty, but it was set amid other features that were rugged and harsh. A craggy brow with bristling tufts of hair overhung deep-sunk eyes and high cheek-bones, the jaw was firm and obstinate above a jutting chin. He was, Stephen reckoned, quite old, for there were deep lines furrowing his face, and the ring of coarse hair about his tonsured skull was grizzled.

"What do you want?"

Cautiously, Stephen moved farther into the little room. "Brother Hilary sent me to you."

"Why?"

"I . . . I was being inattentive."

"Why in the world should that concern me? Can he not look after his own brats? Does he think I am a dry-nurse?" He gave a disgusted grunt. "Hilary must be getting old and weak in the wits. And he's no older than I am. If anything, he's younger by two years or more. Why should he be in his dotage when I'm still sound at sixty-five? If you were being inattentive to his lessons, that's his affair, not mine. Go back and tell him to beat you and to leave me in peace." When Stephen made no move, he said, "Go on, get out of here."

"But – "

Stephen was allowed to say no more. "I told you to go!" Brother Ernulf reached for the nearest thing to hand. It happened to be a paintbrush, and he threw it at Stephen. Stephen ducked and the paintbrush struck the door and fell to the floor.

"Now go!" Then Brother Ernulf seemed suddenly to realize what it was that he had thrown, because he added, "And find that paintbrush for me before you go. You've wasted enough of my time already. I have no wish to spend ten minutes or more searching for a paintbrush."

The brush was lying in plain sight upon the floor. Surely no one would need to search for it, thought Stephen as he picked it up and took it to Brother Ernulf. The monk snatched it from him with a vexed grunt and began gently, with stubby, broad fingers, to smooth out to a perfect point the tapering hairs which had been disturbed by its fall.

Stephen hesitated uncertainly beside him, wondering whether to remain where he was and risk Brother Ernulf's anger, or to disobey Brother Hilary and go back to him. Suddenly he forgot everything else as his eye lighted upon what lay on the desk before Brother Ernulf.

On a sheet of carefully prepared vellum, in the neatest of black lettering, with large red capitals, was that passage from the Gospel according to St. Mark which tells of Christ driving the merchants from the Temple; and above the text, taking up quite half the page, was a coloured picture of the scene described: the Temple, like a large church with tall pillars and a coloured floor; to one side of it, the angry Saviour denouncing the merchants, the twelve disciples near him – including Judas, distinguishable by his red hair – and to the other side, the fleeing merchants, carrying their wares with them; two of the money-changers on hands and knees picking up their spilt gold pieces, and a boy chasing a dove, escaped from its wicker cage. All the robes were in bright colours and all the little details lovingly portrayed.

Stephen had never seen anything like it before – save for his missal, Sir Gilbert's books had had no pictures in them, nor had the ones which Stephen used with Brother Hilary – and he was unable to contain himself. He said with awe, "How beautiful."

Brother Ernulf looked up from his paintbrush. "Eh? What's that?"

"It is beautiful," repeated Stephen, his eyes fixed on the page.

"Oh, that. So you like it, do you?"

"Yes," said Stephen fervently. Then eagerly he asked, "Did you make it?"

"Since the paint is still wet and I am sitting here before it and since there was no one else here until you came in to disturb me, who else do you think could have done it? St. Bennett?" Brother Ernulf peered sideways to look at Stephen's expression of wonder and delight, which even his sarcasm had failed to destroy. Then he asked abruptly, "Why did you say you were sent to me?"

"I was inattentive during our Latin lesson. I was drawing on my slate."

"You were doing what?"

"Drawing on my slate instead of reading in St. Augustine. I was drawing all Pharaoh's horses, his chariots and his horsemen."

"All the what?"

"All Pharaoh's horses, his chariots and his horsemen. You know: *equitatus Pharaonis, currus eius et equites.* When they were drowned in the Red Sea."

"Of course I know. I'm not entirely ignorant." Brother Ernulf glared at Stephen from under his bushy brows. "So that's why Brother Hilary sent you to me." He paused and then said sharply, "Come here and let me have a look at you."

Stephen, who had prudently stepped a few paces back, moved nearer the desk again and found his arm gripped firmly as though the old monk suspected he might try to run away. Brother Ernulf peered at him through narrowed eyes, and Stephen at last realized that he was exceedingly near-sighted. Finally Brother Ernulf freed his arm and demanded, "Have you your slate with you?"

"Yes, sir."

"Then sit down and draw something. And do not say" – he mimicked a boy's voice – "'Please where shall I sit?' There's the floor." He gestured towards it.

Having been so often reprimanded for drawing on his slate, it seemed strange to Stephen to be told to do so, and for a moment he was taken aback. "Draw something?"

"That's what I said. Are you deaf as well as stupid? Draw something. And kindly do not say now: 'Please what shall I draw?' Draw anything. Pharaoh's army, if you like."

Stephen did indeed sit down on the floor, as there was nowhere else to sit, and started to draw. He became so absorbed in his work and the unaccustomed indulgence of being permitted to draw, that he was startled when, half an hour later, Brother Ernulf said curtly, "Bring it here."

"But it's not finished, sir."

"Do you think I care?"

Stephen got up and handed him the unfinished drawing.

"What is it meant to be?"

"Pharaoh's army."

"Not much of an army!" snapped the monk; but he looked intently at the slate for a long time. Then he said – for him, quite quietly, "Yes, I surely see now why Brother Hilary sent you to me. He's not yet in his dotage, after all." He handed the slate back to Stephen and said, "You can stay here until vespers, if you like, and cut some pens for me. I suppose you know how to cut pens?" He hardly waited for Stephen to answer that he did, before waving an impatient hand in the direction of one of the tables. "Over there, in a jar."

Stephen found the quills – goose and peacock wing-feathers, and crow-quills for the fine lines – standing in an earthenware jar at the back of the table, behind the crock of eggs.

"Do only one broad one first and show it to me before you try any of the others. I do not want the whole bunch spoilt. And keep your hands off my swan feathers. I let no one else touch those."

"Yes, sir." Stephen was about to take the knife from his belt when Brother Ernulf said, "The knife is here. Or did you think you could manage the task with your teeth?"

"I have my own."

"You'll use mine. Yours is probably blunt and will split the quills."

Stephen fetched the knife and started work, only to be interrupted by Brother Ernulf saying, "And do not touch that loaf on the table. It's not for eating."

"No, sir." Stephen was not at all surprised to hear that it was not eatable: he had already decided the same himself. It looked thoroughly stale and most unappetizing.

"I'm telling you again, because I know what boys are like, they cannot keep from nibbling at any food in sight. If you eat any of that loaf, you'll be sorry, I can tell you. It's pouncing-bread for smoothing parchment and it's made of powdered glass as well as flour and yeast. So just keep away from it."

Stephen looked at the peculiar loaf with rather more respect for a moment, and then went on with cutting the quill. His first pen was carefully examined and grudgingly admitted to be passable; but he had the feeling that it was better than that, because Brother Ernulf said, "Now go and cut me some others – and carefully, mind you," and Stephen was quite sure that he would not have been allowed to touch a single other quill had his first one not been almost perfect.

The bell for vespers rang all too soon. It was the best day Stephen had had in his three months at Richley. He had not been beaten, he had looked at a painting in the chapter-house, he had seen Brother Ernulf's wonderful work and, best of all, he had been allowed to draw Pharaoh's army.

FIVE

That evening, when vespers were over and the four novices had eaten in silence their light supper of a slice of bread and a cup of ale, in the short interval between collatio in the chapter-house and compline, John and Raimond asked Stephen in whispers how he had fared in the scriptorium with Brother Ernulf. It was only then that he learnt what they had all along known, that Brother Ernulf was the monk most to be avoided of all at Richley. Ill-tempered, crabbed, surly and sarcastic, he was tolerated by his brethren only for his skill as an artist and the perfection of his work – although there were those amongst them who maintained in gentle jesting that they should all be grateful to him for giving them the opportunity to practise so much Christian forbearance. Yet though they might, from the abbot downwards, find it hard to feel charitably towards Brother Ernulf, they were one and all immeasurably – and most improperly – proud of his talent and of having him in their particular house. Remembering both Brother Ernulf's manner towards him, and the beauty of the almost completed page which he had seen, Stephen could well believe all this.

Two days later, at the start of a Latin lesson, Brother Hilary said, "Before we begin, let us guard against interruptions to our studies this afternoon. Stephen, I think that you need attend no more than one Latin lesson every month – though I warn you that I shall expect you to show signs of great proficiency in that one lesson. During the time that you would waste in scribbling on your slate instead of improving your Latin, you will be better employed in making yourself useful to Brother Ernulf."

Stephen went off to the scriptorium with mixed feelings. He was not sorry for the opportunity of seeing Brother Ernulf's work again, but he was very doubtful of his reception. Yet Brother Ernulf only said grumblingly, "So here you come again to plague me! Well, since you are here, you might as well mix some paint for me. Bring me the third jar from this end of the front row on the shelf and the small bowl with the lid from the table, and I'll show you how."

Stephen did as he was told and found that the jar held saffron. The little bowl gave off an unpleasant smell when its lid was lifted, and Brother Ernulf sniffed at it and said, "The glair is getting stale." He peered into the bowl. "There's not much left. You will have to make me some more later."

He showed Stephen how to grind the saffron finely with a small stone muller on a slab of marble and mix the powder with the liquid glair to form a tacky paste. The powder had to be of a certain fineness and the resulting paint of just the right consistency, and it was all less easy than it sounded, but Stephen found it fascinating, even though Brother Ernulf grumbled and nagged at him all the while he was working; and at the end, when Brother Ernulf was at last satisfied with the yellow paint, Stephen was rewarded by being allowed to watch it being used to colour the cloak of one of the disciples. On this next page of St. Matthew, there was only a small drawing, showing the cursing of the fig tree: the Saviour and the disciples on their way from Bethany to Jerusalem, with the Mount of Olives in the background.

Then Brother Ernulf wanted green paint for the Mount of Olives, and Stephen had to take down the bladder from its peg and scoop out some of the sticky green syrup it held. Brother Ernulf told him that it was made from the juice of ripe buckthorn berries mixed with alum, and that this particular green was the only pigment which could be kept ready for use and did not, like all the other colours, have to be dried and then ground and mixed with glair or gum arabic whenever it was needed.

After that, Stephen made fresh glair by beating white of egg into a stiff froth. As soon as Brother Ernulf said that it was of exactly the right stiffness, it was put into a little bowl and left to liquefy, when it would be ready for use. This glair, Brother Ernulf told Stephen, was used for tempering most of the pigments he used, but blue, which, he said, had to be laid on thickly, needed a stronger binder and one less brittle than glair; so for dark blues gum arabic mixed with honey, or size made by boiling scraps of parchment, was necessary. It was for the purpose of making this size that Brother Ernulf saved all his trimmings and oddments of parchment in the basket under the table.

"And mind you let no scraps of parchment go to waste while you are here," he warned. "If yon see any that my eyes have missed – as well you should, having good sight – be sure you pick them up and put them in the basket. 'Waste not, want not,' as my mother – God rest her soul – always said. I'd not wish to be wanting size at any time through your wastefulness."

In spite of Brother Ernulf's surliness, Stephen enjoyed his second afternoon with him in the scriptorium; and he was pleased, and even more relieved, that Brother Ernulf had let him stay and had not turned him away on his arrival – for how could Stephen have known that, on the day before, Brother Ernulf had sought out Brother Hilary after chapter and said shortly, "That boy you sent me yesterday, Stephen Whatever-his-name-is" – it was typical of Brother Ernulf, though himself only the son of a Peterborough mason's journeyman, neither to know nor to care for the name of the convent's most valued noble benefactors – "that boy, he has talent. You can send him along to me whenever you like." And Brother Hilary had said politely – while smiling to himself at the thought that he had not, after all, been mistaken – "I shall be glad to, brother, if you find him of any help to you." "Help!" Brother Ernulf had retorted. "What use could I find for him? I'm only taking him off your hands since you seem to want to get rid of him. Though why I should be so obliging, I cannot think."

From then on, Stephen spent most afternoons in the scriptorium with Brother Ernulf, from three o'clock until vespers at six, and occasional mornings as well.

During the afternoons all the monks of the convent worked. In the early days of the Order, as laid down by St. Benedict in his Rule, where he says: *vere monachi sunt, si labore manuum suarum vivunt* – they are truly monks when they live by the labour of their hands – the black monks had worked in the fields and in their monastery gardens; but those simple times were past, and over the centuries the menial tasks about a Benedictine monastery had come to be performed instead by servants, and the fields to be tilled by villeins and serfs as on any noble's estate; so that gradually the conventual lands with the abbot as their lord had become very like a secular demesne, and in any monastery might be found as many servants as monks – and sometimes more. Instead of fieldworkers and gardeners, the black monks had become fine craftsmen and artists, spending their hours of labour each day in the copying and illuminating of manuscripts, in the writing down of church music, in painting and the making of books.

In spite of Brother Ernulf's temper and the hardly comfortable circumstance of being with him for three hours on end, Stephen looked forward to his afternoons in the scriptorium; though to the end it remained an enjoyment mixed liberally with anxiety, and for much of the time he was on tenterhooks, waiting uneasily for Brother Ernulf to find some excuse – or none at all – for carping at him.

At first Stephen was set simple but not – to him – uninteresting tasks and made himself generally useful: cutting a few new pens, as he had on the first day, or recutting old, worn-down quills; keeping Brother Ernulf's inkwell refilled from the big jar which held the iron-gall ink that was made in the monastery; making fresh glair; and preparing paints.

In time he was to learn about the different colours used by Brother Ernulf, how and of what they were made: orpiment, which was a sulphide of arsenic and came from Asia Minor, saffron, and the juice of unripe buckthorn berries with alum for the yellows; greens from powdered malachite, from leaves of nightshade, elder and mulberry, or iris flowers mixed with alum, and from verdigris – which had been made by hanging sheets of copper over hot apple vinegar – dissolved in wine and left to thicken until the colour was strong enough; orange lead for a bright flame shade well suited for painting a fire; scrapings of brazil wood for a fine red; rich vermilion which was made from mercury and sulphur and was tempered with egg yolk as well as glair to give it added lustre; for black, soot – collected from a cold piece of marble against which the flame of a wax candle had been held – mixed with gum arabic; and the blues – costly ultramarine from ground lapis lazuli, a sky-blue from finely powdered azurite, and, for a darker shade, the dried leaves of woad, whose stems and roots, when the leaves had been gathered, were burnt to make the wood-ash used for lye.

He watched Brother Ernulf gilding his work; first building up the portions to be gilded with glair mixed with chalk, then dampening them and laying on the gold leaf, cut to shape, to fit over the slightly raised surface and give the effect of solid metal. When the gold was stuck firmly and dried, then Brother Ernulf would burnish it with a well-worn dog's tooth set in a handle. Occasionally Brother Ernulf used powdered gold mixed with gum instead of gold leaf, and then Stephen, set to grind the gold, found that it had to be ground with salt which was afterwards washed away – as otherwise the pressure of the pestle would re-weld the already ground particles of gold.

All these things Stephen was to discover and learn gradually; but meanwhile, on one occasion a few days after he had first begun his afternoons in the scriptorium, upon his arrival Brother Ernulf said, "I am busy. I do not want to be plagued with your moving and fidgeting about behind my back. Here's an old piece of parchment good for nothing save boiling up for size. It'll be no loss if you spoil it. Find yourself ink and a pen – not one of my best unused ones – and sit down and draw something. And do not let me hear another sound from you until I have finished what I am doing."

Stephen, who had, two days before, brought to Brother Ernulf's room a stool for his own use, cleared a space on one of the tables and sat down to begin his first drawing on parchment for Brother Ernulf. It would be a quite different matter, he knew, from decorating, for his own pleasure, Sir Gilbert's passages for dictation. But after only a very little thought, he drew a knight riding on a charger, a hawk on his wrist and a hound running at his horse's hooves. The knight was himself – Sir Stephen de Beauville – and the hound was Amile: yet only Stephen was ever to know that. He spent the whole afternoon on his drawing with no interruptions from Brother Ernulf, and the bell ringing for vespers took him by surprise at almost the very moment that the drawing was completed.

Brother Ernulf demanded to see what he had done. Diffidently Stephen offered his work. The monk looked carefully at it and handed it back to him. "It could, I suppose, be worse. But not much worse. When you are here tomorrow, you can colour it, if I have time to show you how."

The next day Brother Ernulf – surprisingly – did have time; and, grumbling and impatient, critical and exacting, he spent most of their three hours together instructing Stephen in the use of a paintbrush. It was an exhausting afternoon for Stephen, and had he not been so eager to learn all he could, and so interested in everything that he was told, he would have been reduced to tears of nervous misery long before it was over. That he did not lose heart utterly at Brother Ernulf's treatment of him was because, knowing what he had been told about the old monk, he was aware that he was not the only one to suffer from his tongue. For the first time in his life, he had been given the chance to discover that it was by no means so hurtful to be railed at by someone who spoke hard words to everyone and found fault with all alike, as to be far more mildly berated by those who spared others their disapproval to spend it on him alone.

After that, Stephen was set to practise endlessly, hour after hour and day after day – copying from large sheets of vellum closely covered with Brother Ernulf's sketches: figures of men and women standing, sitting, running, walking, riding; or portions of people – arms, hands, legs, feet, heads – each sketch subtly differing from the last; and animals, birds and plants; even chairs and tables and homely cooking-pots. First using only a dull grey wash which Brother Ernulf declared would teach him the value of light and shadow, and then in colour, Stephen painted draperies: a black habit, woollen cloaks, a length of silk – hanging from pegs or over stands, thrown upon the floor, flung across a stool or lying on a table – until he was heartily sick of folds of cloth. His efforts derided and grumbled over, he filled scores of square inches of parchment with tiny, intricate diaper-patterns copied from Brother Ernulf's meticulous examples. So long as the summer lasted and the days of early autumn were not wet or windy, he would often be sent out with stool and wooden drawing-board, pen and ink and parchment, to the kitchen garden to draw the gardeners at work with hoe and spade and gathering-basket among the peas and beans, the cabbages and onions; or occasionally to the field just beyond the kitchen garden where there was a stream. Here would repair with baskets of soiled clothes and bed-linen the laundresses who came at intervals to do the convent's washing. They were engaged by the chamberlain, who had charge of clothing, bedding and baths – and he always chose them for their advanced age and the ugliness of their faces, so that a chance sight of them would not tempt any of the brethren to worldly thoughts. Stephen would draw these old women rubbing and scouring the linen with fuller's earth and lye and beating it with their wooden bats and laying it out on the grass to dry in the sun. He enjoyed this sketching in the open air, even though Brother Ernulf almost always disparaged his attempts afterwards.

All the time Stephen strove hard and tried to remember and apply everything that Brother Ernulf had told him; and because of his undoubted talent and his great interest, he made progress, though from Brother Ernulf's comments, no one would have guessed it. Brother Ernulf was never patient, always grudging in his approval, and his faint and reluctant praise was so rare that, on those occasions on which it could not be withheld, it seemed to Stephen a reward of priceless worth, and he could not but conclude – all things considered – that it must have been deserved beyond a doubt.

During all the sixteen months in which he was Brother Ernulf's pupil and, at the last, his assistant, Stephen never realized how apt a pupil he was, nor how useful an assistant Brother Ernulf found him; nor did he know how great a talent he had. From Brother Ernulf's complaining, he might have fancied himself the most heavy-handed and inapt fool that ever tried to handle pen or paintbrush, but he was shrewd enough to know that if he had really been as ungifted as Brother Ernulf made out, the old monk would not have wasted a single minute of his time on him. So, though he did not guess the measure of his ability, he knew that he was by no means unskilled, and this knowledge gave him comfort. Though, had he learnt from Brother Ernulf the truth, that there was one thing which he would probably one day do superlatively, perhaps surpassing even his teacher, a thing which – although it was not that thing which he had so long dreamed of doing – gave him the satisfaction that self-expression always brings, and even, now and then, an odd moment that was almost joy; had he known the truth, his future conduct would undoubtedly have been different. But having all his life been belittled, and being always ready to believe the lowest appraisal of himself, he was unable to guess at what no one told him.

And so, while Stephen learnt and practised, and practised and learnt yet more, the summer had passed into autumn; and on All Saints' Day the fire was lit in the little warming-room beside the frater, where, during the winter months, the monks would resort whenever they might, since, except in the infirmary, the abbot's quarters and the guest lodgings, it was the only fire permitted in the monastery. During the frosty days of winter Stephen's stiff and icy fingers could hardly hold pen or paintbrush; but still, egged on by his own determination and goaded by Brother Ernulf's jibes and grumbling, he struggled with his practice drawings in Brother Ernulf's little room as long as each day's cold north light lasted; for no artificial lighting was ever allowed in the scriptorium for fear of fire and the loss of precious books. But at last the spring came round again, and the longer, brighter days; and at Easter the fire was put out in the warming-room for another six months. And then there was summer again, with bees buzzing among the thyme and the lavender in the infirmarer's garden, budding grapes – which would one day be pressed into red wine – showing like tiny green beads on the vines in the vineyard which lay beyond the south wall of the orchard, and daisies starring the graves in the cloister garth.

SIX

Many of those artists who were the most skilled at decorating manuscripts would do only the drawing of the decorations themselves, leaving the writing of the text of the work they were illustrating, together with its rubrics, to be done by a scribe; and some would even leave the colouring of their pen-drawings to be done by others under their supervision. Brother Ernulf was not one of these. He had, from the moment of beginning his Gospels, which he had determined would be his finest work – as it would also, he knew, be his last – from that first moment he had trusted no one else to have a hand in it. Long hours he had already spent in copying out the text of the four Gospels, placing it exactly where he wanted it upon his pages, allowing himself the precise amount of space he required for the drawing that he had visualized as accompanying it; and he had, until this time, done not only all the pen-work, but the colouring as well, down to the smallest detail and the least important portion of the formal pattern that made up the decorative background to his scenes and figures. He had planned his work as a whole before he ever began it, and had made hundreds of rough sketches which he kept, ready to consult at any given stage of his work, laid carefully between the pairs of wooden boards, corded together, which stood upon his shelf.

100

Of the supremely critical attitude of Brother Ernulf to all artists other than himself, Stephen knew nothing; and therefore when – with more than a year of learning and being grumbled at behind him – after being made to practise for an hour from a copy given to him, he was allowed to fill in with a fine brush the delicate red tracery behind two unimportant figures in the lower corner of a page – though he was fully aware of the honour that was being done him, he did not dream of how immeasurably highly he was being rated.

At first, as he sat over the page at Brother Ernulf's desk on that fine summer's afternoon, with Brother Ernulf's chin pressing into him as the old monk peered short-sightedly over his shoulder, watching jealously and carefully, Stephen's hand was almost too unsteady to use the needle-fine brush; but he managed to control his nervousness and begin. As he progressed, his strokes became firmer and more confident; and when he had finished, Brother Ernulf said, "It will have to do, I suppose. I've no one else to help me and beggars cannot be choosers – the more's the pity."

After that Stephen was allowed sometimes to fill in backgrounds – though never trusted or unwatched for more than two minutes on end. And then one day, once again with Brother Ernulf standing intimidatingly behind him the whole time, he was told to colour in green and red the gown of one of the maidservants of Caiaphas the High Priest – not the important one who was speaking to St. Peter, but one who was merely looking on, holding a jug. Once again he acquitted himself apparently satisfactorily, for he was on several further occasions allowed – always with the colours chosen for him and always with strict instructions which he had to follow – to give further help to Brother Ernulf with the brushwork in minor ways.

And then, on one never-to-be-forgotten August day, Brother Ernulf pointed to a still unfilled space in the least important corner of his otherwise completed drawing for the Crucifixion and said, "I want a little dog and two more skulls there. My eyes ache – they are not growing any younger – and this page must be finished today so that I can begin to colour it tomorrow. I suppose I'll have to let you draw them."

After a practice sketch which Brother Ernulf grudgingly approved, Stephen sat down before the page spread out on the old monk's desk and, every penline supervised, drew a little dog – it was one of his stepmother's Italian greyhounds – sniffing at two skulls at the foot of Golgotha; and when he had finished, Brother Ernulf grunted and said, "Do you call those skulls? But what does it matter? No one will look in that corner when he has my dying Saviour to look at."

Stephen's pride in having been permitted to draw anything, anywhere, on a page of Brother Ernulf's treasured Gospels, could not be wholly dashed, even by that stricture; yet, not knowing how high a standard of perfection Brother Ernulf set not only others, but himself as well; or that until that moment no one else save Brother Ernulf had ever set a pen to any page of this which was to be his finest work, Stephen had little chance of being unduly puffed up.

SEVEN

And so time passed; and as it passed, slowly and imperceptibly the fixed round of Stephen's new life took hold of him. The quiet, ordered routine and the freedom from persecution were not unwelcome to him and, always a biddable boy, it did not matter to him that every hour of his day and night should be controlled and its employment laid down for him by precept. He had even long-since ceased to resent the bell, rung in the dorter by the sub-prior, that roused him at midnight from kindly, oblivious sleep, to drag himself off his bed, grope by the dim light for his shoes and, yawning, stumble wearily from the dorter with the other novices down the night stairs which led them by the shortest way into the church through the side door in the south transept, to take their places in the quire, in the stalls nearest to the altar; to be joined there soon after by the monks themselves, treading softly in their night shoes, two by two, following the young brother who lighted them on their way with a lantern.

Not only had Stephen grown used to his sleep being broken, but sleep itself was no longer the merciful release from cruel reality that it had at first been: for now reality was failing to seem so cruel.

Stephen loved the large monastery church. Even at night, dimly lighted and filled with shadows, the candles bright about the altar, the lowest stalls of the quire sufficiently illuminated for the novices to follow the words in their books and make the right responses; the monks behind them, darker shapes in the darkness – for they were expected to know the responses without the aid of written words – even at night he thought it beautiful. But by daylight, with the sun shining through the Rhenish stained glass of the windows and throwing patches of coloured light on to the already brilliant hangings, on to the brightly painted walls and the glazed green and yellow tiles of the floor, then it seemed to him like a glimpse of paradise. And as if all that were not enough, in the church as well, a thing of interest not only to Stephen but to many of the monks besides, was housed that new-fangled wonder, a large mechanical clock of wrought iron, in an iron framework, which chimed the hours. It had only recently been set up there, to the great comfort of the sacrist, whose duty it was to ring the bell punctually for the daily offices.

Lessons with the novice master, his long hours of instruction on the Rule of St. Benedict and on all that would be expected of the novices once they were professed – at no time had Stephen really disliked these things; and once his afternoons with Brother Ernulf in the scriptorium had begun and he had found a place where he was not only permitted, but actually expected, to draw, he had ceased to scribble on his slate and had begun instead to pay full attention to Brother Hilary, and had found the things which the old novice master had to say and teach more interesting than he had ever thought they could be. All of this Brother Hilary had noticed, congratulating himself secretly on the way he had handled Stephen, whom he personally considered a most promising novice, in spite of his youth.

As for his hours of leisure: even the games of checkers or bowls played by the novices and the younger monks in the time allowed for their recreation, were calm and orderly. There were none of the unfriendly rivalries, the acrimonious disputes as to who exactly was the winner, that had accompanied too many of the games of Stephen's childhood; games from which he had, since early years, usually been excluded, save when he was needed to make up the numbers required – and then he had usually drawn back of his own accord. Here at Richley, bowls was a means of exercising young limbs tired by long hours of sitting in church or at a desk; and for those a little older, checkers was a way of passing the time pleasantly – whoever won.

Even had there been no afternoons in the scriptorium, Stephen would slowly have become reconciled to his new life. It would have taken many, many months; yet, because of his temperament, it would ultimately have happened. But the satisfaction and the feeling of personal liberation which he attained when drawing, hastened his acceptance of the way of life that had been forced on him. It was not that he no longer dreamt of being a knight and winning the approbation of his family; that was a desire too long sustained to be relinquished easily – and, besides, he had no thought of abandoning it – but it was a dream less frequent now, a desire less compelling. He still, each time he knelt to pray, implored divine aid for his ambition; but now the appeal was gradually ceasing to be more than a form of words. No longer felt with his inmost being, it was, rather, something which he did today because he had done it the day before. Stephen's cry for aid, formerly felt with every nerve in his body, had become a habit, a customary ritual that, had he been given time, would one day have ceased to have any meaning for him, and so, unnoticed, have come to an end.

But he was not given time.

EIGHT

Early that autumn, when he had been nineteen months at Richley Abbey, Stephen was told one morning to go to the guest parlour where visitors awaited him. It was the only time in more than a year and a half that he had had either word or visit from the outside world, and, having believed himself forgotten, he was pleased and excited. At first the preposterous idea came into his head that perhaps it was his father who, having had second thoughts, was come to take him home. But this unlikely happening was instantly dismissed as folly. Making his way towards the guest parlour which lay between the guest lodgings and the church, he wondered eagerly who his visitors could be. Some members of his family, without a doubt. But which of them? He had believed that none of them cared enough about him to travel even from his father's manor at Burnwick, near the Northamptonshire border, to see and speak with him; and he felt cheered at the thought that someone – one of his brothers, probably – had considered him worth an eight-mile ride.

At first, when he went in, the little guest parlour with the benches round its walls and the two stools drawn up to the table in the middle, seemed full of de Beauvilles; then he saw that there were only three of them. His eighteen-year-old half-brother Thomas was sitting on the table, swinging a leg and slapping his gloves impatiently upon the table top. He stayed still and stared as Stephen entered. Edmund was by the window which faced out across the courtyard towards the almonry and the gatehouse; while twelve-year-old John was sitting on one of the benches. Edmund turned round and John got up and all four looked at each other. Except for John, they were those of his family whom Stephen would least have expected to put themselves to the trouble of visiting him, and he was taken aback.

Thomas spoke first. "Well, Stephen, I wager you never thought to see us today."

"Did my father send you?"

"Heavens, no! Why should he do that? We came out of brotherly – and cousinly – affection. Did we not?" He turned, smiling derisively, to the others.

"We did indeed," said Edmund, grinning.

"We wondered how you were," said John. Then he burst out laughing. "You look so funny, Stephen, dressed like a monk."

"John's quite right, Stephen. You do look rather absurd." Edmund was now walking all round Stephen, examining his appearance with exaggerated interest and astonishment.

Thomas laughed, "He'll look even funnier when they shave his hair off." With condescension he inquired, "How are you, Stephen?"

"Thank you, I'm very well." To himself, the words sounded stiff and stilted, and his voice unlike his own. And try as he might, Stephen could not smile; nor could he make even the weakest attempt to appear at ease. The sight of the three of them had brought back, with all its attendant heartache, the memory of those things – his by right of birth – of which he had been deprived. Their gay clothes and their air of consequence, their casual manners, their easy assumption of their own superiority, were as much a mockery of him as their stares, their smiles, their words. He moved closer to the table and held to its edge, and endeavoured to speak calmly. "How is my father?"

"Oh, in his usual health and humour," said Thomas. "We are at Burnwick with him until the end of this month."

"And my stepmother?"

"Just as ever."

"Give her my greetings when you return to Greavesby."

"If I can remember until then," said Thomas carelessly.

"I have a new horse, Stephen. A bay gelding. I rode him over here today," John broke in eagerly.

"Do they give you enough to eat, cousin? Or is every day a fast day here?" asked Edmund with pretended solicitude.

"He has two white forelegs and he goes like . . . like a swallow. Do you know what happened when I rode him yesterday?"

"He looks whey-faced enough at the moment to have lived on beans and cabbage since we saw him last," remarked Thomas to Edmund.

Stephen, standing by the table, heard them and could not answer them: John rattling on about his new palfrey – not because he wanted to share his joy and excitement over it with his half-brother, but because there was no one else who was not heartily tired of hearing its praises; Edmund, with his jeering questions; and Thomas's open contempt. They had not come to see him out of affection, nor even out of pity: they had only come to jibe and to laugh. They had ridden eight miles to make a mock of him, and to remind him of all that he had lost. And now they would ride back, he knew, and tell the others of how Stephen had looked, how he was even more tongue-tied and spiritless than he had been before; and of how suited he was to the monkish life.

Suddenly he was unable to bear it any longer. His knuckles whitening as he gripped the table edge so hard it hurt, he burst out, "Go away! Go away from here. Why did you have to come to torment me? I hate you all. I hate you! Go away from here."

There was absolute silence for a moment or two. Thomas recovered first from his surprise. He got off the table with a falsely injured air and said in a tone of hypocritical disappointment, "If that's all you can say to us when we've taken the trouble to ride eight miles to see you, I think it is indeed better that we should go away." He began to draw on his gloves.

John said in a sulky voice, "You might at least have let me finish telling you about my horse."

Edmund made a shocked, clucking noise with his tongue against his teeth in imitation of Lady Elinor, and shook his head in feigned disapproval, though his eyes were gleaming delightedly at this successful result to their mission. "What an outrageous thing to say, Stephen! I thought that monks were filled with Christian charity and loved everyone. I'd have thought that it would be a sin for them to hate. And we your own loving kinsmen! Shame on you, Stephen."

Led by Thomas, they went out by the door to the guest quarters, John calling out good-bye, but Thomas kept a dignified and displeased silence. Edmund went last. In the doorway he turned and said in an unctuous voice, his eyes downcast and his hands held palms together before him, "Remember us in your prayers, Brother Stephen. Remember to pray for us poor sinners left in the wicked world." He began to laugh at his own jesting as he followed the others, slamming the door close after him to cut them off from Stephen; but not before Stephen had heard the other two join with him in his laughter.

The room was very silent after they had gone. Stephen still stood by the table. Looking down, he saw that his hands were shaking. I will not stay here to be mocked, he thought. I will not stay here. Somehow, he must get away and find a knight who did not know who he was and therefore did not despise him, a knight who would let him take service with him. With a sudden shock he found that he was saying the words aloud: "I will not stay here. I will not stay here."

The sooner I go, the better, he thought. I shall go tomorrow. And may God help me.

NINE

All through the day that morning's episode was heavy on his mind. He thought exclusively of it in lesson time – and was twice punished by Brother Hilary, which did not serve to make him less unhappy. He brooded on it while he ate his Wednesday dinner of salt cod – which he disliked. Nothing tended to make him change his mind and repent his decision to run away.

It was the afternoon of his monthly Latin lesson, so he had not even the consolation of working in the scriptorium; though he did make his way there during the hour of recreation, hoping to find Brother Ernulf and to be allowed to help him in some task. Even if Brother Ernulf were not there, he thought, he would at least have the comfort of looking at the Gospels. Usually the older monks spent their recreation time in resting, but often Brother Ernulf worked. He was working on that day. Once again, events conspired to strengthen Stephen in his resolve to run away. If anything could have kept him at Richley, Brother Ernulf and his Gospels could have done; but Brother Ernulf was in a yet more surly mood than usual.

"Am I not even to be free of you this afternoon? You told me you'd be with Brother Hilary, and I was fool enough to think that I'd not have to waste any more of my precious time on you until tomorrow. Soon I suppose you'll come to plague me all day long," he grumbled. "What have I done to deserve to have to bear with you, a tiresome brat who fancies himself an artist? Go and play bowls or find someone else to put up with you and get out and leave me to work in peace."

Stephen stood very still and straight in the little room, looking at Brother Ernulf's back. He wanted to weep; but he did not. You will be rid of me soon enough, he thought bitterly. You will be rid of me forever after today. He turned away and without a backward glance he went out and closed the door.

He lay awake for most of that night, planning his escape for the morning. He had run away once before – and failed. This time he was not going to fail. But this time it would be infinitely more difficult to get away. This time he would have no horse – and no Amile to go with him. He had no money, no food save the piece of bread which he had saved from his supper; and, worst of all, his own clothes were locked away somewhere in the storeroom of the chamberlain.

By the time he had to rise at six for prime, Stephen had reached the conclusion that there was nothing else for it, he would have to go as he was, in his novice's habit, taking with him only his knife and the slice of bread.

He had also decided that the best time to go would be at that hour during the morning when the almoner received the poor and the sick in the almonry beside the gatehouse. The gates would be open, the poor and the sick would be about awaiting attention, the almoner and his two assistants would be busy doling out food and medicines, and it would be conceivable – unlikely, he admitted, but possible all the same – that Stephen the novice might be presumed to have been sent with a message to the almonry. The thing to do, he was sure, was to be calm and unhurried, to look as if he were on a legitimate errand, and to be ready, if questioned, to lie quickly and convincingly. Once at the gates, he would then have to choose his moment to slip through them and along the road.

When the time actually came, it proved easier than he had expected. He made his way out through the church by the main west doors which gave directly on to the courtyard of the guest quarters. In the church doorway he paused a moment to look carefully about. The gates were thronged, as he had hoped; there were a number of the monastery servants around, going about their tasks; and one of the young monks who assisted the almoner was distributing food outside the almonry, while the other assistant and the almoner himself were within. Stephen had only to cross the courtyard and go out through the gates. It sounded so easy if one thought of it like that – but what if he were questioned?

Then he saw two pails standing outside the stables, empty and unattended. He came down the steps from the church door, went unhesitatingly to the pails and picked them up. Hurrying in as unhurried a manner as possible and trying to look as though it were the most natural thing in the world for him to be carrying two pails towards the gates, he crossed the courtyard. The assistant almoner glanced at him as he passed by, but looked back again at once to the basket from which he was distributing left-over bread.

Stephen put down the two pails carefully beside the gate-house door, as though that had been their intended destination. Then, forcing himself not to turn and look back guiltily over his shoulder, he walked slowly towards the gates. There were several folk coming in for alms and several going out with their hands, platters or baskets filled. The porter was chatting to two old men and seemed unlikely to notice him.

His heart hammering, Stephen stepped under the gateway. As he did so, he came abreast of an old woman hobbling along on a stick, clasping a full pitcher to her breast and clutching a basket of broken meats awkwardly in one gnarled hand. Just as Stephen passed her, she dropped her stick with a cry of dismay. He stopped, took two paces back and picked it up for her. She thanked him, but in taking the stick from him, she almost dropped the pitcher.

She grinned gap-toothedly at him. "It's none too easy this morning. My good neighbour usually lends me her arm to lean on, but today she's sick in her bed and I'm taking her this cordial. But it seems I'll be lucky if I get the jug home in one piece, let alone full of medicine."

"Where do you live?" asked Stephen, as a sudden idea presented itself.

Her hands being full, she nodded in the direction with her head. "Along the road, a little way beyond the village."

Stephen seized the opportunity. "I'll carry the jug for you and you can lean on my arm."

She was delighted. "Now, that's what I call a real kindness. But then, you're all dear, good folk inside there" – she jerked her head backwards towards the courtyard – "so it's no more than I'd expect from any of you – may the sweet Lord bless you all."

Stephen took the earthenware pitcher and she grasped his arm firmly with one skinny claw and they set off slowly along the road, the old woman chattering all the time.

Surely, Stephen thought, no one seeing him now would dream of calling him back?

They made only slow progress through the village, and it was quite ten minutes later that they reached the old woman's tiny cottage; and by that time Stephen had heard, in brief, the story of her life and widowhood, and, in detail, the symptoms of the sudden illness of her neighbour. Yet at least, he thought, he was on the right side of the village: for it was eight miles in the other direction that his father's manor lay; and that was the last place for which he wished to make.

Outside her cottage the old woman wheedled and coaxed. "You'll be a dear, good angel from heaven, will you not, and take the cordial over to Meg for me? That's her home there. Leave the jug with her and she'll bring it back herself when she's well again."

Stephen took the pitcher. He gestured towards the highway that ran on southwards from the village through the lush grasslands of the Ouse Valley. "To where does the road lead?"

"To Bedford, and after that to London, I believe, though I've never been so far. But Bedford is a good town and I've had some fine times there when I was young."

Followed by her thanks and her blessings, he carried the pitcher to her neighbour's rather larger cottage and knocked on the door. A voice bade him come in.

Inside the one room of the cottage a young woman lay on a straw-stuffed mattress on a bed, a patched coverlet over her. She looked, Stephen thought, as he came near with the pitcher, very ill; but in answer to his inquiries she tried to smile.

"It's nothing but a bit of a pain inside me. It'll be better directly, I do not doubt, once I have drunk the good monks' medicine."

Stephen found a wooden cup and poured out some of the cordial and raised her head while she drank it slowly.

Then she lay back once more and smiled at him again – this time less wanly.

"Is there anything else I can do for you?"

She shook her head. "My man will be home soon, thank you kindly all the same."

Stephen left her with the cup and the pitcher close beside her on a stool, where she could reach them, and went from the cottage. Outside, he looked back the way that he had come. There was no one from the monastery in sight. He began to walk quickly along the road towards Bedford. Two hundred yards or so away, he broke into a run. He ran on and off for the next two miles; then, thinking it safe to stop for a few minutes, he sat down beside the road beneath an alder-tree, and taking his knife from his belt, he cut short his novice's habit to just below the knees, so that it might look a little more like the tunic of a country lad. The piece he had cut off, he tore into strips and these he wound crosswise about his legs, over his hose, as a protection against brambles, nettles and the like; for he could foresee an immediate future in which he might have to do a fair amount of hiding in ditches, and a good deal of walking over rough ground away from frequented paths. He resisted firmly the temptation to eat his only piece of bread, while thinking regretfully of all the broken victuals he had seen given away that morning, and got up and set briskly off along the road, striding with determination towards a definite goal, though with no fixed destination in mind.

TEN

Ten days later, Stephen was in Berkshire, having put some sixty miles between himself and Richley Abbey – sixty miles as the crow flies, that is, for he had walked many more miles than that. He was weary, footsore and dirty; his habit and his hair were grey with dust, and he was hungry. Above all, he was hungry. An incessant pain gnawed at his empty stomach and he felt lightheaded, weak and faint. He had tried begging without much success; with even less success had he tried bargaining – offering to work at some task for an hour or two in exchange for a meal. He had searched for berries and mushrooms, and in that he had been fortunate, as it was the right time of year for such things. At first he had asked for alms at the religious houses he had passed – but not for five days now; not since he had noticed the almoner in the last abbey – a Benedictine convent – looking at him, as he had thought, strangely. Since then he had lived on blackberries, rose hips and raw mushrooms, and two hen's eggs which he had managed to steal from a nest; and for his drink he had had water from streams and horse-troughs. At night he had slept in barns and ditches and been thankful for the mild, dry weather.

Stephen's quest for a knight with whom he might take service had been temporarily relinquished in the face of his more compelling need for food and clothing – indeed, in the face of the necessity for merely keeping alive.

That evening, near a town, Stephen passed the buildings of a priory. The gates were hospitably open and he longed for the courage to go to that guest lodging which was set aside for the poorer travellers, where he would be sure of a meal and a pallet to sleep on – but he dared not. He found, instead, not too far from the highway, a sheltered place beneath a bush where he could sleep. He was by this time too tired and dispirited to search for blackberries and other wild fruits in the fading light, so he lay down and fell asleep.

At the first glimmer of the next day he trudged on towards the town, hoping to find there a few eatable scraps of refuse, thrown out from the houses, that had not already been devoured by the pigs which roamed the streets. Half an hour later he was through the gates of the town and prowling about the awakening streets. He managed to snatch a half-eaten cabbage stalk from the very jaws of a pig, but it was barely edible and sickened even his – by now far from fastidious – taste. He tried begging and asking for work from two housewives whom he saw opening their front doors to let in the fresh early morning air; but with a busy day's work ahead of her, neither was inclined to be kindly or encouraging. One of them threatened to call her husband and the other picked up the pail of slops which she had brought with her to empty into the gutter and made as though she would empty it over him instead, so he gave up his attempt and wandered on.

He found his way to a public water-supply and drank. Even cold water inside one was better than nothing, he had found. It meant that one was at least less empty. Then he washed some of the dirt off his face and hands and sat down on the steps of the conduit.

Two women and a small boy came to fetch water. One of the women was yawning and both were still only half dressed, but they were triumphant at being first with their buckets and at not having to wait their turn. When they saw Stephen they told him roundly to be off. He started to ask them if they knew of anyone who might give him food in payment for woodcutting, for carrying water – for doing anything; but they refused to listen to him and again told him to go. When the small boy, shouting shrill abuse, started to throw handfuls of dried horse droppings at him, Stephen got up despondently and walked away.

There were a number of people about the streets by now. The shopkeepers were taking down their shutters and setting out their goods in their houses. Street vendors with their wares were beginning to go about, to be ready to catch the first customers before their rivals appeared.

Farther along the street a baker was opening his shop and the sweet, fresh smell of new-baked, still warm loaves seemed everywhere. Stephen approached him. The man had a mean and calculating look and it would probably be useless, he thought. But all the same he said, "Please, I have eaten nothing for days. Have you any stale bread you could spare?"

The man frowned at Stephen. "I never have any bread to spare, I'm always sold out by midday. And let me tell you that my bread never goes stale – it's too good. It always gets eaten up long before it's stale, every crumb of it. I'm not the best baker in this town for nothing." He looked Stephen up and down. "Another filthy beggar." He spat. "Why do you not go to the priory outside the gates? They'll give you something to eat there – small thanks to them, encouraging your kind! There are too many good-for-nothing boys like you around the streets. Something should be done about it. Now take yourself off and stop pestering an honest tradesman." When Stephen did not go at once, he began to curse him. "The devil run away with you and all other wheedling beggars." He raised his fist menacingly and took a step towards Stephen.

Stephen walked away then, but he did not go far; the almost painful smell of the new bread was unbearable, but he could not tear himself from it. As soon as he saw that the baker was paying him no more attention, he came back and stood in the entrance to a house across the narrow street opposite the man's shop.

Two women came and bought loaves, one soon after the other. Stephen asked them both in turn to spare him a piece of bread. One of them berated him loudly, so that he hastily stepped back against the doorway of the house, hoping that the baker would not hear her and notice that he was still there. The second woman was afraid, bade Stephen keep his distance as though she thought he was about to attack her, and gripping her loaf firmly and holding up her skirts with her free hand, she hurried off, glancing back nervously over her shoulder at every other step, to make sure that he was not following her.

Then came two small children. They took their purchase and ran home laughing before Stephen had time to speak to them. After that there was a longer pause and Stephen began to grow desperate. Then a large, red-faced woman with a basket bought two loaves, jested with the baker for a minute or two and started home again. Stephen put himself in her way. "Mistress," he said recklessly, "you have two loaves. I have not eaten bread for days. Please spare me a little of yours."

"Lazy young scoundrel!" she exclaimed indignantly. "You should be working, not begging for bread."

Stephen said eagerly, "I'd willingly work. Are there any chores I could do for you?"

"There most certainly are not!" Had she gone on home then and left him, so much that happened to him later would not have happened, and Stephen's whole life might have been very different: but she did not go. She chose instead to stand in the street, one hand on her hip, her basket hanging over her other arm, and tell Stephen exactly what she thought of him and of all hale and sound young beggars. The smell of the loaves in her basket was too much for him. He suddenly grabbed one, turned away and ran wildly off along the street in the direction of the gate through which he had passed an hour earlier.

The woman shouted out that she had been robbed and set off gamely in pursuit. Anyone who heard her took up the cry, "Stop thief!" and everyone who had nothing better to do – as well as several apprentices who, at any rate in their masters' opinions, had any number of better things to do – joined in the chase.

Stephen fled down the street, holding to the loaf as though everything depended on it, and managing somehow to evade for a time not only those who followed him, but those who hearing the cries, came running at him from either side of the street to try and intercept him. But the street was too narrow for him to escape them all for long; and fifty yards or so from the gates someone tripped him up with a staff so that he fell. He was on his feet again almost at once, still clutching the loaf; but by that time he was surrounded and many willing hands reached eagerly for him. Someone dragged the loaf from his grasp, and Stephen, as though it were life itself that was being taken from him, gave an anguished cry, "No! No!" and then he was down again on the ground, being kicked and struck at with fists and sticks.

ELEVEN

Two horsemen, coming from the priory where they had spent the night, the second of them leading a laden pack-horse and a handsome charger, passed through the town gates, only to find, a little farther on, that their path was blocked by a noisy and excited crowd which appeared to be beating something in its midst. Having tried unsuccessfully to make himself heard above the din, after a word over his shoulder to the other, the first man set his horse at the crowd and began to force a way through. The crowd parted slightly and a little of the noise died down, so that the young man on the horse was able to make himself heard. He said, "My good people, I've no doubt that your town is a very fine one, but I've no wish to spend the day in it. If you would be so obliging as to let me pass, I could be on my way without trampling on any toes."

More of them moved aside, and the young man smiled good humouredly. "I thank you." He glanced at the knot of folk still standing about whatever it was on the ground and said with amusement, "There seems to be some trouble. What is happening?"

A man answered him, "It's a thief, good sir. We've caught a thief."

"We're taking him to the Justice," said another.

"Whatever's left of him when we've finished with him, we're taking," a stout man, who was holding a huge cudgel, added with a grin.

"Stole a lot of jewels, he did," shouted a woman.

"And bags of gold as well, I've heard," another woman informed her.

"Is that so?" said the young man on the horse. "I'd dearly like to see this bold robber of yours before I go. He must be quite an enterprising rogue, from all you say."

The knot of people parted, and he moved his horse forward and looked down with curiosity at the heap of dusty rags below him.

Feeling the crowd draw back from him, Stephen raised his head a little to see why he had been given this respite. He saw his attackers still there, but no longer so close, and, right beside him, the hooves and legs of a horse. His eyes moved upwards and he saw that it was a lively bay, well groomed and finely caparisoned. He raised himself painfully a little higher, leaning on his two hands, and looked up at its rider, a slim young man with fair hair and expensive, fashionable clothes, who was looking with grave amusement down at him. As Stephen glanced up, the young man smiled. For a moment their eyes met, then the stranger raised one thin eyebrow and inquired conversationally, "What did you really steal?"

"A loaf of bread."

The young man chuckled. "What a sad disappointment! I'd hoped to see some truly desperate character." Then he added, "But perhaps you are indeed desperate?"

"Yes, sir. I think I am." Stephen tried to stand up, but got no further than his hands and knees. His whole body ached and his head was swimming. He gave up his attempt, sat down in the street and put his head into his hands.

"This should pay for a number of loaves." A shower of silver halfpennies fell amongst the crowd, causing an undignified scramble.

Stephen's head cleared a little and he was aware that the stranger had dismounted and was standing beside him.

"Do you think any bones are broken?"

"I . . . I'm not sure."

"Well, try to stand up and we'll soon find out." One slim, gloved hand at the end of a delicate wrist was held out to him. He took hold of it with both of his and found himself drawn, in one quick movement, to his feet, feeling astonishment that there should be such strength in so slender an arm.

They stood together in the street, Stephen still panting a little and finding it difficult to hold himself upright; though there seemed to be no bones broken, after all.

The stranger, with his horse's reins looped over his left arm, held Stephen's elbow lightly with his right hand, ready to grip firmly should Stephen show signs of falling. While Stephen recovered himself, the young man studied him out of a pair of gay but shrewd hazel eyes and noted the refined features, the beautiful but over-sensitive mouth, the blue-grey eyes set wide apart: no common thief he decided. Rather a most uncommon one.

Something warm and wet tickled Stephen's cheek and he put up his free hand to brush it away and then saw that it was blood.

"Does that hurt you much?"

"Not much."

"You'll not fall down if I let go of you?"

"I think not." Stephen was a little doubtful even though he was certainly feeling steadier and his legs were beginning to seem more reliable.

The young man took his supporting hand from Stephen's arm and moving aside the hair above Stephen's temple, examined the source of the blood. The skin had been split by a glancing blow from a stick. "It seems to me," he said cheerfully, "that there's more blood than wound. How are you feeling now?"

"Much better, thank you."

"Then I think that food is the next thing to be considered. Is your home in this town?"

"No, sir."

"Then we'd best find somewhere more private to have our breakfast. At the moment," he glanced about him at the gaping crowd, one eyebrow raised amusedly, "at the moment we seem to be providing a spectacle for the honest citizens of this town. Do you think you can walk a little way? Or would you rather ride?"

"I can walk, sir – I think."

"No doubt a wise choice. If you are going to fall down, you'll have that less far to drop. So let's be off, shall we? By the way, I am Pagan Latourelle, knight, from Worcestershire, and this" – he waved a hand in the direction of the older man – "is my servant Humphrey. What is your name?"

"Stephen d–" He stopped himself just in time. "Stephen," he repeated with finality.

Sir Pagan gave no sign that he had noticed Stephen's reticence. "Let's go, shall we?" he said pleasantly.

They set off slowly, Sir Pagan leading his horse and Stephen holding tightly to its stirrup; Humphrey, with the charger and the pack-horse, riding behind. Sir Pagan chatted easily about nothing in particular as they went along. He was an amusing and tireless talker, as Stephen was soon to discover. Later, he was to prove himself a good listener as well: but that was still to come. The crowd followed them for some of the way, growing ever thinner as the hope of further halfpence lessened; and by the time the street ran into the marketplace, with the parish church to one side of it, there were only a few children left with them, and one ever hopeful old man. Beside the church three hobbled cows and a horse grazed in the churchyard. They stopped there, Humphrey tethered the four horses to the gateway and Sir Pagan sent him off to buy hot pies and ale, while he and Stephen waited.

The two of them sat down on the grass near the church wall, in the sun. Stephen, whose legs were still weak, was glad to be off them. Sir Pagan talked on, though Stephen was hearing only about one word in three. At one point Sir Pagan spoke jestingly about something or other – ten seconds afterwards Stephen could not have told what it was that had been said, but at the moment it seemed to him very amusing. He smiled and then began to laugh, and having once begun he could not stop; and then suddenly he found that he was not laughing any longer but crying instead. He put his hands over his face and rested his head on his drawn-up knees and wept helplessly, shaken by deep sobs.

When it was finished, Stephen was left wondering how it had ever happened, and feeling rather foolish. He wiped his face with his hands and his sleeves and glanced sideways at Sir Pagan to see how he had taken it.

Sir Pagan was regarding him with friendly sympathy. He smiled. "Feeling better?"

"Yes, thank you." Stephen looked away again. "I'm sorry. I cannot think what came over me. You said something funny and I wanted to laugh, but somehow I wept instead."

"A hardly complimentary manner in which to receive a jest. How lucky for me that I'm not more conceited, or I should be feeling properly set down by such discouraging criticism." Sir Pagan looked across the churchyard. "Ah, here comes Humphrey with the pies."

Humphrey had brought three pies and a leather bottle of ale. While Stephen ate and drank – and never had any meal tasted better – Sir Pagan left him to himself and went to speak with Humphrey, instructing him to open the baggage and bring out a cloak. Stephen had just finished the last crumb of the third pie when Sir Pagan strolled back to him, and they shared what was left of the ale.

"You told me," said Sir Pagan, "that you did not live in this town. Where, then, do you live? For I'd like to see you safely home before I go on my way."

"I do not live anywhere. I have run away." The second he had said that, Stephen regretted it. He hastened to make amends for his honesty. "I'm an apprentice. I've run away from my master."

Sir Pagan received this calmly, as though running away were something one did every day. "You are an apprentice, are you? To what trade?"

For a moment this had Stephen at a loss. He looked about him for inspiration, saw the horses at the church gate and said, "My master was – is – a saddler."

Sir Pagan gave a quick, unnoticed glance at Stephen's hands as he said approvingly, "A most useful and necessary trade. But one, I presume, which you did not find to your liking? Well, I cannot say that I blame you. I do not think that

I'd have cared to be apprenticed to a saddler myself." He was silent for a minute or two and then he asked, "Have you plans as to what you are going to do now? Are you making for any particular place?" This time he spoke in French, and Stephen, noticing nothing, fell into the trap.

Relieved that his lie had apparently been accepted, and glad to be able to get back to the truth, he replied in French, "I've made no plans as yet, sir, and I do not know this part of the country." He looked inquiringly at Sir Pagan. "Perhaps you'd be good enough to tell me something about it, sir. It would be a help to me."

Sir Pagan gave no sign of being aware that Stephen had betrayed himself by both understanding and using quite naturally that language always used at court and by the nobility and gentry; but, still in French, he began to speak of the various towns near by, and of the condition of the roads in Berkshire, and other matters likely to interest a traveller; while Stephen listened and asked occasional questions.

Then Sir Pagan said casually, "We are on our way home to Lower Avonden, in Worcestershire, from a tournament near Reading. If you are not making for anywhere in particular why do you not travel with us for a little way? It's always safer to travel in company, and besides, from time to time, Humphrey and I – we eat, you know." He paused and gave Stephen a sideways glance, eyebrow raised, eyes twinkling, and chuckled infectiously, so that Stephen found himself smiling back at him.

"Come with us," Sir Pagan went on, "until you have decided where you wish to go. It would relieve my mind to have you under my eye. I'd not like to think of your stealing loaves in every town through which you pass. That sort of thing can lead to trouble, as you've already found."

This was an opportunity not to be missed. Not to have to worry about food for a few days was undreamed of good fortune. Stephen accepted the offer with gratitude; though at the same time wishing that it had not been necessary to lie to such a kindly young man.

As soon as Humphrey had rejoined them after returning the bottle to the ale-house, they set off, Stephen wearing a green cloak belonging to Sir Pagan and mounted on the bay, while Sir Pagan rode his charger. They spent that night in the guest house of an abbey near Newbury and Stephen was able to enjoy a hot bath in a wooden tub and a bed to sleep on. He awoke in the morning feeling more hopeful than he had felt since leaving Richley. Surely, he thought, his luck was changing and things were now beginning to improve.

After breakfast they set out again, Stephen in a pair of Sir Pagan's hose and a smart blue tunic. Although Sir Pagan was no taller than anyone else, and he was certainly not fat, they were not a particularly good fit; but Sir Pagan said cheerfully, "It need not be for long. We'll be passing through Oxford on our way, and we may as well stop there a day or two and have a tailor make you some clothes."

TWELVE

Sir Pagan's kindness had very soon begun to make Stephen feel guilty about deceiving him; and on the third morning, as they were making ready to resume their journey, Stephen – against his better judgement, but unable to resist any longer – said impetuously, "Before we go, may I speak to you, sir?"

Sir Pagan, arranging the long liripipe of his head-gear into a bunch of folds on the top of his head according to the latest fashion, until it resembled a cross between the turban of a Saracen and the comb of a cock, said, "Of course. What is it?" and paused expectantly.

126

Not looking at him, but plunging into the words before he should have time to regret them, Stephen said, "You've been kind to me and I ought to have told you this before. I lied to you. My name is Stephen de Beauville, and I'm not an apprentice." He stopped short and waited nervously to be taken to task.

But Sir Pagan said composedly, "I'm glad that you've decided to tell me. It was beginning to be difficult to remember that you believed I thought you were a runaway saddler's apprentice."

"Then you knew that I had lied?" Stephen was astonished that Sir Pagan should not disapprovingly have mentioned his suspicions before.

"Of course I knew. But if you chose not to trust me, that was your right. It's very wise not to trust strangers. But," here Sir Pagan stopped to smile, "I do beg of you, another time, to remember that a saddler's apprentice is unlikely to speak French."

"I never thought of that, sir," Stephen admitted ruefully.

"The next time such an occasion arises, you must be on your guard," warned Sir Pagan with mock gravity. "By the way," he added, "you said de Beauville. Are you kinsman to old Greavesby?"

"He's my father."

"I've met him once or twice at court. He seemed to me as bristling and as fierce as the boar on his own arms. I'm not surprised you ran away from him."

Stephen smiled at this disrespectful but not unapt description of Earl Robert. "It was not my father from whom I ran away, sir, but from a monastery. He wanted me to be a monk."

"Great heavens! I should hope you would run away from such a fate as that. For myself, I think I'd almost rather be apprenticed to a saddler." Sir Pagan returned to his inter-

rupted dressing, adjusted the very end of the liripipe to hang
over his shoulder and said, "Well, I suppose we'd better go.
Humphrey will think we are never coming."

Thus easily were Stephen's transgressions dismissed,
and he went out with Sir Pagan to where Humphrey and the
horses waited for them with a heart lighter than it had been
for very many months.

THIRTEEN

Stephen enjoyed the leisurely journey into Worcestershire.
Sir Pagan was a cheerful, pleasant companion, and Stephen
was soon quite at ease in his company. He was some nine
or ten years older than Stephen, but treated him like an only
slightly younger brother – yet far from the manner in which
Stephen's own brothers would have treated him – taking it
as the most natural thing in the world that he should show
Stephen both kindness and generosity, and cutting short
with promptness all Stephen's attempts to thank him. A few
weeks later, when Stephen was once again to try and speak
of his gratitude, he was to say, "Nonsense. I like you, Stephen, so I'm only being self-indulgent. One cannot be kind
to people one likes. One can only be kind to one's enemies
or to strangers or to those unattractive folk for whom one
feels Christian charity." Yet, in truth, Sir Pagan was kind –
though this was no virtue in him, but rather only a natural
inclination.

Sir Paine Latourelle – or Pagan, as he called himself, preferring the Latin form of his name – though possessing no
wide lands, was a comparatively rich man, being far better
off than most mere knights. He held a small estate in Worcestershire directly from the crown; and his father having died
while he was still a child, he had grown up in the court of
his royal overlord, where he had served as page and squire.

Amusing and witty, a skilful jouster and a fine horseman, he was always welcome at court; and though he was himself not one of their adherents, he was on good terms with the Despensers' party, which was still high in favour with the King.

Stephen soon found that though Sir Pagan's outward manner might be gay and careless, underneath the apparent superficiality he was as shrewd as anyone – Sir Pagan was indeed no one's fool. He might spend long minutes each day making choice of what to wear, as though he considered clothes of the first importance; and he could contrive, even at the end of a hard day's journeying, still to look as elegant and unruffled as when he had set out; but, as Stephen was to discover one day, when on a lonely stretch of road three mounted highway robbers attacked them, he could handle a sword with rapid efficiency and most deadly consequence, as the robbers learnt to their cost.

In appearance he was pleasing rather than handsome. After the French fashion he wore no beard, and though his nose might have been considered a shade too long and his mouth a shade too wide, his hazel eyes were beautiful and always sparkling merrily, and the smooth, well-combed hair that hung almost to his shoulders, with its ends carefully curled, was the colour of ripe corn and might well have been the envy of many a vain young woman.

At Greavesby, Stephen had always heard so much ill spoken of the King that it seemed strange to him to hear Sir Pagan praise his royal lord, whom he liked and even admired. "He is a fine, tall man and very strong. I know of no better judge of a horse or a hound. And if he chooses to dig ditches, play the farrier and thatch roofs, in a manner more fitted to a farmer than a king, that's his concern and he does no harm by it. He is good-natured, easy-going, generous, and loyal to his friends – and what more can one ask of a man?" He might have added, but did not, that King Edward the Second was so easy-going that he spent as little time as possible in meddling in affairs of state, was generous to the degree of giving away his own crown jewels and his wife's family treasures to a friend, and would carry his loyalty to the point where he endangered not only his throne, but his life as well. Yet to Sir Pagan, himself kind-hearted, extravagant and a good friend, none of this mattered.

He told Stephen many entertaining stories of the gay, carefree life at court: about the plays and the music and the merrymaking; about the King's white greyhounds, and his Welsh harriers which – or so the King himself swore – could discover a hare sleeping and were cared for and trained by little fierce Welshmen who gabbled away together in their own outlandish language; and about the King's magnificent horses which he so much loved – Sir Pagan's own fine chestnut charger had been sired by one of the King's stallions, and he was justly proud of it.

By the time that they reached Worcestershire, Stephen and Sir Pagan were on excellent terms and there was little formality between them. All talk of Stephen's journeying with Sir Pagan only while he made up his mind as to where he wished to go, had days since been abandoned; and without there having been a mention of it on either side, it was tacitly understood that Stephen would not only go to Lower Avonden, but stay there as long as he cared to.

Without realizing it, Stephen had found his knight.

FOURTEEN

They came to Lower Avonden on a sunny early autumn afternoon as the shadows were lengthening, riding down the gentle slope of the valley where the manor lay near the River Avon; so that Stephen's first sight of the house – standing encircled by its stout stone wall, its field strips about it, the village with its cottages of wattle and plaster and its stone-built church to one side and the water-meadows and the river to the other – Stephen's first sight of it was an almost enchanted one, seen in a genial glow of golden light: golden walls of warm Cotswold stone and a tawny, lichen-covered roof, golden stubble in the fields, the faint yellowing of the willow-trees on the river-banks, scarlet hawthorn berries and laden apple-trees, and the sun gilding the whole long, twisting ribbon of water. To Stephen it seemed compact and kindly and infinitely welcoming, so unlike the huge grey castle of Greavesby which perched like a proud, unyielding eagle on its rocky crag.

Riding beside Sir Pagan along the track that led to its gates, at that point where the track bent and the house first came into view in the distance, Stephen was struck by its beauty and loved it instantly. Because of the bend in the path, they had both caught sight of it suddenly and in the same moment; and though to Stephen it had been a surprise, while for its master it had been an expected and awaited prospect, it was a scene that reached to both their hearts.

At the same second they turned and looked at one another and each knew what the other was feeling; though Stephen said nothing and Sir Pagan, after a moment, only remarked lightly, "Welcome to Lower Avonden. I shall be glad to see my supper."

FIFTEEN

Though each day's acquaintance had increased Stephen's liking for Sir Pagan, and though he found him in no way intimidating or repressing, he had so far told him very little about himself. He had mentioned neither his family's opinion of himself nor his own ambition to prove his family wrong; and Sir Pagan, lacking this intelligence, would naturally assume, Stephen supposed, both that he had received at least some training in arms and that he was as bold and spirited as any other fifteen-year-old of his rank. Some day, he knew, Sir Pagan would have to learn the truth about both these facts, and he was not looking forward to that day. And since the more he was with Sir Pagan, the more he found to like about him, so the worse it seemed to him to go on – as he considered it – deceiving him. Sir Pagan might have proved himself both kind and understanding, and he might appear tolerant of the failings and faults of others; but would he feel so ready to be indulgent when he found out he had offered his protection to the misfit of the de Beauville family, a despised and disregarded coward?

It was with the thought of making trial of Sir Pagan's probable reaction to the truth about himself, that he had dared to tell him, rather tentatively, one day while they were still on their way to Worcestershire, about his former fear of dogs; for, shameful as this fear might have been, it did not show him in too bad a light, since he had conquered it.

"Dogs?" Sir Pagan had broken in on Stephen's faltering narration to remark. "That's an unusual thing to be afraid of – and cursedly inconvenient, I should think, since the creatures are everywhere – but then all men are afraid of something: God, death, hell, the plague, the Devil, or a nagging wife." He had then smiled with mock ruefulness. "I do not mind admitting it to you, I myself am lamentably afraid of growing old. Toothless, hairless – possibly even witless – with shaking shanks, tottering around on a stick, unable even to mount a horse. Dear heavens! What a fate! May the Lord preserve me from it." He had then light-heartedly laughed at himself, before going on to ask, "But tell me, are you still afraid of dogs? For I've seen no sign of it."

Encouraged by Sir Pagan's undeprecating acceptance of his weakness, Stephen had told him about Amile – right to the very end of the story. Hearing the tremor in Stephen's voice as he had come to the close of his recital, and realizing that sympathy might well have been fatal to his careful self-control, Sir Pagan had only said quietly, "You know, Stephen, you did the right thing. One must never desert a friend." And he had stretched out a hand and laid it briefly on Stephen's shoulder in a faint pressure of understanding, before turning to talk of other things.

Stephen had been greatly heartened by Sir Pagan's reception of his account of a weakness overcome, yet so far he had dared tell him no more of the discreditable truth. But soon after they had reached Lower Avonden, one evening sitting in the solar beside a blazing fire which crackled and sparked on the hearth below the carved and painted chimney-piece that was ornamented with Sir Pagan's coat of arms, a tall, slim golden tower on a field of green, Sir Pagan broke a comfortable silence to ask, "What made old Greavesby decide that you should be a monk? Are you unnaturally and monstrously learned, or did you at some time show misleading signs of undue piety?"

Stephen sat very still. It had come, the question he had been dreading, and at a time when he had least expected it. He hesitated, trying to bring himself to answer, wishing that he could have been spared the question a little longer. Lower Avonden was a good place to be in and Sir Pagan was kind to him: would he still be kind when he knew the truth? Or, almost worse than unkindness, would he be pitying? But because he both admired and respected Sir Pagan and was growing to be so fond of him, it never entered Stephen's mind to lie to him. He replied at last in that flat, unemotional voice that was with him always a sign of the deepest emotion, and not looking at Sir Pagan but staring into the fire: "He said that I was fitted for nothing else because . . . because I was . . . " – it was very hard to say it – "because I was a coward." It was out now and spoken and nothing could take it back; and he waited for scorn or condemnation or whatever would come. But let it not be pity, dear God, he pleaded. Let it not be pity.

He had not long to wait. Sir Pagan asked almost immediately, "And is he right? Are you a coward?" in the tone of voice in which one might inquire: "Do you like venison? – or raisins?" or, "What colour are your eyes?"

Stephen looked from the fire to his hands and found that he was twisting his fingers together painfully. "Yes, I suppose so," he almost whispered.

Still in the same tone, Sir Pagan asked, "Would you like to be really brave?"

"Of course!"

"Then in that case you are fortunate in being a coward," said Sir Pagan with cheerful conviction. "Only a coward can ever be truly brave."

Stephen was startled into turning his head to look straight at Sir Pagan. "What do you mean?"

"Why, what I said. One's valour is in proportion to one's fear. The man who is always entirely unafraid can never be brave. He has nothing to be brave about. One can only show real courage if one is afraid. The coward, therefore, being afraid of nearly everything, is alone capable of the highest courage."

The paradox was too much for Stephen. He stared incredulously at Sir Pagan. Sir Pagan was smiling, but he had spoken quite seriously: he was not making a jest of Stephen in any way.

"Think it over quietly by yourself sometime," he suggested, "and you will see what I mean." He considered Stephen searchingly for a while in silence, and then he asked – for him, almost earnestly, "You're quite sure, are you, that you really do not want to be a monk?"

Stephen's reply was immediate. "Quite sure. I am going to be a knight. I decided that long ago."

Sir Pagan lifted an eyebrow. "On the first day that someone told you that you'd never make a knight, I suppose?"

"Yes, just about then. How did you guess?"

Sir Pagan smiled but did not answer. Instead he asked another question. "How much do you know of being a knight?"

Stephen looked away again. "Nothing."

"Then it's time you began to learn, is it not? Fortunately, I am competent to help you. Shall we start tomorrow?"

Sir Pagan, who took life lightly and had always found it good, was shaken by the look which Stephen turned on him. Like a sinner in hell who sees the gates of heaven opening for him, was the fanciful comparison that sprang into his mind. To cover a sudden and most unwonted embarrassment, he bent his head and reached for a dried apricot from the silver dish beside him and tossed it towards Stephen before taking another for himself. "Here, we'll need to feed ourselves up if we're to begin tilting in the morning," he said.

SIXTEEN

From then began what were to be for Stephen the happiest days of all his life. Years after, he was to achieve content – that most valuable of conditions, which is to happiness as a homely, serviceable lantern is to the stars – but at this time he was happy. He was so happy that he deplored the ending of each day, even though he knew the morrow was to be its replica. He had achieved one half of all that he had ever desired: a home where he was cherished; a loved and trusted friend in whom, without fear of ridicule or censure, he might confide; and the chance to learn proficiency in arms. And the other half: knighthood and the adulation of his – by then no longer doubting – family, would, he was convinced, be his in due course.

Stephen had no secrets from Sir Pagan. Once he had told him what he considered to be the worst about himself, there seemed no point in holding back anything else; and for the first time in his life he enjoyed the luxury of being able to talk endlessly about himself to a sympathetic and dependable listener. He told Sir Pagan of everything: of all his doubts and difficulties, of his family and his life at Greavesby, of the months at Richley and Brother Ernulf and his drawing lessons; and to all Sir Pagan listened with interested and affectionate understanding, until Stephen had talked himself out and, having made up an arrears of being of importance to someone, could turn his attention to his present circumstances.

Nowhere could Sir Pagan have found a more eager pupil or one more insatiable in his quest for fighting skill; and Stephen, though he was to grow tall enough, was always, like Sir Pagan, to be slim and small-boned, and was therefore fortunate to have as teacher one who had a mastery of many clever tricks and feints by which a quicker, more slightly-built man might, both mounted and on foot, outwit a heavier, slower adversary. Stephen was altogether lucky in his instructor, since Sir Pagan, for all his air of inconsequential levity, had remarkable aptitude for feats of arms. Just how well versed he was, Stephen, by reason of his own previous ignorance and inexperience, was not to know until much later, when he had other standards by which to judge Sir Pagan's ability.

But there were other things than fighting skill – things no less valuable – which Stephen learnt from Sir Pagan in the happy days at Lower Avonden: self-respect, self-reliance and a large measure of self-confidence. For it was Sir Pagan – soon himself convinced by Stephen's conduct – who finally persuaded him of the untruth of the legend of his cowardice; though it took a long time for Stephen to accept that his family had been mistaken and that Sir Pagan was not merely being considerate of his feelings and indulgent towards his faults.

Stephen was never to lose his reserve, never quite to overcome his sensitive fear of being slighted, he was never to show at his best in lively, boisterous company – one cannot, after all, change one's temperament at will; or, as Sir Pagan put it, "One is as God has made one, and it's small use trying to be someone else." But, thanks to Sir Pagan, where he was not able to conquer an inconvenient trait, Stephen acquired the ability and the assurance to conceal it successfully.

Yet another thing Stephen learnt: Sir Pagan taught him how to laugh – and not only at things outside himself, but at himself as well. So that never again, even in his saddest and darkest moments, was he to fall a victim to self-pity.

And so for Stephen, living ecstatically from hour to hour, the full days passed, one after the other, bearing with them nothing but the promise of further such days of happiness to come; and not once in all that time did Stephen, who had at Richley found such solace in it, set pen to parchment or draw a single line – and not because he lacked the opportunity at Lower Avonden; for, had he felt the need to express himself in drawing, he would only have had to say so, and Sir Pagan, in no way conventional, would have been ready to indulge his whim and provide him with the means; no doubt merely remarking, as he remarked of some of the King's pursuits, "An odd way of passing the time, but it harms no one." No, Stephen did not draw because he neither wished nor needed to: he was too happy in the realities of life to need to substitute for them the consoling make-believe of art.

SEVENTEEN

The autumn of 1324 passed into winter and then Stephen spent his first spring in Worcestershire. In March – while at Lower Avonden the valiant little daffodils thrust up their pointed tips through the cold earth and the dead branches of the willows along the river's edge began to glow with life – at this time Queen Isabella sailed for France to try to settle personally the differences between King Edward and her brother, Charles the Fourth of France, over the possession of Gascony: an event that was to prove of grave import for England.

Throughout that summer of 1325 Stephen's happiness was unabated. He had been at Lower Avonden for exactly one year when a friend of Sir Pagan, travelling north, stayed two nights at the manor and told them the news from London. The Queen had been successful in her mission in France, and the King's eldest son, the thirteen-year-old Lord Edward of Windsor, had sailed to join her at the French court, that he might do homage, on his father's behalf, for Gascony.

The visitor seemed pleased at this outcome of the wrangling over England's possessions in France, but Sir Pagan said thoughtfully, "I wonder if it was wise to let the boy go to the Queen. She hates the Despensers, and may use him to their hurt."

"What hurt could she do to them, when they have the favour of our lord the King?" scoffed his friend. "Besides, it was they who persuaded the King to let Lord Edward go."

"She can do no hurt, I trust," said Sir Pagan. "But I do not like it."

Sir Pagan's forebodings proved not unfounded. Once she had the heir to the throne of England with her in France, the queen refused either to bring him home again or to let him return alone, in spite of the King's demands. At the French court, too, she was openly in the company of the traitor, Sir Roger Mortimer, whose life the King, after his victory at Boroughbridge, had generously and rashly spared. Some two years before, Mortimer had escaped from the Tower of London and made his way to France; and he and the Queen now plotted together as to how best they might use their control of the young prince against his father and the Despensers.

The spring of 1326 was one of fear in London and the south, for many expected the Queen to persuade her brother to invade England. But in the end he refused her his help, and she was forced to look elsewhere for troops. In the September of that year, with a small army of men of Hainault, Queen Isabella and Roger Mortimer and certain other malcontents set sail and landed on the Suffolk coast. Within ten days they had been joined by a number of the lords of England who saw in this rebellion an opportunity to rid themselves of the hated Despensers. The King, unable to raise the city in his defence, left London for the west, pursued by the Queen's army. Amongst those who made haste from the north to support Isabella when she reached Gloucester, were Stephen's father and his three eldest brothers.

As soon as the news reached Worcestershire, Sir Pagan, who had for some weeks been expecting the worst, set off at once to join the King; and Stephen went with him. They were both prepared for fighting: but there was no battle. The rebels marched to Bristol, where the elder Despenser, unable to muster any troops, was forced to surrender and was immediately put to death. The King, with too few supporters to attempt resistance, parted from most of his remaining adherents and fled into Wales with only the younger Despenser and his still faithful chancellor, and one or two clerks. There, on November the sixteenth, they were captured at Neath; the King was taken to Kenilworth Castle in the custody of his cousin Henry, brother of the executed Earl of Lancaster, and the rebellion was over – and successful. The King's cause had been lost through the unpopularity of his favourites.

The more important of those still loyal to the King were hunted out and put to death. Sir Pagan, wandering about on the borders of Wales, said to Stephen, "They'll hardly consider me worth taking and killing, but for all that, we'd best not return home yet. The Queen might just possibly decide to send to Avonden for me." But when he heard that the King was in Kenilworth, he made his way there, in search of the latest news.

After two attempts to make him resign the crown in favour of the Lord Edward had failed, the King was told by a deputation from Parliament that unless he gave way to their demands, the people of England would repudiate not only him but also his two sons and offer the throne to one not of royal blood – since Roger Mortimer had been behind the sending of the deputation, no doubt it was he himself who was meant. To save the crown for the son who was afterwards to deal so leniently with his father's murderers, with tears the King resigned it, to be known henceforth as plain Sir Edward of Caernarvon. The fourteen-year-old prince began his reign at the end of January with his father still a prisoner in Kenilworth Castle, and Henry of Lancaster and the Queen – and through her, Mortimer – as regents.

"Earl Henry is a far better man than his brother," said Sir Pagan. "I do not think that he will treat our lord the King too ill. There's nothing we can do here, so we may as well go home. At Avonden my friends will know where to find me, if I am needed. And if the Queen and Mortimer – may the devil take them both – overreach themselves, they may well lose their present popularity, and then will come our chance to aid the King."

So Sir Pagan and Stephen returned to Lower Avonden. Even the troubled state of the country and the misfortunes of the King could not entirely spoil Stephen's own personal happiness; besides, Sir Pagan was optimistic that Roger Mortimer, who had already obtained possession of his father's confiscated estates and was now looking covetously at the vast Despenser lands, would quickly make himself detested by his greed; and that he and the Queen, whose guilty love for one another had already caused a scandal at the French court, would soon outrage opinion in England also.

EIGHTEEN

In April the King was moved to more secure confinement in Berkeley Castle in Gloucestershire, under other guardians. As the year advanced, discontent against the true rulers of England – the Queen and Roger Mortimer – increased; in the southwest especially there was great unrest, with plotting, spies and rumours everywhere, and little bands of desperate men who sought, whether for their own advantage or for his sake, to restore Edward of Caernarvon.

One such group gathered about Sir Pagan at Lower Avonden, and there was another a few miles away at Upper Avonden, in the castle of a neighbour, a baron who had no reason to love Mortimer. When the time was ripe and their strength sufficient, Sir Pagan and Baron Geoffrey had determined to combine their forces and make an attack on Berkeley Castle. Meanwhile, they collected arms, horses and supporters, drawing as little attention to themselves as possible.

Lower Avonden became more full of men than it could hold, and all living at Sir Pagan's expense, so that he had never had greater need of his wealth. A very few of these men were, like Sir Pagan himself, moved by loyalty to the deposed King; some were of that type of born rebel who will always be against whoever is in power; others were lawless rogues, a few such as will attach themselves to every cause; a number were frankly mercenaries caring for no cause and with no interests but their own gain; but most of them were, like Baron Geoffrey, enemies – for one reason or another – to Roger Mortimer and his party and cared only to see his downfall.

With Stephen, and to his own few, trusted friends who shared his loyalty to Edward of Caernarvon, Sir Pagan would shrug his shoulders, raise an eyebrow and say, "We must be thankful for all support, and not despise any help God sends us – even though we may wish He saw fit to be a little more discriminating!"

Throughout the weeks he remained calm, good humoured and apparently hopeful; and he was in daily communication with Baron Geoffrey. And then, in July, came the startling tidings that there had been a successful attack on Berkeley Castle and the King was rescued. There had been other, similar rumours before, so at first no more reliance was placed on this latest report than on the others. But then word came to Baron Geoffrey from a spy of his in the castle itself, that the King was indeed gone from Berkeley after an attack by a strong band of men led by two brothers named Dunhead – one of them a Dominican friar – and that although the castle had been plundered and the King released, the fiction was being kept up by his gaolers that he was still at Berkeley in their charge.

This was indeed good news. It was succeeded, naturally, by countless rumours: the King was still with the Dunheads, the King had been recaptured, the King was at the head of an army of Welshmen, the King was at Corfe Castle, at Bristol, at Bridgwater. And then the King was in fact retaken; and by the time the true intelligence of this reached Lower Avonden, he should have long been back in his prison at Berkeley, but that, having denied he had ever been gone from there, his captors had to replace him covertly and discreetly.

Yet a band of well-armed men, acting as if with authority and guarding a prisoner, cannot move far about the countryside without attracting attention, and the news that Thomas of Berkeley's men had indeed recaptured the King and were bound for home, with word of the route they seemed to be taking, reached Sir Pagan and Baron Geoffrey independently from two trusted spies.

So far, they had between them had insufficient support to make possible an attack on a well-defended castle, but an ambush along a road was a different matter. After a hurried council of war, they set out from Upper and Lower Avonden, guided by the spies: Sir Pagan with some forty men and Baron Geoffrey with twice that number.

For a scheme carried out on the spur of the moment, it was not ill-contrived. They made for that stretch of road between Evesham and Tewkesbury where it had been considered an ambush could best take place. They rode hard and on arrival at the highway were told by the man sent on ahead as a scout, that since he had been there, the King and his guards had not come by.

Hastily they set the ambush. To one side of the road the land was level, with trees and undergrowth affording cover for any number of men, some fifty yards in. On this side Baron Geoffrey concealed his larger band. On the other side the ground sloped down to the road for a short distance; here there was less cover, but the benefit of a downward attack and a better sight of the enemy approaching. On this slope Sir Pagan and his forty men lay hidden. Because of his superior view, it was arranged that he should give the signal to attack by one blast on a horn, and that as soon as his men broke cover and the King's captors turned to meet them, Baron Geoffrey would give the word to his men and they would charge from their side.

Waiting, it was impossible not to feel anxious, and Stephen, beside Sir Pagan, wondered how it would end. There was a good chance of success. According to the spies, the enemy was no more than a hundred and fifty strong – while they were a hundred and twenty and had the advantage of surprise. Sir Pagan himself still seemed calm and confident enough; and though he said little while they waited, he turned and smiled encouragingly at Stephen now and then, when he could take his eyes from the road.

They had not been waiting long, however, when a peasant pushing a handcart piled with hay came in sight – one of Baron Geoffrey's grooms who had been sent to watch, higher up the road. As he passed the waiting men, he stopped, sat down by the roadside and took off one shoe, shook out an imaginary stone, put the shoe on again and went on his way: this was the agreed signal that the enemy was no more than half a mile away.

He was hardly out of sight before two outriders cantered up the road, glancing from side to side. One of them reined in his horse and scanned the wooded slope on Sir Pagan's side. The sun was shining directly in his eyes as he looked up. Sir Pagan had ordered every man to keep his weapons covered lest the glint of metal through the foliage should betray them; but for all that, the man's scrutiny was unnerving to Stephen, and he prayed silently that he would not take it into his head to ride up the hill.

Both men, however, seemed satisfied, and after a minute or two cantered on.

"Incompetent rogues – God bless them!" whispered Sir Pagan to Stephen with a quiet chuckle.

Soon after them came the prisoner's escort – far larger than had been expected. Sir Pagan, rapidly counting heads, calculated it to be at least three hundred strong: the men-at-arms must have been doubled since the spies' report of their numbers. Obviously they were expecting trouble. Looking down on them as they approached, a compact body of men, well armed and bristling with lances, it was possible to see their prisoner in their midst, a tall, plainly dressed man on a tired, old, stumbling hack which went with drooping head. It was this glimpse of his King that roused Sir Pagan. For the first time since he had known him, Stephen saw him angered. He heard him murmur, "The devils. The cruel devils. He who so much loves horses." And then Sir Pagan began to curse them, quietly and intensely, under his breath, his hands in their chainmail gauntlets clenched about his horse's reins.

Then the enemy was directly below them and Sir Pagan turned to Stephen who held the horn. "Now!" Stephen, feeling sick with apprehension, blew a single blast, and then his horse was thrusting a way down the slope through the bushes and undergrowth beside Sir Pagan's.

There was not one of Sir Pagan's men – for whatever reason they had chosen to support his cause – who did not follow him down into the road; but, had they known what was to happen, it is probable that there would have been only Stephen to go with him.

For, although the sight of the doubled numbers against them had troubled, but not deterred, Sir Pagan, a hazard that might leave loyalty and personal regard undaunted is likely to prove fatal to a more ignoble sentiment. Baron Geoffrey, inspired only by his loathing of Roger Mortimer and resentment of his rule, had no mind to lose his life in gratifying hatred. He gave no signal to attack. He had made up his mind to this as soon as he had seen the strength of the enemy. If he could have warned Sir Pagan of his intention, he would have done so; and, to do him justice, he fully expected Sir Pagan to have decided, as he had, that the undertaking was too dangerous, and he was almost as surprised by the assault as were those who were its object.

The endeavour was doomed and hopeless from the start. Though the attackers gave as good an account of themselves as they might, they were overwhelmed long before they had fought even a few yards towards the King. Stephen engaged a man-at-arms, sent him sprawling in the roadway, managed to unhorse a knight and then turned his attention to another who had set upon him; but, tightly hemmed in as they were between the slope behind them and the almost impenetrable wall of armed men before them, there was little room for effective encounter. He fought on doggedly and not unskilfully, so long as Sir Pagan fought; and Sir Pagan fought until he had seen almost all those who remained of his band – all those of the forty who had not fled as soon as they realized that they were not to be joined by Baron Geoffrey's men – dead or down; then, calling to the others to fly, he forced a way to Stephen, grabbed at his horse's bridle and said, "Come quickly. There's no use in staying longer."

They thrust their way from amongst the enemy, together with three others: a knight and his son from Wales and one of the mercenaries, a man named Ranulf, a tall, loose-limbed fellow, with a huge hooked nose and an old puckered scar that ran down one cheek. As they broke through the horsemen who tried to prevent their escape, Sir Pagan struck at a knight in his path and the man exclaimed in astonishment, "Why, Pagan Latourelle!" as he struck back. But before either could do the other any hurt, they were separated by the stress of fighting all about them.

Together the five survivors won free at last and galloped wildly down the road and off into the woodland, pursued by a number of knights and men-at-arms. Baron Geoffrey and his men had fled, without striking one blow, over ten minutes before.

About half an hour later, in more open country, the fugitives seemed to have, temporarily, evaded their pursuers – at least, there was no one of them in sight. They paused to look back the way that they had come and to decide what they should do. The knight and his son were for returning to Wales, and left them, to ride towards the River Severn; but Ranulf, though inclined to be angrily disparaging about what he considered the mismanagement of the ambush, ended by shrugging his shoulders and deciding for the time being to remain with Sir Pagan and Stephen; and the three of them rode on across country in a roughly southwesterly direction and finally came on to a road, where the going was easier for their by now exhausted horses.

NINETEEN

Towards dusk, somewhere between Tewkesbury and Gloucester they halted in their flight near the outskirts of a village.

"We seem to have shaken them off," said Sir Pagan, "which is as well, for the horses must rest."

Ranulf objected, saying that it was unwise, and when Sir Pagan said, "Go on alone and leave us, if you think your horse can carry you," Ranulf exclaimed angrily, "It's all very well for you. You are a friend of his." He jerked his thumb over his shoulder in the direction from which they had come. "I never saw him in my life before today and I do not care what becomes of him. I'm only in this for the price of a new hauberk."

"Which you have had already," said Sir Pagan without heat.

"Only half of it!" Ranulf retorted.

"The other half was to be given only if we were successful. You agreed to that." Sir Pagan added with a slight laugh
which somehow managed to rob the insult of its sting,
"There had to be some way of keeping you mercenaries on
our side."

Ranulf continued to grumble half-heartedly; but being
as tired as the other two, he finally gave way, and they found
a deserted herdsman's hut in which they could spend the
night. Ranulf looked about it disgustedly. "We shall need
food," he said.

Sir Pagan took a coin from the purse which he had
brought with him in case, after a successful rescue, there
had been anyone who had insisted upon being paid off immediately. "Here, see if there is anything to be bought in the
village."

Ranulf's eyes narrowed a little at the sight of the money,
though neither of the others noticed; and it was in slightly
better spirits that he set off on foot for the village, a mile or
so away. While he was gone, Stephen and Sir Pagan watered
the horses from a stream near by, rubbed them down and
set them to graze on the grass around the hut. It was almost
dark when Ranulf returned with two loaves and some
cheese. As they ate, they made plans for the morning.

"So far," said Sir Pagan, "they seem to have lost track of
us, but we cannot be sure of that. Unfortunately, I was recognized, so they know for whom they are looking." He added
with, for him, unusual bitterness, "He used to be one of
Arundel's men, too. His master died for our lord the King.
Can no one in England now stay loyal for more than half
a year?"

After having eaten, Ranulf seemed to have recovered his
temper completely and he agreed to Sir Pagan's suggestion
that they should make for Gloucester.

148

"It's near enough to Berkeley for us to hear the rumours from there," said Sir Pagan. "And it may be a good spot in which to find a few willing helpers for our next attempt. We'll need far more men next time, because I doubt if we'll have another such chance as today's. Next time we may well have to attack the castle."

Ranulf did not raise a murmur at this high flying, and Sir Pagan went on, "But we can think about all that later. Meanwhile, we must lie low, and Gloucester is as good a place as any in which to do that. It is a town which is large enough to boast an inn where one can lodge – the Golden Lion near the South Gate – and we shall have to put up at an inn. One can hardly stay longer than two nights at a religious house without arousing comment, and, anyway, innkeepers ask fewer questions than guest masters."

Again Ranulf made no objection. He yawned, stretched and said, "Now that that's settled, let's get some sleep. I'll take the last watch, I cannot keep awake a moment longer."

Though there was little room for them, they brought the three horses into the hut in case they should be seen and arouse the suspicions of any passer-by.

Sir Pagan said, "You take the first watch, Stephen, and then you can get an unbroken sleep."

Stephen tried to smile and speak lightly. "You forget. It would be no hardship to me. I'm used to being woken up for matins."

"That was a long time ago. Besides, I know you monks." Sir Pagan chuckled. "You sit in your stalls, mumbling paternosters and looking pious, and all the time you're fast asleep and dreaming. No thank you. You'd never notice even if we were surrounded by Mortimer and all his men, and all you'd say if you did wake up would be '*Deo gratias!*'"

Stephen wondered how Sir Pagan could contrive to jest even at a moment like this; and though he could not see Stephen's face in the darkness, Sir Pagan seemed to know how he was feeling, for he laid an arm across his shoulders and said, "Cheer up, Stephen. We may have failed, but we'll try again. And we have escaped with our lives when all those others – God rest their souls – are dead."

When Sir Pagan lay down to sleep, Ranulf was already snoring. Stephen stood outside the broken-down doorway of the hut and watched the roadway, every so often walking right around the hut. The moon was rising and the land looked very peaceful. Sir Pagan was right, he thought. They were still alive, the two of them, and together, and nothing else mattered. Not even the unfortunate King.

Sir Pagan relieved him long before his time. When Stephen protested, he said untruthfully, "I doubt if I could get to sleep again, so I might as well watch. Go and lie down."

Stephen was heavily asleep almost immediately he lay down on the hard, damp earth-floor of the hut, and he only woke for a moment when Sir Pagan, some two hours after midnight, roused Ranulf and lay down beside Stephen. "All well?" Stephen asked him.

"All well," he answered, "but it's growing chilly. It's nearing morning."

Stephen moved closer to him for warmth and Sir Pagan laid one mail-clad arm across him protectively, and then Stephen was asleep again at once.

The next thing he knew was the violent upheaval of his uncomfortable bed as Sir Pagan thrust him aside and snatched up his sword. Stephen heard voices, Sir Pagan's and Ranulf's, and the startled horses neighing and stamping. His first thought was that they had been taken by surprise. He sat up and groped for his weapons. It was dawn and a cold, white light was coming through the broken door. There was no one else in the hut beside himself and Sir Pagan and Ranulf. Ranulf was lying where he had been flung, his dagger in his hand, and Sir Pagan was standing over him with his drawn sword. The purse containing their funds was on the ground beside Ranulf.

"If you needed money badly enough to steal it, you should have asked me for some. I would have given it to you." Sir Pagan struck Ranulf with the flat of his sword. "Get up and take your horse and go."

Sullenly and furiously Ranulf rose. By this time Stephen was on his feet and armed and at Sir Pagan's side. Ranulf made no attempt to resist the two of them. They watched him saddle his horse in silence and take up his weapons. He led the horse out of the hut and they followed him. As he was mounting, Sir Pagan took a handful of coins from the purse and held it out to him. Take this, if you think you've been underpaid."

Glowering, Ranulf took the money and rode off in the direction of the village. The sun was just appearing on the horizon and the saffron sky in the east was beginning to be banded with gold.

"We, too, had better go soon," said Sir Pagan.

TWENTY

They entered Gloucester that afternoon by the North Gate and made straight for the Golden Lion near the South Gate, as arranged. The landlord provided them with a good meal and even better ale, and grateful hot water to wash in.

Late that evening, after dark, in the upper room of the inn, they found that there were five other guests to share the large bed with them. Three were merchants of varying degrees and the other two were master craftsmen. The five men, who had become acquainted over their supper, were continuing their talk as they prepared for the night by the light of two inadequate tapers.

Sir Pagan yawned and smiled at Stephen. "A real bed will be pleasant after last night, even if we have to share it with half the tradesmen of Gloucestershire."

Stephen knelt down and pulled off Sir Pagan's boots, while Sir Pagan dragged his tunic over his head. Hoping to pass as peaceable travellers, they had already hidden their weapons, their hauberks and the padded gambesons which they wore under them, wrapped up in their cloaks to look like baggage.

The sudden sound of loud voices in the inn-room below came to them through the floor boards. Sir Pagan, in shirt and hose, began to replace around him his belt with the purse for safety during the night. The voices below continued, and he said, "I hope they'll not keep up that carousing, or whatever it is, all night."

Footsteps creaked on the wooden steps which led up to the sleeping quarters, and the landlord's voice, agitated and loud, came to them above the other sounds, though slightly muffled by the door.

"This way, sir, this way. I assure you, this is an honest house."

"Dear saints! It sounds like genteel company, and a lot of it. Well, we were here first. They'll have to take the floor," said Sir Pagan.

The door opened and the landlord came in with a taper, obsequiously lighting the way for the ten or twelve men who followed him: a knight and a band of men-at-arms. Since four of them carried flaring torches, the landlord's poor taper was hardly necessary.

"Here you are, sir. These are all my guests tonight. I assure you, I am of good repute and well known in the town. Many people will vouch for me. This is a respectable house. I harbour no traitors."

The room seemed suddenly very brightly lit. The five tradesmen stopped their talking and drew away into the shadows nervously. Stephen stood very still and Sir Pagan made no other move than to feel with his foot for the bundle of their weapons and coats of mail which was lying on the floor beside the bed.

The knight stepped into the room. He was tall and thin, with a stiff, self-conscious manner. "In the name of our lord the King: which of you is the traitor, Paine Latourelle?"

No one answered. Sir Pagan very gently pushed the bundle under the bed with his foot.

"We know that he is here," said the knight – but he did not sound entirely convinced. "Now," he went on briskly, "which of you is he?" He motioned to one of the men-at-arms to go and stand in front of the small, shuttered window, and to another to bring a torch closer.

The men moved into the room; the one with the torch going from one to another of the guests, so that their faces could be seen quite clearly by his leader. When he came to Stephen, who was standing with Sir Pagan across the room from the door, on the farther side of the large bed, the knight said, "This Sir Paine has with him his squire, Stephen de Beauville. Bring that youth here."

The man-at-arms pushed Stephen across the room towards the knight, who looked closely at him.

"What is your name?"

Stephen could think of nothing but that his presence seemed about to prove a danger to Sir Pagan, and that it would therefore be best to deny acquaintance with him. He said as quickly as possible, "John of Warwick. I am travelling alone. I am a clerk. Do you want me to prove it?"

He was not given a chance to prove that he could read, for one of the merchants, eager to keep out of trouble, his voice high and trembling, said, "He's lying. He's not alone. He's with the fair young man."

"Is that true?"

"No. We met here for the first time tonight. I am John of Warwick, a clerk."

A third man-at-arms, who had moved to his side, suddenly grasped one of Stephen's wrists and twisted it behind his back. "Answer the truth," he growled in Stephen's ear. Taken by surprise, Stephen gave a gasp of pain.

Sir Pagan stepped forward and said sharply, "Take your hands off him. I am Pagan Latourelle." Carrying his tunic, he came round the end of the bed to stand on the same side as the knight and the rest of the men-at-arms. He seemed quite at ease.

The knight waved Stephen away and gave his attention to Sir Pagan. "I am here to arrest you on a charge of treason," he said stiffly. "You and your squire will accompany me now, if you please."

"Treason?" commented Sir Pagan, an eyebrow rising. "You surprise me. I had thought that it was those like you who were the traitors."

"Enough of this. Put on your clothes – or do you want me to take you as you are?"

"I might find it a little chilly." Sir Pagan unhurriedly put on his tunic and began to refasten his belt.

With some thought of reaching their weapons on the other side of the bed, Stephen began cautiously to move across the room past the bed's foot. The two men-at-arms beside him, one still holding his torch, did not try to prevent him, but they moved with him as though to keep an eye on him. There was no hope that he and Sir Pagan could win their way out against so many, Stephen thought. But with swords in their hands they could at least die together, fighting.

"You were expecting me to come to this place. How did you know I'd be here?" asked Sir Pagan easily – almost conversationally – as though he were questioning a guest as to how he had found the way to his house.

The knight in charge said, "There was a message brought by a lad from Norton that you would be here this evening or tomorrow."

"Who sent him?"

The knight shrugged his shoulders. "He could not say who sent him, only that a stranger had paid him to bring the message. We thought at first that he was lying, but questioning failed to shake his story. He was a very stupid lad – too stupid to be able to hold to a lie – so at last we believed him and let him return home."

"Then you never discovered who sent him?" Sir Pagan's questions were still casual.

"No." The knight gave a brief laugh. "But whoever he was, he did us a service, though I, for one, did not have much faith in this mysterious stranger's information. But I was, it seems, wrong." He looked his prisoner over with satisfaction.

Sir Pagan said slowly and clearly, "Beside myself there was only one person who knew that I proposed to lodge here tonight. Only one person could have betrayed me. And there he stands." Sir Pagan swung around and looked at Stephen. "There he stands," he repeated, shooting out one hand dramatically to point at him, "the only one I trusted with my plans."

Stephen was too shocked to make any protest. He could only stand watching Sir Pagan, horrified and wondering if their misfortunes had sent him mad. Sir Pagan gave him no time to recover.

"Now I know why it took you so long at Norton to buy food, and why a miserable loaf of bread and some rotting meat cost so much. You were looking for a messenger and it was on him you spent the money." He gave a harsh, mirthless laugh. "You paid for my betrayal with my own money. How you must have smiled behind my back. How clever you'll have considered yourself – but all the same, you dared give your name to no one in case your plot miscarried." His eyes narrowed as though he were remembering the events of the past two days. "Oh, I see it all now! You had to keep with me, to make sure I came to this place at the appointed time. When I spoke this morning of going instead to Tewkesbury, it was you who persuaded me not to." He exclaimed with bitterness, "To think that I so nearly defeated your aims!"

Sir Pagan paused for breath and the knight asked Stephen, "Is this true? Was it you sent that lad to us?"

Stephen found his voice at last. "No! No, I did not!"

"Liar!" shouted Sir Pagan. "Who else could it have been? Tell me that!"

Stephen opened his mouth to say, "Ranulf knew," but he never spoke the words, because Sir Pagan, taking by surprise the men-at-arms who now stood on either side of him, sprang across the room – leaping up on to the wide bed and down off it again in no more than three seconds – and flung himself upon Stephen, carrying him by the force and fury of his attack backwards beyond the reach of the two men who guarded him, to hurl him against the wall.

"Cursed traitor! After all that I have done for you!" He struck Stephen savagely across the face. Under his breath, urgently and rapidly, he said in French, "For the love of God, say that it was you!" Aloud, he almost screamed, "What did you hope to gain by betraying me? Answer me that!" He clutched at Stephen's throat as though he would have throttled him. Then there were men-at-arms behind him pulling him off Stephen and dragging him away, still cursing and reviling Stephen.

Stephen, eyes wide with horror, looked on speechlessly, one hand to his smarting cheek, the other at his bruised throat; his appalled indecision at the choice that was being forced on him, appearing not too unlike guilt.

His whole nature revolted from the part Sir Pagan was asking him to play. For the last months he had shared the risks and the dangers dared by the man he loved and admired and to whom he owed so much. Now that the worst had happened and Sir Pagan was taken, all Stephen wanted to do was to share his fate, to die by his side if it came to death – as it undoubtedly would. And now Sir Pagan, caring nothing for his own plight, was working to save Stephen's life. How could he bring himself to take the chance that was offered him, Stephen wondered. Yet it was what Sir Pagan wanted him to do, and love and gratitude demanded it of him.

The knight came over to Stephen. "Did you send us the message?" he asked. Stephen, still staring at Sir Pagan, ten feet away with his arms firmly held, never heard him and he had to repeat his question twice before Stephen turned to look at him dully.

"Did you betray him?" said the knight impatiently. "Yes or no?"

It was a terrible thing to ask of anyone, this thing that Sir Pagan was asking him to do; yet he owed it – and far more – to his friend. Stephen looked again at Sir Pagan, imploringly; only to see the appeal in Sir Pagan's own eyes, though his mouth was still fixed in an ugly sneer.

"What are you afraid of, Stephen?" he mocked, "See, they are holding me fast. I cannot get at you, so you might as well tell them the truth and earn their thanks."

This aspect of it had not before occurred to their captor. "That is so," he said to Stephen. "You can safely tell us the truth. We'll not let him hurt you now and he'll have little opportunity after today."

The room was unnaturally silent as everyone, guests, men-at-arms, the landlord and all alike, awaited Stephen's answer. Stephen himself never took his eyes from Sir Pagan. Though he should live to be a hundred or more, he would never be called upon to make a harder decision in all his life; and it seemed to him – as to Sir Pagan also – that he was taking a lifetime in making it. At last, still looking only at Sir Pagan, he said in a voice that no one would have known as his, "Yes. I did it," and he saw Sir Pagan's strained face relax in an expression of relief for one short moment before he had his emotions under control again. Love and gratitude had conquered.

"That settles that, then," said the knight and turned his back on Stephen.

Sir Pagan, making as though he were restraining his anger only with difficulty, said, with bitter hatred in his voice, "May the devil take you to burn in hell for ever, Stephen."

The knight said to his men, "There's nothing to keep us here any longer. Bring the prisoner and come."

One of the men-at-arms, who had been searching the room and had opened the bundle of weapons, now took it up to carry with him; and another, looking at Stephen, said to his leader, "Do we take the squire as well, sir?"

The knight hesitated, weighing the matter; then he gave Stephen a contemptuous glance. "What do we want with him? He's served his purpose, let him have his reward. He can go free."

Sir Pagan, as if the struggle with himself was now almost over and his natural optimism was being recovered, said lightly and tauntingly to Stephen, "What will you do now, Stephen? You can hardly go home. By the time you get there, I've no doubt that madam the Queen will have given Lower Avonden to one of her Roger's hangers-on." Smiling ironically, he remarked to the knight with now apparently almost completely restored good humour, "A boy I took out of the gutter to be my squire, and this is how he repays me."

The knight did not answer him save by a curt, "Let us go now, if you please," but his demeanour showed the sympathy he did not utter.

"Let me at least put on my boots," said Sir Pagan calmly. The men-at-arms having by now released their hold of him, he sat down on the bed to pull on the boots, ignoring his captors while he did so. When his boots were on, he asked, almost cheerfully, "Is this to be a hole and corner affair, a killing in the dark, or am I to be honoured by a show of justice?"

The knight said stiffly, "You will have all the justice which a traitor to our lord the King deserves."

"Your lord the King he is, perhaps, but he's not mine. My lord the King – God keep him safe – I shall be dying for: which is a pity when he has so great a need of friends." He went on calmly, as he stood and took up his surcoat, "Oh, I have nothing against the Lord Edward. He is the King's son and one day, please God, he will be a good ruler. But the regents" – his head disappeared into his surcoat and then reappeared – "the regents are another matter." The surcoat adjusted to his satisfaction, he dismissed the Queen and Mortimer with a careless wave of his hand and a ribald jest.

Two of the men-at-arms had laughed before they realized that his remark had been not only ribald but treasonable as well, and they hastily changed their guffaws into the angry growls of loyal subjects at the words of a traitor.

The knight frowned and bit his lip, but he only said, "We are wasting too much time. Landlord, lead the way and get your door unbolted for us."

The innkeeper made haste down the stairway with his taper, followed by several of the men-at-arms, and then the knight signed for Sir Pagan to go next.

About to set his foot on the first of the steps, Sir Pagan stopped as if on a sudden thought and turned back towards the room. He unfastened the purse from his belt. "I was forgetting. You'd best have this. I'll find no further use for it and my enemies are unlikely to pay you any more for your pains." He tossed the purse to land, clinking, at Stephen's feet and gave a disdainful laugh. "My sincere apologies, but I doubt very much if you'll find as many as thirty silver pence still left in it." He turned and went out through the door, followed by the remaining men-at-arms and the knight.

When they were gone, and all but the two poor tapers gone with them, movement and sound returned to the other patrons of the inn. Slowly they drew together in the comfortingly dim light, whispering, no longer fearful now that they knew the danger was nothing to touch them but, instead, agog with curiosity and speculation, glancing every now and then at Stephen, who was quite unaware of them.

He stood where he had been left, stunned and numbed by what had passed; and it was only by slow degrees that he came back to a realization of where he was and what he should have done. He should have followed to see where Sir Pagan was being taken. As though suddenly restored to life, he began to make hastily for the door. His foot struck against something. Looking down, he saw Sir Pagan's purse. It had been so like Sir Pagan, quick-witted as always, he thought, to find a way, not only of saving his life, but of warning him against returning to Lower Avonden and of giving him the remainder of their money. He picked up the purse and ran for the door, observed attentively and with interest by all in the room.

Downstairs the landlord and two or three other men were talking in low voices. They looked up as Stephen came headlong down the rickety steps into the room.

"Open the door for me!"

Without a word the landlord went to the door, unbolted it and stood aside, not even making mention of the unpaid reckoning. But one of the other men, as Stephen passed him, said, "Good night, Master Judas," and spat.

Stephen stepped through the door and stood in the shaft of yellow light that spilled out from the fire and the tapers within; then the light narrowed until it was cut off entirely as the door was closed, leaving the night so much the darker by contrast.

There was no sign of torchlight in either direction: the men-at-arms with their prisoner had long been out of sight; and with the sound of bolts being shot to behind him, Stephen stood in the darkness outside an inn in a strange town, looking up and down the street, holding Sir Pagan's purse in his hands.

TWENTY-ONE

Three days later, in Gloucester Castle, charged not very specifically with taking up arms against the King, Sir Pagan was granted the pretence of a brief trial; and at its end Paine Latourelle, knight, of Lower Avonden in the county of Worcestershire, was condemned to that death reserved for traitors and was taken back to his prison. There he was told that his execution would be on the following morning.

He laughed. "Our present rulers are indeed in a hurry to send us all to heaven. But the Lord Edward will not be a child for ever. One day, God willing, he'll be a man and catch up with them. And then it is they who'll find they were the traitors."

By then Stephen had discovered that Sir Pagan was being kept in the prison below the castle. Slowly and with difficulty, using their money, he had bribed his way past porters and guards as far as the castle gaoler himself. From him he learnt that Sir Pagan was to die in the morning.

"Why do you want to see him?" asked the gaoler suspiciously.

"I'm his squire."

"That's what I mean. I thought it was his squire who betrayed him."

Despair lending him inventiveness, Stephen said, "That's why I want to see him. I want to ask his forgiveness for what I did. He cursed me. I cannot live with his curse hanging over me. I must ask his pardon before it is too late. For God's sake let me see him."

"Let's see your money first."

Stephen offered him all the remaining coins.

"That's not very much for what you're asking me to do."

"Please!"

"I see no reason why I should put myself out to help a pair of traitors – for when all's said and done, you're no better than he is, even if you managed to wriggle out of your desserts – and for so little money." The man grumbled on; but all the same he finally took the purse and said, "Come back after I've had my dinner. I'll find it easier then and I'll see what I can do for you. Mind you, I make no promises, but come back just the same. Though," he added, "I doubt if he'll be all that pleased to see you, if I do manage to let you in to him."

Even after a good dinner the gaoler was still inclined to cavil, though he did not offer to return Stephen his money. But at last he said, "Very well, I'll do it. Though, as I've said already, I doubt if he'll be glad to see you. I know I'd not feel too kindly towards the one who'd betrayed me." He spat, then shrugged his shoulders. "But if you're so set on it, and since there's something in it for me . . . " After a moment he added warningly, "Yet I'll not be able to give you long with him."

Stephen followed him down a spiral stairway, across two rooms and into a narrow passageway, dimly lighted. The walls were damp and dripping and the whole place stank. The gaoler stopped before one of the doors along the passage and turned his huge key in the lock. Pulling back the heavy bolts, he said, "You've not long, mind. I've no wish to take any risks for you. So say what you've got to say and do what you've got to do and get it all done quickly." He swung open the door and Stephen stepped into the small room.

It was even darker inside than the passageway had been, so that at first he did not see the figure standing against the wall to his left, under the one tiny, high-up window. Sir Pagan, his eyes used to the gloom, recognized him at once, and Stephen turned his head in the right direction only when the chains clanked with Sir Pagan's shocked recoil. "Stephen!" It was breath forced through clenched teeth, rather than his name.

"Now, you've not got long, remember. I'll be back to fetch you directly, so do not think you can take your time about it." As an afterthought, the gaoler added, "He's chained to the wall, so if you stay where you are, out of his reach, he'll not be able to do you any harm." He went out and closed the door behind him.

"Pagan!" Before the bolts were shot home, Stephen was across to the wall and their arms were about each other.

"God be praised! For a moment I thought that I'd failed after all, and you were a prisoner, too. How did you manage to persuade them to let you in?"

"With the money you left with me. I told them I wanted to ask your forgiveness for betraying you."

Sir Pagan spoke as lightly as ever. "How I wish I'd been there to hear you ape the penitent. We're a clever pair, are we not?"

Stephen's hands clutched at Sir Pagan's arms as he broke in, "Is it true that . . . ? Will they really . . . ? Oh, dear God, have mercy! Will it really be tomorrow?"

"So I've been told."

"So soon!" Stephen's voice was a cry of pain. "If there were only more time – a few days even – I could have tried to get help. Someone of importance to speak for you . . . Oh, why have we not longer!"

"Even had we a month or more, Stephen, I do not think that there's anything which you could do. All my powerful friends fell with the King. They could do nothing for me now."

They clung to one another in silence for a few moments; then Sir Pagan said, "I'm sorry that I'll not be able to make another attempt to free our lord the King. I think he is in great danger now. They will not dare to let him live much longer."

There was so much that Stephen wanted to say, and so little time in which to say it; and he could not even begin, he could only remember that after today he would never speak to Sir Pagan again.

"Stephen, when . . . when you are alone, what will you do?"

"Does it matter what I do? I wish I might die with you."

"No! At least let me know that I saved your life. I have to leave you without money, a home or friends; do you think I find that easy? But at least you have your life. By the way," Sir Pagan gave a little chuckle, "I hope you admired my play-acting. I considered it rather good, myself."

Into Sir Pagan's shoulder, Stephen said, "I have nothing left to live for, I would rather die."

"You are young, you have everything to live for." Sir Pagan gripped Stephen by the shoulders and held him away from him for a moment, so that Stephen was forced to raise his head. "And if you care for nothing else, then you can at least live for my sake, because I wanted it. This may be unbearable now, Stephen, but one day it will seem no more than a sad story to remember: a sad story which happened in another place, to someone else." He drew Stephen close to him again. "And you have no need to pity me." He was managing to speak almost gaily. "I am lucky. My teeth will never fall out, my hair will never grow grey, or my hands become too feeble to hold a sword. I'll never be called upon to face the thing I fear." Stephen knew from the way his voice sounded that he was smiling.

After a little while, Sir Pagan said, "Listen to me, Stephen, this is important." He moved his hands to grasp Stephen's two arms above the elbows. "Do not let other people make your decisions for you. Live your life as you want to live it, not as others think you should. Be yourself; and whatever you want to do, do it with all your heart and soul." His thin fingers bit into Stephen's flesh. "Above all, always be yourself. Do not be afraid to do what you want to do, so long as it hurts no one else. We are each of us as God made us, and if God has seen fit to make you in an uncommon mould, be brave enough to be different. Promise me that, Stephen."

"I promise."

They said no more for a moment or two: then Stephen, at a sudden thought, looked up and said, "Have they let you see a priest?"

"There was one here earlier today. A well-fed little fellow, speaking most singingly through his nose. I'd not be surprised if his name were Hewel or Llewellyn – one finds them everywhere these days, the Welsh – but I dare say that God will care nothing for the way he speaks. He says he will come to me again. Oh, never fear, he'll pray me into the next world all right, I do not doubt – but I'd rather have your prayers."

"You will. Always. Always."

"And take care of yourself, Stephen. Keep away from anyone who is likely to displease the regents. And do not stay in Gloucester. They might have second thoughts about you, even yet. Go today, the moment you are outside this place."

"No. I could not leave you before . . . before it's over. I shall be there tomorrow."

There was a moment's silence and then Sir Pagan said quietly, "I wish you would not. But I'll not pretend that it will not be a comfort – and a help – to know that you are there."

They both heard the muffled sound of the bolts as they were drawn back on the other side of the door. Stephen's arms tightened about Sir Pagan as though he could never let go; but Sir Pagan, almost brutally, broke his grip, saying urgently, "God keep you always, Stephen," kissed him, and quickly thrust him away from him. Stephen staggered backwards into the middle of the little room, and when the door swung open a second later, he was standing where the gaoler had left him.

"Time's up. Out you come. Quickly now! So far all's well, but I've no wish to be caught at the last moment." He took hold of Stephen's arm and pulled him outside into the passageway and closed and locked the door. "Hurry, lad, hurry." He pushed Stephen before him along the passage towards daylight and freedom.

TWENTY-TWO

Very early the next morning Stephen was at the place of execution outside the town. A space had been roped off and was guarded by men-at-arms. Stephen could see those things which waited for Sir Pagan: the crossbeam and the ladder, and one of the executioner's assistants blowing up hot coals in a brazier with his bellows.

How he had lived through the last four days, where – if at all – he had eaten and slept, Stephen could not have said. Yet somehow he had found the strength and the courage to endure and to do what had to be done; and now, for this last ordeal of all, he would need, he knew, even greater strength and courage. After that, there would be no more strength needed, no more courage – his world would have come to an end.

There was quite a large crowd – for a criminal whose trial had been so secret and whose offence so vague – and all in a holiday mood. Even in such times of upheaval and fear, it was not every day that one could watch a traitor die, and the crowd was prepared to enjoy itself. Water-vendors, pedlars and sweetmeat-sellers went about hawking their wares, always thankful for an opportunity to sell a little more than usual.

It was those on the outskirts of the crowd who first saw the arrival of the company of men-at-arms from the castle. "Here he comes!" they yelled. Their shouts were taken up by others who could as yet see nothing, and a shudder of delighted expectation ran through the crowd.

Stephen, in the very front, near the barriers, where the crowd was thickest, between a young woman who carried in her arms the infant she had been unable to find anyone at home to mind, and two men who had, until this moment, been discussing the weather and the season's crops, and jostled forward from behind by half a dozen other eager folk, felt his throat go dry and his legs go weak; so that, for a moment, he feared that he might fall. He had no need for concern: however weak his legs, so long as the crowd stayed still, there was no danger of his falling; he would be held up firmly by the press of bodies all about him.

God have mercy on him, he thought. God have mercy on him. He tried to remember a suitable prayer from his days at Richley; but none he knew seemed fitted to an occasion such as this. All he could recollect was the hundred and twenty-ninth Psalm, and he repeated to himself under his breath, fervently: *De profundis clamavi ad te, Domine; Domine, exaudi vocem meam. Fiant aures tuae intendentes in vocem deprecationis meae. Si iniquitates observaveris, Domine, Domine, quis sustinebit?* until the moment when he was able to see Sir Pagan, and then the Latin died away on his lips.

At the end of this, his last journey – short as it had been – Sir Pagan was for once unable to look elegant and unruffled. Dragged through the streets behind a broken-down old nag and pelted with filth by the onlookers, with his clothes torn and stained, his hair uncombed and uncurled, and a four days' stubble of yellow beard, he looked very unlike the carefree, extravagant, rich young courtier that so many people – today so far away – remembered. But, whatever his condition, his wonted, irrepressible air of cheerfulness had not deserted him. Even if he walked slowly and stiffly, once he was standing still he looked about him with detached amusement at the crowd and, as always, raised an eyebrow.

A woman behind Stephen, with pleased anticipation, exclaimed, "Why, by all the saints, he's quite young, poor wretch!"

Sir Pagan's careless glance moved over the folk who had come to enjoy his death – and then he saw Stephen. His smile was immediate and unforced, gay, affectionate and encouraging. But Stephen, his jaws as immovable as stone, could not smile back, try as he might. He saw Sir Pagan's smile begin to fade in distress at the sight of his own unconcealable sorrow, and then he managed – somehow – to part his stiff lips and twist his set mouth into the appearance of a smile, to which Sir Pagan instantly responded, almost happily. Then for a while the burly form of the executioner blocked out Stephen's view of him.

But a little later, from the rungs of the ladder, before he was thrust off, Sir Pagan, with the rope around his neck, managed to turn his head for one last, quick smile at Stephen. And Stephen, the full horror of what was about to happen flooding over him, began to pray desperately: Dear God in heaven, let him die before the rope is cut. Let him die now. Then he remembered. Why should He listen to me? I refused to be a monk and serve Him. Into his distracted mind came the wild thought of a bargain with heaven. I cheated you, Lord. I ran away from Richley. Let him die now and I'll go back and be a monk. I'll go back if you let him die quickly. Oh, God, have mercy. Holy Virgin, help him. Let him be dead before he is cut down.

Stephen's prayer was not answered. Sir Pagan was still alive and conscious when the rope was cut. He was still alive all through the long minutes that followed; minutes during which Stephen stood watching, the side of his left hand wedged between his teeth – without even knowing what he was doing he had bitten to the bone and was to carry the scars for the rest of his life. Sir Pagan was still alive until the moment when the executioner hacked off his head and death mercifully ended the torture.

When the man, his arms red almost to the elbows, held up Sir Pagan's head by the bright hair to show it to the people, Stephen lost his senses; but, supported by the tightly packed crowd, he remained on his feet.

Ten minutes later, the spectacle once over, the folk began to disperse. The shifting mass surged and swayed, Stephen fell and the crowd closed over him. He would undoubtedly have been trampled to death very soon, had not a certain fat woman, clinging to her husband's arm so that she should not be separated from him, found Stephen beneath her feet. For all that she had come to gape at an execution, she was a kindly soul, and insisted that her grumbling husband should help her carry Stephen to safety. Together they heaved him to his feet, and supporting him between them and thrusting and elbowing a way, they dragged him to the outskirts of the crowd, the fat woman sweating and panting, and her husband cursing her soft-heartedness. They finally propped Stephen, still senseless, against the wall of an ale-house a short way off, and left him there.

One of the ale-wife's customers – the execution had brought her much welcome additional trade – told her about Stephen and she came out to have a look for herself. Hands on her hips, she considered him, then she shrugged her broad shoulders. "He's no one I've ever seen before. I suppose he was hurt in the crowd. His clothes must have been fine enough once, though they're in a sorry state now. Oh well, he's doing no harm there, whoever he is, so he might as well stay till he recovers." She went in again to pour her ale and bully her overworked serving-wench.

Stephen came to himself for a little while later in the day. He stared uncomprehendingly about him, began to remember a little; and then kindly darkness came down upon him once more.

He was still there, propped against the ale-house wall, when the ale-wife came to the door and looked out before locking up for the night. She saw him in the shadows and went to him, shaking his shoulder to rouse him. "Come along, lad. You cannot sit there all night." As she released his shoulder, Stephen fell sideways. An unpleasing thought came into the woman's head. "Bring a light, Doll," she shouted. She knelt down and thrust one large, work-roughened hand down the neck of Stephen's tunic. He was still warm and she could feel his heart-beats. By the time the yawning girl had come with a taper, the ale-wife had heaved herself to her feet again. She jerked her thumb at Stephen. "Help me carry him in. We cannot leave him out here all night. A plague on him! Why he had to choose my house to fall sick outside, the good Lord only knows."

THOMAS

Part Three

ONE

Stephen, once again alone in the world, lay ill at the ale-house for days – how many, he was never to know. For most of that time he remained like a log on the heap of straw in the storeroom where they had put him on that first night. He had periods of consciousness, but afterwards he remembered nothing of them and had no idea of how long he had been there when he finally came to himself sufficiently to notice his surroundings. To begin with, he was too weak to move, but slowly he regained the strength to walk; slowly, too, to his numbed mind returned the remembrance of what had happened; though for a long while yet he seemed to be living in a dream – a grey half-world of unwaking where the reality that lived and breathed about him was no more real than the mercifully blurred memories and images which drifted through his mind. And thus, gradually, in a fashion his faculties returned, with one exception: he was unable to speak.

With his air of dull apathy, his torpid, uncomprehending stare and his lack of speech, the ale-wife took him for some poor, dumb half-wit who had come to watch the execution and been injured in the crowd. She pointed him out to her customers as a sort of curiosity of her house; and spoke of him in his presence as though he could not understand her – as indeed, for much of the time, half-unaware of others as he was, he could not. For all her loud vulgarity, the close-fisted care with which she measured her ale – so that she should not pour a drop more than she had been paid for – and her incessant nagging and browbeating of the sluttish Doll, she had the compassion to allow Stephen to remain with her even after he would have been capable of walking away. She let him sleep in the storeroom, gave him just enough food each day, and set him various tasks to do that he might earn his meagre keep: cutting wood and fetching water, shifting barrels of ale and, later, running errands for her in the town. The stronger he got, the more she expected from him.

In time his strength came back in full; and, more slowly and haltingly, his power of speech; though he spoke little and never of himself – he told her only that his name was Stephen and that he came from Worcestershire – and he still seemed to her to be half-witted. When not at work, he would sit on a stool in a corner of the ale-house room, staring silently before him, seemingly oblivious of what went on around him and lost in some distant region of his own, so that it often needed a blow or a shout in his ear to bring him back to the present. Day after day passed for him in this manner. He had neither the will nor the inclination to do otherwise than as he did, and he knew and cared nothing for what went on about him.

In the outside world, unknown to Stephen, events moved on. In September, when word of a Welsh plot to rescue him came to the ears of the apprehensive regents, unhappy Edward of Caernarvon, on the orders of his wife and Roger Mortimer, was murdered in Berkeley Castle. It was given out that the King's father had died from natural causes – he who had been so strong and fit – but few people were deceived. Three months later he was buried magnificently in the church of Gloucester Abbey with a great show of gilt and grief – golden lions painted on his hearse and the four Evangelists in effigy upon it, leopards emblazoned on the trappings of the horses, an escort of knights all in new robes, and no expense spared to do him honour now that he was conveniently dead. And for chief mourners, the widowed Isabella with her husband's embalmed heart in a vase of silver, and his eldest son – now king indeed. Stephen heard this pomp and splendour talked of in the ale-house; but he did not associate it with the prisoner on the road to Tewkesbury.

Throughout the winter Stephen remained at the ale-house; and he might have stayed there for many winters more, sunk in a stupor of grief, but for a fortunate chance in the spring.

He had been sent on an errand early one May morning, and was walking unheeding through a narrow street, quite unmindful of the sound of horses' hooves that grew ever nearer behind him, and unmindful even of the shouts of warning directed at him. Then he felt a hand on his shoulder, pulling him rapidly and roughly aside. "Stupid fool! Do you know no better than to get in the way of the gentry? They'd ride any of us down and care nothing for it, as quick as you could spit."

Stephen murmured his thanks to the man who had dragged him aside to stand against a house wall, out of the path of the oncoming horses; and then he was aware of the horsemen whose passing filled the narrow way between the buildings on either side. He looked at them uncaring; and the richly dressed man with an air of authority, who rode amongst his followers, caught a casual glimpse of his up-turned face and then, suddenly frowning, turned his head and stared.

Stephen never even noticed that he had been remarked, but a few moments later, as he was going on his way, he found beside him a smart squire who said disdainfully, "My lord wants to speak with you."

The cavalcade had stopped in the market-place and Stephen was led up to the horse of the man who had sent for him. About fifty years of age, tall and dark, with blue-grey eyes like Stephen's own, he was no one whom Stephen had ever seen before. He was still frowning, but in puzzlement, not anger, and his eyes were not unkindly. He observed Stephen in silence for some moments before asking, "What is your name?"

Stephen stared back at him without comprehension for a few seconds, then, as though it were a name which he had had to dredge up from some forgotten corner of his mind, he said, "Stephen de Beauville, sir."

The man nodded thoughtfully, and then he smiled. "I was certain that I could not be mistaken," he said, speaking now in French. "You are Greavesby's son, are you not? The child of my sister Orabel. My little sister Orabel." His voice grew strangely gentle. "I do not mind telling you that I wept for a whole day when I heard that she had died, though I had not seen her for three years and more. She was always my favourite sister." His manner became brisker. "You have been ill, have you not?"

Stephen nodded.

"I thought as much. She was never very strong and it gives you a look of her. You are very like her at this moment, for all your rags." Then his voice dropped so that only Stephen might catch what he said. "I'd heard rumours that my nephew had been in Gloucester and associated with a knight, one Paine Latourelle, who had made an attempt to . . . to gain possession of the person of the father of our lord the King. I have, of course, kept these rumours to myself. Are they true?"

The question had been worded with either tact or caution, which, Stephen did not know – or care. He only said, "Yes, sir."

"What have you been doing since that time?"

"There was a woman in an ale-house, she took me in. I am still with her."

If his uncle was surprised, he concealed it well. "I see. I think perhaps you'd do best to come with me. Guy, whom I sent to fetch you, is soon to be knighted and I shall need another squire. It seems to me that my own nephew would be a good choice. I'll inform your father, of course. You can come with me now. We have passed two nights with the Grey Friars near the South Gate and we are on our way towards Cirencester. I have a small manor, Longbourne, east of that town."

"But what of the ale-wife, sir? She sent me with a message. She has been good to me, I cannot leave her without a word."

"Tell me her direction and I'll send her a purse of money." He turned to order someone to find a horse for Stephen; and Stephen, for whom events were moving too fast, dazedly did everything he was told.

They rode out of Gloucester and on to Ermine Street by the East Gate. It was the gate above which Sir Pagan's head, on a stake, had been set; but this Stephen did not know.

When they stopped for the night, Bartholomew Boncourt, Earl of Manningfield, sent for his nephew and spoke to him alone. He questioned Stephen about his escape from Richley Abbey and his reason for it; then he said, "There's no necessity for Orabel's son to be a monk, if he'd rather not, whatever Greavesby says. He did wrong to force you against your inclination, and I'd not scruple to tell him so. Well, you have no need to fret about it any longer; I'll handle your father if he raises objections."

He talked of several other matters; but he did not mention Sir Pagan until the very end, when he said, "We shall not speak of it again after today, but I have heard that it was you who betrayed this man, Paine Latourelle." He paused and looked at Stephen, who said nothing. "As I said, we shall not speak of it again, but I'd like to say this to you now: I do not believe that little Orabel's son would ever betray the man he served."

He dismissed Stephen with a gesture of his hand, and Stephen was suddenly intensely grateful to him, yet all he could say was, "Thank you, sir."

TWO

It took time for Stephen to adjust himself to life in a great household once again. But his circumstances in his uncle's Berkshire castle of Manningfield were very different from his case in Greavesby. Apart from the facts that he was now older and wiser, and that, unlike his father, his uncle took an interest in his well-being and progress, as soon as his first bewilderment was over and the initial adjustments made, the measure of assurance and self-respect which Stephen had acquired at Lower Avonden stood him in good stead. Sir Pagan might be dead, and his head, over Gloucester's East Gate, little more then a dried skull to which a few strands of corn-gold hair still clung, but the good he had done for Stephen remained. Fate might have taken Sir Pagan from him, but nothing was ever to take from Stephen Sir Pagan's gifts. With the state of his mind as it had been when his uncle had discovered him, he might well have become the timid, diffident and easily repressible Stephen of his boyhood years at Greavesby for at least a period – if not forever – but it did not work out that way. For, in those early, difficult days, first at his uncle's manor of Longbourne, near Cirencester, and then in Manningfield Castle, Stephen had only the memory of Sir Pagan to cling to, and he desired above all not to disgrace that memory. It was Sir Pagan who had given him self-confidence – therefore he must be confident; it was Sir Pagan who had woken his courage – therefore he must be brave; and it was Sir Pagan who had taught him his skill at arms – therefore he must not fall below others in that respect.

His fellow-squires received Stephen in the way they would have received any untried newcomer amongst them, with hectoring and ungraciousness and, at moments, downright cruelty – tempered a little, perhaps, in Stephen's case by the fact that he was the nephew of their lord. But it was for Sir Pagan's sake and not for his own, that Stephen stood up to them and did not take their testing meekly. As a result, they thought no worse of him than they would have thought of any youth of tougher fibre and far less sensibility than Stephen; and when they were to discover his skill at arms, they were to think considerably better. Stephen was as surprised as they at the standard of his ability, for it was only now that he learnt, by the disclosure of his own superiority, just how great had been Sir Pagan's skill. His first dagger fight with another of the squires, prompted by a particularly offensive practical joke, taught both Stephen and the others a great deal about him; a lesson that was completed when, two days later, he joined them on the tilting-ground. After that, they felt for him, not only respect, but a degree of liking to which Stephen – still shut up within himself, and reserved as he was always to be – was never able to respond. Yet, for all his sensitive reticence which the others were unable to understand, Stephen was accepted by them and, no longer an untried newcomer, was molested no more.

It was at this time, at Manningfield, that Stephen discovered that, though skilled, he actually cared very little for tilting and jousting and feats of arms. He put this down to the fact that he no longer had Sir Pagan to practise with: he was wrong, but it was some time – several years, indeed – before he was to realize this.

The two squires whose duties it fell to Stephen's lot mainly to share were Renier, one year older than Stephen, and Gerald, who was a year younger. Renier was cheerful and high-spirited and given to falling in love – and out again – regularly every other month. He was never without a lady to sigh about and to praise – whether she was some countess glimpsed from afar at a tournament or a pretty kitchen-wench whom he could kiss in a corner of the great hall.

Gerald, an earnest youth, was a great admirer of Stephen's fighting skill, and was always begging to be shown this or that trick with sword or lance. Since Stephen was always ready to be obliging, Gerald was permanently grateful to him. With his admiration and his gratitude – both offerings until then foreign to Stephen – Gerald must unwittingly have done Stephen a great deal of good.

Accepted, respected, admired and even liked in spite of his unresponsiveness, Stephen was neither happy nor unhappy in his uncle's service. His past was over and done with, his present was busy and useful, and his future – that future towards which he had always aimed – was marked out and undisputed. But in a teeming household where at least a score of those with whom he was in daily contact were agreeable and dependable, Stephen, mainly by reason of his temperament, was still alone. However much he might share their lives and their pursuits and appear on the surface to conform, he was still walled off from his companions by his unsurmountable reserve. And just as no other hound could ever have been to him what Amile had been; so, for all the wide choice of friends about him, there was no one who could fill, even partially, Sir Pagan's place in his heart.

His days were always fully occupied, either with his duties or with joining in the pleasures and pastimes of his companions; but there were times – and they continually increased – when, either because some sight or colour had reminded him, or because his mood was pensive or melancholy, or else for no reason at all, he would remember Brother Ernulf and his Gospels; and, contemplating in his mind's eye the old monk at his task of creating beauty, Stephen would wonder what the Gospels looked like at that very moment and if they were nearing completion; and he would long to hold once again a pen or a paintbrush in his hand and to be allowed, albeit grudgingly, to furnish a few square inches in the least important corner of a page; and then, having enriched that empty space to the best of his ability, with his task achieved and seeming not too ill, to have felt again an infinitesimal fraction of that upsurge of joy which, he sometimes thought, God Himself must have felt on the sixth day of the creation: *viditque Deus cuncta quae fecerat; et erant valde bona.*

Et erant valde bona: would he ever be able to think that of anything he ever did, Stephen wondered.

Naturally, Stephen never spoke to anyone of this, for there was no one to whom he would have dreamt of unburdening himself and confessing such incongruous longings; nor did he ever attempt to draw, because such practices were unfitted to one who would, in not too long a time, become a full-fledged knight.

THREE

In the summer of 1329, when Stephen was nineteen, part of Earl Bartholomew's household passed through Reading on its way back from one of his hunting-lodges. Clattering through the streets of the town beside Renier, Stephen suddenly saw a horseman passing them, going in the opposite direction. The man looked with interest at the Earl's train, but he did not notice Stephen. Stephen caught his breath. There was no mistaking that large eagle-nose and the long, puckered scar down the left cheek. Ranulf was already past when Stephen recovered from his shock of surprise. Without a word to Renier he urged his horse on to catch up with his uncle. Breathlessly he said, "Please, sir, will you give me leave to absent myself on a private matter for an hour or two?" He added, "It's very important and urgent."

Stephen never asked for favours nor presumed in any way upon their relationship, and so the Earl, looking at his disturbed, white face, only hesitated for a moment before saying, "Very well. I shall expect to see you at Manningfield tomorrow morning."

Thanking his uncle, Stephen turned his horse's head and made off along the street, back the way they had come, calling out to Renier as he passed only that he had the Earl's permission to be absent that afternoon.

"Great heavens!" exclaimed Renier jovially. "You are in a hurry." He turned round in the saddle to shout after Stephen "If it's a pretty girl you've seen, I hope you catch her! But you might have taken me along with you."

By the time Stephen reached the end of the Earl's cavalcade and could see clearly along the street, Ranulf was nowhere in sight. He asked the man who rode on one of the horses pulling the last of the baggage wagons, if he had seen a horseman with a scar.

"He went past a moment or two ago, sir. I noticed the scar and wondered how he had come by it."

Stephen continued on his way, keeping a careful watch out. He asked several people if they had seen Ranulf and – though most of them had been too taken up with their own affairs or had still been gaping after the Manningfield baggage-wagons and pack-horses to have noticed a single unimportant horseman – thanks to Ranulf's scar, there were three who were able to tell him that he was going in the right direction. And at last one of two women, who were gossiping outside a shop-door, said to him, "He went into the tavern across the way."

Outside the tavern a boy was walking two horses. One of them would be Ranulf's, Stephen supposed, though he had not at the time noticed the colour of Ranulf's horse.

He dismounted, gave the reins to the boy and made his way to the door of the tavern. On the threshold he paused. He had never, before this very hour, given any thought to avenging Sir Pagan because he had never expected to see Ranulf again. Revenge was a compulsion which had sprung into his mind at the sight of Ranulf. And now, at the very moment of encountering his quarry, he paused to consider that he might never come out of the tavern again. He turned back to the boy. "If I do not come to claim my horse, take it to the Earl at Manningfield Castle and tell him how you came by it. He will reward you."

The boy looked at Stephen, goggling and open-mouthed, as though he did not understand a word; but a moment later he was grabbing, alertly enough, the silver halfpenny which Stephen gave him. "The Earl at Manningfield and a reward," he said, and grinned. "I'll remember, sir."

Stephen entered the tavern. There were altogether seven men already in the room, gathered about a long table. Five of them seemed to be acquainted and were sitting in a group, talking to the tavernkeeper, who was holding a jar of wine balanced on one shoulder, while he stood, hand on hip, giving his loud opinion upon something or other. The sixth customer sat a little apart from the others, yet conscious of their talk, as though he were a stranger, but ready to join in, confidently, at any moment. It was Ranulf, drinking wine.

As Stephen walked towards the table, his eyes on Ranulf, the tavernkeeper saw him and broke off what he was saying. At one glance he took in Stephen's clothes and bearing and hurried forward. "Good day, young sir. What can I do for you? A cup of my best Rhenish? Or something even better, perhaps? I have an excellent vernage from Tuscany, fit for a king."

"I want nothing, thank you." Stephen went past him to stand opposite Ranulf at the farther end of the table. Ranulf was tipping his cup to his lips for a long draught of wine. As he righted his head and set down the cup, he saw Stephen. For a moment he showed startled surprise, then he grinned. "By all the saints! Stephen! Well met."

Stephen, very pale, his hands gripping the side of the tabletop, said slowly and very quietly, "Yes, I, too, think it is well met."

Still grinning, Ranulf said, "Why, you must be one of the last people I expected to see in a tavern in Reading – or in a tavern anywhere else, for that matter. I thought that you had been – " He broke off and his grin spread as he glanced at the other customers and the tavernkeeper who were watching and listening to the two of them with frank curiosity. "Well, since we are not alone, perhaps I'd better say: I thought that you were dead."

Still quietly, Stephen said, "No, I . . . survived. But that was no thanks to you."

"Your survival deserves a celebration." There was a half-sneer now behind Ranulf's grin. "You must drink a cup of wine with me, for old time's sake." He beckoned. "Landlord – "

"No!" For the first time, Stephen raised his voice. It was shaking a little and his face was, if possible, even whiter than it had been before. "Can you dare to sit there and pretend you do not know why I followed you in here?" It was at this

186

point that Stephen remembered that, as it was a peaceable journey the Earl was making, and since in any case the train was well guarded by men-at-arms, his own sword was with his other baggage, strapped to the back of a pack-horse. He was wearing only a dagger. He drew the dagger. "You had better stand up, Ranulf, if I am going to kill you."

Instantly the tavernkeeper was at his elbow. "I cannot allow brawling. I must ask you to go, sir. This is a respectable house."

Stephen was suddenly reminded of another landlord whining those very same words in a room filled with torch-light. He swung round to the tavernkeeper. "If this is a re-spectable house, why do you allow scum like this to drink in it?"

"Devil's whelp!" Ranulf jumped to his feet, stepped back-wards over the bench on which he had been sitting, and drew his sword. Instantly he found his right arm taken in a grip like iron and his sword removed from his grasp. One of the other drinkers, a huge, black-bearded fellow, taller even than he was, stood behind him. This man flashed his teeth in a broad grin that split his beard across his face and said, "Oh, no! None of that. Fair's fair. The youngster has no sword, so you'll not use yours on him."

Two of his companions ranged themselves beside him, and Ranulf, scowling, saw the folly of trying to get back his sword. He cursed them, but made no move against them.

The tavernkeeper, with no more than a worried glance across the table, continued to protest to Stephen. "I cannot have you coming in here and picking quarrels with my guests."

"Our quarrel was picked two years ago," said Stephen, "and today we are going to settle it."

Ranulf drew his dagger. "By heaven, we are! You talk loudly enough, Stephen. Let's see what you can do."

Another man, with a small, round head and thin, bird-like legs, laughed. "That's the spirit! There's no need to let the lad have it all his own way."

"Not in here!" shouted the tavernkeeper. "Not in my house!" He turned to his other five customers. "Help me throw them both into the street."

Stephen took the purse from his belt and laid it on the table. "That's yours if you let us stay here."

The tavernkeeper hesitated. He picked up the purse and weighed it in his hand. "Why should I take a chance for two strangers?" He looked from one to another of his friends, read the agreement on their faces, and said, "Very well. Shut the door, Will."

The little man darted to the door and bolted it, and the tavernkeeper jerked his head towards the other end of the room and said, "Not in here. There's a yard outside."

They went into the yard; Ranulf pushing his way out first to look around the small enclosed space contemptuously. There was a bench by the house wall and one or two empty barrels in a corner.

As the others followed Ranulf out, the big man said to Stephen, "You're a game young fighting-cock, but you'll have no chance against him. I know his sort, they're hard fighters. Go now, while your skin's still whole, and I'll see he does not follow you until you're well away."

Stephen shook his head. "It's something which has to be done." He sat down on the bench and pulled off his riding boots.

Ranulf took up a position with his back to the afternoon sun. He was a good head taller than Stephen, and his long arms had a wider reach; he had, too, the advantage of age and experience; but Stephen was lighter and far quicker. Stephen stood with the sun in his eyes and wiped the palms of his hands on his tunic. He took a firm grip on his dagger and judged with his eyes how far Ranulf was from him. Dear God, let me kill him, he prayed silently. And then he was relying on himself, thinking with unexpected calmness that the first thing to do was to get the sun out of his eyes, and the second, to remember about Ranulf's longer reach.

The tavernkeeper and the other five men settled themselves on the bench and prepared to enjoy the fight. From time to time they applauded a move or called encouragement to one or other of the antagonists – all except the big, black-bearded man; he had set himself up as Stephen's champion, and shouted only for him.

"What are you waiting for?" taunted Ranulf. "A moment ago I thought you were so keen to join him in hell."

Stephen started to move slowly to his right, forcing Ranulf to turn with him in order to keep him in sight. When Ranulf was almost facing the sun, Stephen, while appearing still to be moving only to the right, began to edge nearer to Ranulf. When be was still out of Ranulf's reach, he suddenly leapt forward, fast as a cat, his dagger flashing up and down. Ranulf was only just too quick for him. He jumped aside and Stephen's dagger missed his breast, but caught him in the shoulder, leaving a patch of red. As Stephen leapt backwards after the stroke, Ranulf lunged at him, his dagger raised, but he failed to touch Stephen. There was a long-drawn "Aah" of satisfaction from the six watchers at the sight of the first blood. Ranulf cursed; and he and Stephen started to circle round and round each other warily. Hoping that Ranulf was not noticing, Stephen began again to edge closer and closer in, trying to get within Ranulf's reach without its being apparent. Ranulf seemed not to have noticed, then, just before Stephen judged it to be the moment to leap in and strike, Ranulf flung himself forward. Stephen, on his unshod feet, leapt lightly back, and Ranulf's dagger missed him by inches.

"Well dodged, little one," the big man called.

They circled each other again; and again Stephen crept closer, though he now knew that Ranulf was well aware of his ruse. He did not come so close this time, but leapt forward sooner, right arm raised. Instead of jumping backwards, as Stephen had expected, Ranulf stepped forward, and taking advantage of his greater height and reach, shot his left hand upwards to catch hold of Stephen's wrist in a grip like a vise. There was an expectant hiss of indrawn breath from the onlookers.

"Got you now," said Ranulf between his teeth, his right hand poised to strike neatly under a rib.

Stephen went limp at the knees and let the weight of his whole body hang from his wrist, at the same time throwing up his left hand to protect his face. This gave him the moment's respite that he needed. His weight dragged Ranulf's left arm down so that the grip on his wrist was loosened a fraction. But only a fraction: Stephen needed to exert every ounce of strength in his arm as he straightened up and wrenched his wrist outwards and down. He broke Ranulf's grasp – and it felt as if he had broken his own wrist as well – and leapt backwards a split second before Ranulf's dagger came down and cut into his shielding left arm, an inch or two above the elbow.

There was a buzz of excitement from the watchers; and the big man said softly, "Bravely done, lad. Bravely done."

They began to circle around one another again, breathing heavily, seeking for an opening. This time Stephen made no attempt to attack for several minutes. He was waiting for the burning pain in his right wrist to ebb and leave him feeling as though he once more had the strength to strike with it.

When he felt that he dared again rely upon his wrist, he made a quick dart at Ranulf, trying to get under his guard.

As Ranulf stepped swiftly to his right and countered this attack with a forward thrust of his own, Stephen leapt nimbly back, avoiding him. He did this, at intervals, three times more, until he judged that Ranulf had grown used to the pattern of attack. The fifth time that Stephen darted in – as Ranulf was beginning the movement that would carry him to his right and forward, his dagger raised against Stephen – in a flash Stephen's wrists met in front of him and his dagger changed hands. His empty right hand feinted at Ranulf's left side, his left hand went up and, as Ranulf completed his sideways step and lunged forward, Stephen ducked under his upraised arm and the dagger in his left hand went into Ranulf's throat.

It had been so quick that no one had realized what was happening before it was over; and then a hoarse gasp followed by shouts of admiration came from the tavernkeeper and the five other men.

Ranulf dropped his dagger and his hands went to his neck and clutched at it, as though he would have held back the blood that oozed between his fingers. He bent over and staggered forward, as if to hurl himself at Stephen; but Stephen stepped back and Ranulf fell to his knees at Stephen's feet, his hands still at his neck and the breath whistling and gurgling in his throat.

Stephen looked down at the writhing and heaving figure crouched at his feet and felt nothing, not hatred, nor pity, nor triumph; nothing but an immense weariness. His own breath was coming in gasps. He said, half to Ranulf and half to himself, "It was he who taught me that trick. I wish he could have seen the use I made of it." Then he found that his legs would hold him up no longer. He staggered over to the wall and sat down on the bench, his head in his hands. He was obscurely aware of the others carrying Ranulf to the wall near the door and spreading his cloak over him, and of the tavern keeper flinging a pail of water over the place where Ranulf had lain, washing the blood away.

Then one of the men slapped him on the shoulder. "You'd best come in, lad. You're all sweaty, and it's growing chilly."

He looked up and saw that the sun had indeed gone from the high-walled yard and so must be nearing its setting. He stood up and found that he could walk. Ranulf was lying just outside the doorway; Stephen went past him and in and sat down at the table. The little bird-legged man handed him a cup of wine. When he lifted the cup, Stephen's hands were trembling, so that the cup rattled against his teeth. He drank the wine and laid his head on the table. Suddenly he looked up and across to the door to the yard where Ranulf lay so still. "Someone should go for a priest," he said.

The big man came over to him. "It's too late for a priest, lad." He added with a laugh, "That is, unless you're needing one. Let's take a look at your arm." He pulled Stephen's torn sleeve away and looked at the wound. "A good, clean cut," he said with satisfaction. "You'll take no hurt from that." He bound it with a piece of cloth and arranged the sleeve over the rough bandage.

One of the other men came up to Stephen and handed him his dagger. "You dropped this outside." As Stephen took it, he noticed that it had been wiped clean. He sheathed it and stood up. "I shall have to report the death. Whom should I tell?"

The tavernkeeper looked at the others, then back at Stephen. "There'll be no need to say anything about it. He's a stranger here, just like yourself, and no one will miss him."

"But –" began Stephen.

"You'll not have to worry about a thing," interrupted the big man. "Me and my friend here," he nodded towards the man who had returned Stephen's dagger, "me and my friend, we'll see to it for you, and glad to oblige."

The tavernkeeper said, "There's a gate leads from the yard straight down to the river. As soon as it's dark, Wat and Adam will take him down and drop him in."

Big Adam nodded cheerfully. "That's right. We'll wrap him up in a couple of old sacks as neat as a babe in swaddling bands, and a few stones in with him. No one will be any the wiser."

Seeing Stephen's look of shocked surprise, the tavernkeeper came closer. "Never you worry. It's not the first . . . accident . . . I've had here, sir. I can trust my good friends," he looked at the others, "can I not?"

"That you can!" They laughed; and someone brought Stephen another cup of wine.

"Will, go and open the door or we'll have people wondering why it's locked. Adam, you and Wat go out to the yard and do what's needful. You'll find some sacks in that corner." The tavernkeeper pointed to the farthest end of the room. "And you, Jack, go and see to his horse and gear. Later, we can sell it and split the profit." Having put them all to work, the tavernkeeper wiped the top of the table with a cloth and set out some empty cups. Will, who had by this time opened the door, came back with a pair of new customers. The other men greeted the newcomers – all save Wat and Adam, who had gone out to the yard with the sacks. Stephen sat down again and began to drink the second cup of wine; and then the tavernkeeper was at his side with a hunk of bread and a piece of cheese. "Get that inside you," he invited, and was off again before Stephen could thank him.

A few minutes later Adam came up to him and said in a low voice, "All wrapped up as snug as you please. As soon as it's good and dark we'll go down to the river. Now, as for you, you'd best be going home."

"I'll wait until . . . until . . . " Stephen looked towards the yard.

"No, you'll not. What do you think you can do?"

"There might be difficulties."

"No fear of that. We're not fools, Wat and I. Off you go now."

Stephen looked around for the tavernkeeper, found him at his elbow and said, "Shall I go?"

"You do as Adam says. We'll see to the rest."

Stephen stood up. "Thank you, all of you. You have been very good to me. My name is Stephen de Beauville. If there is any trouble, you can always find me in the household of the Earl of Manningfield."

"There'll be no trouble," said Adam. "I promise you."

"Adam's right," the tavernkeeper assured him. "There'll be no trouble."

Stephen started on his ride to Manningfield while it was still daylight; but by the time he reached the castle it was quite dark. For most of the journey he had been half asleep and swaying in the saddle, but he arrived without mishap. By the light of a taper held for him by a yawning serving-lad, he found his way to the room where Renier and Gerald were already sleeping. He pulled off his clothes and dropped them on the floor; then, so heavy-limbed that he could hardly move, he climbed into the bed and was asleep almost instantly.

In the middle of the night he awoke and remembered all at once what had happened during the day. Ranulf was dead and Sir Pagan was avenged. At the thought of Sir Pagan, he did what he had not done in the whole of two years: he began to weep for him, passionately, uncontrollably.

His sobs awoke the other two. Renier raised his head sleepily. "What the devil's the matter?" he asked.

"It's Stephen," said Gerald.

Renier listened for a moment or so; then he said, with much worldly wisdom, "He must be in love, and the lady's not being kind to him. Poor Stephen." He turned over and went to sleep again.

But Gerald propped himself on one elbow and laid a hand on Stephen's heaving shoulder in the dark. "If there's anything I can do to help, just tell me," he said.

Into the pillow, Stephen murmured his inaudible thanks, and went on sobbing.

FOUR

As Sir Pagan had once hoped, Roger Mortimer eventually overreached himself. By the autumn of 1328, he was Earl of March and ruler of far wider lands than had ever been held by the detested Hugh Despenser. He entertained lavishly. He held at Hereford an extravagant tournament to celebrate the marriage of his daughter; and, at Bedford, another which he described as a Round Table, in reference to the claim of the Mortimer family to be descended from King Arthur, as well as from the Trojan Brutus. Queen Isabella's greed was almost as great as his; and she did not scruple to stoop even to demanding from the Master of King's Hall at Cambridge the return of some books which had been a gift to him from her murdered husband.

Naturally the great lords of England were resentful and restless; but, save for Henry of Lancaster, who made a cautious and halfhearted attempt to check Mortimer, they preferred to bide their time and wait for the King to grow older and assert himself, as they knew he must one day.

Earl Bartholomew deplored the behaviour of the rulers of England and was deeply shocked by the treaty of peace – so advantageous to the Scots and so humiliating to the English – which they made with Scotland; but, like so many others, he believed the state of affairs could not last forever, and he had great hopes of the young King. "It will not be long, please God," he said, "before our lord the King proves himself a worthy grandson of old King Edward – God rest his great and noble soul; he was a warrior whom any young knight might have rejoiced to serve, as I did – but meanwhile I would prefer to see as little of England's shame as I may. I've always hoped to go on pilgrimage before I grow too old. I think that now would be as good a time as any for such a venture. When I return, God willing, the time may be ripe for driving away these thieving kites."

Leaving his lands to the care of his two capable sons, Peter and William, early in 1330 he set off for the Holy Land, taking with him only a few companions, amongst them Stephen.

For the first time in his life Stephen saw the sea – and sailed on it. He saw its ever-changing colours and marvelled at its vastness, and experienced the discomforts of a voyage. He saw France and Italy and the blue Mediterranean; he saw the bright, strange fruit and gaudy flowers that did not grow in England, the golden sands of Syria, the dark-skinned Saracens; and he saw Jerusalem and the Church of the Holy Sepulchre. It was a new world which he had never imagined to exist; and all the varied sights of it held him spell-bound – the shapes and colours which he knew he would never forget, and which he longed, impotently, to be able in some way to perpetuate.

To their disappointment, the pilgrims from Manningfield had been unable to visit Rome and St. Peter's. With the Pope resident at Avignon, the city had been in a turmoil: the great noble families quarreling amongst each other, and rival factions fighting in the streets, seizing gates and bridges and holding them against all comers. Having heard so many tales of what had happened to other strangers who had ventured into the city on their own peaceable concerns, regretfully Earl Bartholomew had pronounced it foolhardy for them to risk their lives.

"It is a sad comment on this world of ours," he remarked, "that we have more fear of the Christians in Rome than of the unbelievers in Jerusalem."

At that time the Holy Land had been for forty years once more in the hands of the Saracens, but Christian pilgrims were tolerated for the sake of the tolls they paid as well as for the money they spent on food and goods. For they were taxed on entering Jerusalem and they had to buy their way into the Church of the Holy Sepulchre, which brought much profit to the revenue.

Stephen had always imagined all Saracens to be monsters – cruel, savage, ruthless and dangerous monsters – and he was surprised to find this was not so. Most of them were courteous and helpful, and some were even hospitable. And though there were those who, on seeing the pilgrims approach, would call out "Dogs of Christians!" and spit on them as they passed by, there was little enough of that, and on the whole the folk they met with were either kindly or indifferent.

Earl Bartholomew and his companions entered Jerusalem by the Pilgrims' Gate, near the Tower of David, to which the road from Joppa, where they had landed, led; and they spent their first night in the Holy City at the pilgrims' hospice which had formerly been the house of the brethren of St. John of Jerusalem. It was said to be large enough for the use of a thousand guests at one time; and each pilgrim had to pay two silver pence to stay there, whether he remained for one night or one year.

Early the next morning they made their way to the Church of the Holy Sepulchre. There was but the one door in the high wall which surrounded the crusaders' church and the many chapels and other buildings grouped about it, for the west door had been bricked up nearly a hundred and fifty years before on the orders of Saladin, when he had taken Jerusalem. Along the lane at the foot of the wall beggars, both Christian and Saracen, were gathered, calling for the pilgrims' charity as they passed by.

Earl Bartholomew and the others went through the doorway and down the steps into the courtyard below, where a score or so of pilgrims were already assembled. More beggars crouched on these steps; and in the courtyard were sitting with their wares the sellers of food – bread, eggs, dates and other fruit – with which the pilgrims could fill their scrips to last them until the next day; and hawkers who sold little ornaments and works of craftsmanship, that the pilgrims might buy gifts for those whom they had left at home. Water-sellers went about, and men offering their services as guides to the holy places. With the cries of the vendors, the chaffering of the buyers and the excited chatter of the expectant pilgrims, it was, thought Stephen as he bought a bunch of grapes for his uncle, for all the world like any market.

On two sides of the courtyard were little chapels dedicated to the saints, and on a third side was the wall of the church with a door in it. On either side of this door, on stone benches, sat the guardians of the church, elderly, grave-faced, bearded Saracens with their long, flowing robes and their turbans. When some three score or more of pilgrims had collected in the courtyard, the guardians unlocked the door of the church and let them through, counting them carefully and taking from each of them the entrance price of five ducats: for entry was free only at Easter and on the feast of the Invention of the Cross. When all the pilgrims had filed through out of the sunlight into what seemed at first, by contrast, like black darkness, the door was locked upon them and they were free, for four and twenty hours, to wander where they would amidst the holy places.

There was so much there to look at and admire, to wonder over with awe and reverence: the monuments of the Christian kings of Jerusalem; the round, domed chapel of the Holy Sepulchre, with its sixteen marble columns and its sparkling mosaic likenesses of the twelve apostles, St. Helena and the Emperor Constantine; the chapel of St. Helena herself, with, down a flight of stairs, the rocky grotto where she had found the Cross; and, up a dim stairway in a small chapel, that place which, of all others, must be to Christendom the holiest in the world – the hill of Calvary, with the cleft in the rock into which the Saviour's Cross had been set on Holy Friday. Up and down countless steps, along dark and twisting passages, from shrine to shrine, carrying lighted tapers went the pilgrims and their guides; until their eyes were weak with the marvels they had seen and their hearts were filled with gladness.

But to Stephen, as no doubt to so many others, the most sacred spot of all was the Saviour's Tomb within the chapel of the Holy Sepulchre. Under the dome of the chapel, beneath a marble canopy fretted with arches, lay the plain white Tomb of marble over the rock where Christ had lain until Easter morning. In turn the pilgrims went forward to kneel at the Tomb and pray.

When it came to Stephen's turn, there, in that spot where a man might pray for forgiveness for his sins – and feel certain of receiving it; or for the strength to live a godly life – and not doubt it would be bestowed; or for his heart's desire – and be confident of its being granted him; all Stephen could think to do during the moments that he knelt there, was to pray for the soul of Sir Pagan.

At daybreak, summoned by a wooden clapper, the pilgrims gathered together to celebrate mass in the chapel on

Calvary; and then the guardians unlocked the door, and the pilgrims, counted carefully as they went by, streamed out once again into the bright light of morning, weary but elated.

Earl Bartholomew and his companions rested for that day in the hospice, and on the following morning they set off to climb the Mount of Olives. Leaving Jerusalem by the Gate of Jehoshaphat, they went down the dusty road into the Kedron Valley with the walls of Jerusalem towering above them, and before them the Mount of Olives, a harsh ridge of rock with a few stunted olive-trees growing on its bare sides. Past the walled garden of Gethsemane with its cypresses and the old olive-trees which were believed to be the very ones beneath which the Saviour had walked, they went up the hill, past old Jewish tombs, past shrines and chapels and ruins, while the heat shimmered on the rocks beside the track; and all the way up the slope, to anyone who looked back, with every step that he took, more of the city would become visible.

From the top, when they stopped to rest, they could see Jerusalem spread out before them across the valley – perched on steep rocks and standing, at its loftiest point, almost as high as the Mount of Olives – with its firm wall all about it and its buildings, some of new white stone, others sand-coloured or darker brown; and, directly opposite, the Saracen's holy place which no Christian might enter, the Dome of the Rock, with a crescent upon its pinnacle, built upon the spot where once had stood Herod's Temple.

Seeing it all there before him across the valley in the cruel midday sunlight, under a brazen sky, a few grey olive-trees here and there, a flock of sheep on the road below the city walls; seeing it as he supposed that Christ must so often have seen it, Stephen felt that it was the most wonderful sight of his life, and he suddenly remembered Brother Ernulf who had had to imagine this scene for himself, and he wished that the old monk, grumbling and testy, might have been there with him to see it. In that memorable moment of his life, it was not Sir Pagan, whom he had so much loved, whom Stephen would have had there to share the moment with him, but crabbed old Ernulf of Peterborough for whom he had never felt any affection, but who had taught him how to paint.

During the days that they remained in Jerusalem, they saw as many of the sights and holy places as were permitted to Christian pilgrims, before setting off on their return journey, travelling northwards to Damascus and taking ship at Tripoli. And, almost a year after they had started out from Manningfield, they were home again, weary, sunburnt, with their pilgrim's garb ragged and travel-stained, but entirely satisfied. One of the servants had died of a fever in Italy on the way back, and they had lost six horses – four of them at once as the result of a stormy crossing between Corcyra and Brindisi – and they had been obliged to replace them with inferior beasts, purchased here and there; but otherwise the little band of palmers was intact. It had been, in Earl Bartholomew's opinion, a very successful pilgrimage.

FIVE

For several months in 1330, Henry of Lancaster and the young King had been plotting together to rid themselves of Roger Mortimer; and in October, when Mortimer and Queen Isabella were in Nottingham Castle, they struck. The castle was well defended, but Edward, with a small company of supporters, entered secretly by night through an underground passage and made his way up to Mortimer's apartments. There he and his friends killed the knights who guarded the door and entered to capture Mortimer himself. They hurried him down the stairs – while Isabella cried after them imploringly, "Have pity on gentle Mortimer!" – and out of the castle to London. A few weeks later Roger Mortimer suffered the fate he had dealt to the Despensers and those others who had stood in his way, and King Edward the Third was at last the ruler of his own kingdom.

In the spring of 1331, while England was still rejoicing at the triumph of the young King, Stephen, just twenty-one, was knighted, and his years' long ambition was thereby fulfilled.

Beside the alterations which it brought to the duties and employment of his daily life, being at last a knight made another difference to Stephen. He now no longer only thought of Brother Ernulf and his Gospels and remembered with a faint regret his own days of drawing practice at Richley, he actually obtained for himself an inkwell and a supply of pens and parchment, and on occasions – not very often, it is true, but every now and then – he would find himself some quiet corner as far away from others as was possible and draw, quite as assiduously as he had ever done at Richley, hands or arms or folds of drapery, a sleeping hound or a busy servant-girl, or a repeating pattern suitable for a brocade gown or a decorative background; or he would copy the illustrations in a breviary borrowed from his uncle's chaplain. After an hour or so occupied in this manner, he would lay down his pen and roll up his parchment and arise strangely refreshed and nearer contentment.

Perhaps it was that, being now a knight and more important than a mere squire, he could afford to be a little unconventional; or perhaps it was that, having safely reached his goal, he could dare to do a thing which might, before, have jeopardized the achievement of his old ambition. Had he been asked, Stephen would not have been able to say which it was, for he had no idea that any unconscious reasoning lay behind the sudden lifting of the self-imposed ban on drawing.

His fellow knights – of whom Renier was now one – knowing that he could read and write, presumed that he was writing letters to his family at Greavesby, or poems to some lady whom he loved, and made only a few chaffing comments on his clerkish skill and, partly from good nature and partly from a desire to respect the well-known reserve of their lord's nephew, let him be; and no one, strangely enough in such a crowded household, discovered his secret.

SIX

For the greater part of the next two years, Stephen's life was uneventful. He attended his uncle at Manningfield or at one or another of his manors, he took part – not without honour – in tournaments, he hunted, hawked and jousted; and sometimes he drew. As in his earlier years with Earl Bartholomew, he was neither happy nor unhappy; and if life had little to offer him, he was not even aware of the fact, since he had learnt as a child to expect nothing from life. Once the first glamour of having achieved knighthood had worn off, there was a vague, half-felt dissatisfaction with his mode of living always present in his heart; but he accepted it as the natural lot of every man in an imperfect world and paid it no attention; and he had long ago ceased to hope – as he had once hoped at Richley – that somewhere in the future there might be happiness for him. He had had his happiness – at Lower Avonden – and no man could expect happiness to seek him out twice in one lifetime.

In 1329 Robert Bruce had died, to be succeeded by his five-year-old son David, and Scotland passed into the hands of regents. King Edward the Third, who loved war and conquest as much as had his grandfather, took advantage of the opportunity offered by Scotland's weakness. In 1332 he moved the seat of government to York, where it was to remain for the next five years; and in December of that year, with the defence of the Border and the claims of Edward Balliol, pretender to the Scottish throne, as his excuses, he began to prepare for war.

Glad to think that at last the shame of the unpopular peace treaty with Scotland might be wiped out, Earl Bartholomew willingly sent his due number of knights and men-at-arms, led by his second son, thirty-year-old Sir Peter, to join the King's army at Newcastle-upon-Tyne, and with them went Stephen, to war for the first time, in the spring of 1333.

On the march north, Stephen had been bidden to part from his companions at Nottingham and, going a little out of his way into Lincolnshire, to break his journey at the castle of a certain baron who was an old friend of his uncle, though some fifteen years older than the Earl. Charged with numerous messages and bearing gifts, he set off eastwards from Nottingham with his squire Walter and six men-at-arms. Walter Boncourt, a distant kinsman of the Earl, was a steady, rather slow youth of seventeen, who much admired Stephen and was – though in a very restrained fashion – enthusiastic about going to war in Scotland. Stephen could not imagine Walter ever making a stir in the world, but he would always, he thought, be a worthy, upright man; meanwhile, he made an admirable squire, well-behaved, quiet, eager to please and efficient.

At the castle of Baron Simon FitzAmory, Stephen was received with great kindness by the baron and his very much younger lady; they both insisting that Stephen should stay with them for at least three nights. Baron Simon – a tall, broad man, whose grey hair and beard still showed tawny streaks here and there – attempted unsuccessfully to hide a good nature beneath a bluff manner. He walked heavily with the aid of a stick, being troubled with an old wound in the leg, gained in the Scottish wars under King Edward the First. He took to Stephen at once, and told him endless tales about the old warrior king's campaigning in Scotland. By his first wife, Baron Simon had five daughters, now all married and with children of their own; but by his second wife, the still pretty Lady Alis, he had only the one child, his son Thomas, now fifteen, his disappointed hopes in whom he confided at length to Stephen. Thomas, it appeared, only a week before, had been sent home in disgrace from the household where he had been a squire, after some particularly shocking misdemeanour which had surpassed even his previous escapades.

"I was too old when he was born to be as strict with him as I should have been," said the baron regretfully. "We spoilt him, I admit it. I should have sent him to your uncle when he was seven, but he was my only son and we could not bear to let him go so far away from us. When he was twelve I sent him to be page to Baron Richard, a neighbour and an old friend, not ten miles away; and he was sent back after three months as unmanageable and always in mischief. It was a shock to us, his mother and me, since we had never known him to be like that, or seen him through others' eyes. Oh, heaven knows I've beaten him hard and often enough since then: but I'd left it too late, I fear. Finally, last autumn, Richard agreed to give him another chance, but the wretched boy was back here within six months. A week ago, when he got home, I beat him until my arm ached, and now he's under lock and key, on bread and water for a month. Perhaps that will bring him to his senses."

Stephen said all the polite and consoling things that were necessary, assuring the old man that his son would surely settle down in time; and Baron Simon went on to relate certain of the boy's worst escapades. Throughout the recital his wife – except when he demanded her agreement on some point – spoke very little, only nodding her head sadly now and then in silent accord with her husband's assertions, and occasionally wiping away an unobtrusive tear. She obviously loved her child; and Stephen could not help feeling that the baron, too, for all his talk, was still fond and even, he suspected, proud of his only son, making, wherever he possibly could, a virtue out of the boldness which prompted his disobedience and led him into spirited pranks, and out of the hardihood with which he survived repeated punishment to think up and commit new misdeeds.

Privately, Stephen decided that Thomas sounded a most disagreeable youth, and he was glad that he would be spared meeting him. Among Thomas's exploits were poaching the deer from the lands of a nearby abbey; cutting half through the saddle-girths of various people, so that when their horses began to gallop they found themselves on the ground; egging on a bunch of young companions to help him rob a merchant whom they met along the highway; freeing from its chain a pet bear in Baron Richard's castle and goading it into chasing the servants; and – a deplorable offence – throwing a dead sheep down the well in Baron Richard's kitchen, to see how long it would take to pollute a water supply.

On Stephen's second day with Baron Simon, two messengers, come after him with great speed from Berkshire, brought word that Walter's father, a knight who held an estate from Earl Bartholomew, had been taken ill with a sudden stroke and was dying. For Walter, the Scottish adventure was over before it had even begun. Stephen said good-bye to Walter and sent him back to Berkshire with the two messengers, downcast and tearful not only for the loss of his father and for his mother's grief, and for the knowledge that now to him, as the eldest son, would fall a large measure of responsibility, but as well for the dashing of his hopes of fighting in Scotland. He was also genuinely sorry to leave Stephen, whom he had found unexacting and considerate.

His host and hostess commiserated with Stephen on losing his squire at the very outset of his journey, and Stephen smiled and made light of it. But he did not notice the glances that passed between them as they offered him their sympathy. Had he done so, he might not have been so surprised – or so dismayed – when, quite casually, a few hours later, Baron Simon suggested that, as Stephen was now without a squire, he might perhaps care to take Thomas with him to Scotland.

On Stephen's polite but non-committal answer, the old man abandoned his pose of casualness and said frankly, "It's what he needs, the discipline of a campaign. It would give him a lawful outlet for his high spirits."

And Lady Alis, leaning forward in her chair, laid a gentle hand on Stephen's arm and said, her voice trembling a little, "Please, please, Sir Stephen, do take him with you. It may be his last chance."

The baron said gruffly, "Lick the lad into shape, and I'll be everlastingly grateful to you. I'm too old to manage him."

In the face of their importunity and his own lack of a squire, it would have been impossible for Stephen to have refused with courtesy the request of such kindly hosts. Very averse, but with a show of willingness, he agreed to do as they asked.

Thomas was immediately sent for and presented to Stephen. He turned out to be a rather thickset boy with a mop of dark-red hair and heavy, red, frowning eyebrows, and his full lips had a sullen droop at the corners; though – possibly a little subdued by his recent punishment – he was quiet and respectful enough. And when told of his father's plans for him and hearing the baron's demand that this time he should behave himself, he only cast one resentful glance at

Stephen from eyes that were as dark as bluebells and said unenthusiastically, but in a tone which could otherwise give no possible offence, "Yes, sir."

But for all that, Thomas looked, Stephen thought, every bit as intractable and troublesome as he had been described; and Stephen did not contemplate with the slightest pleasure being given charge of him. He felt himself entirely unfitted to handle the boy and to succeed where others had failed, and there was nothing about Thomas's appearance which in any way suggested that he might be a congenial companion for someone of Stephen's temperament; and Stephen found himself regretting Walter Boncourt even more than he had expected to. His sullen air, his Judas hair – even Thomas's very name was repugnant, recalling to Stephen, as it did, not the popular saint of Canterbury for whom so many Englishmen were named, but that one of his half-brothers whom he had always found the least likeable.

It was, thought Stephen, the devil's own luck that Thomas FitzAmory had come his way. With his gentle, sensitive nature, and with his imagination, he was entirely unfitted to manage a boorish young scapegrace. Sir Pagan, he reflected, would have known exactly how to handle Thomas and would have found the situation amusing – but then Sir Pagan, with his good humour, his common sense and his knowledge of the world, would have had any wild beast eating from his hand in a week. Stephen could see the joke of his predicament all right; but though that might make the situation a little more bearable, it resolved nothing.

Before Stephen left the castle, the baron said to him, "Be as rough as you please with Thomas. I do not care how you treat him, so long as you get at least some good out of my son."

But Lady Alis, as she gave her guest the customary kiss of farewell, blinking back her tears, whispered, "You'll do what you can for him, please? And not be too hard on him? It's not all his fault, you know."

"I'll do my best, I promise," said Stephen, inwardly cursing his ill-fortune.

They rode off for the North, the men-at-arms sorry to leave a place where their entertainment had been so good; Stephen full of misgivings and Thomas following him on his father's best horse, a stubborn set to his jaw and his blue eyes smouldering rebelliously.

SEVEN

Although on that first day of their journey – and indeed for several days afterwards, until they were settled in camp – Thomas was well-behaved enough in spite of Stephen's apprehensions, he was neither willing nor affable. He did as he was told, but with no show of readiness, and he accepted with ungraciousness the part that had been thrust on him. Quite properly, he spoke only when he was spoken to; yet it was not the silence of courteous respect but only the muteness of resentment. Stephen – no one better – could respect reserve when he met with it, but he was certain that Thomas's uncommunicativeness was due neither to reticence nor to shyness. Even had this not been plain from the youth's manner, nothing he had heard of him could possibly have led him to believe that Thomas was by nature as quiet and restrained as he now appeared to be.

Presuming that Thomas had met with little but disapproval and censure for the past three years, and knowing only too well from his own boyhood experience that if one hears nothing of oneself that is not disparaging, one will in the end believe that there can be no good in one, Stephen, from the outset, tried to behave towards Thomas as though he had heard no ill of him, hoping by a friendly approach to gain a response. But Thomas did nothing to help him. To all Stephen's well-meant questions on a variety of subjects he merely answered, "No, sir," or "Yes, sir," or "I do not know, sir," until his indifference would have damped the most ardent well-wisher; while Stephen's encouraging smiles and his attempts at an informal, amiable manner drew from Thomas no single smile in reply, nor any lightening of his sullen, heavy expression.

At the end of his second day's failure, Stephen wondered if perhaps complete frankness might not be more successful. With a smile he said, "Thomas, you have made it perfectly plain that you deplore your father's decision to send you to Scotland with me. Believe me, I have every sympathy with your attitude and I probably wish for your company as little as you wish for mine. But for the sake of your parents, for whom – short though the time I've known them – I feel a great respect and regard, there's nothing we can do about the matter. We must both make the best we can of the situation until it can be honourably ended, so we might as well call a truce and try to tolerate each other. What do you say?"

If Thomas found his unconventional approach surprising, he gave no sign of it. He looked at Stephen steadily from under frowning red eyebrows, then he shrugged his shoulders very slightly. "I have nothing to say, sir. It is for you to give the orders."

It was unpromising; but Stephen was too tired after a long day's riding to care about making a further effort, and he let the matter rest. In the days that immediately followed, he continued to be kindly, friendly and even-tempered; while Thomas remained distant, unenthusiastic and apparently still resentful.

After the delay in Lincolnshire, Stephen made good speed, and he arrived at Newcastle only two days later than the others. All the roads to the town were crowded with men going and coming on the King's business: knights and their attendants riding to join the army, messengers, strings of packhorses, and baggage-wagons laden with supplies of provisions and fodder being brought in from the surrounding countryside.

The army, already large and growing daily larger, was encamped outside the walls of Newcastle and along the banks of the river, where it sprawled over a large expanse of countryside, noisy, colourful and smelly. Among the twisting lanes of tents, the groups of baggage-wagons, the rows of tethered horses, the squires and servants scurrying here and there, and the pedlars and merchants – who came from Newcastle every day, hoping to relieve the King's army of all its spare money – shouting out their wares, Stephen foresaw difficulty in finding his companions from Manningfield.

One of the men-at-arms, a seasoned campaigner, seeing Stephen at a loss, said helpfully, "They'll not have got here long before us, sir, so they'll not be too far in. We'll find them somewhere near the edge and probably somewhere near this very road, since it was this same road they'll have come by."

This was so logical that Stephen wondered why he had not thought of it at once for himself; and after that it was not very long before he saw his uncle's golden swan on its azure field fluttering above a group of tents, and could begin to look for Renier, who had promised to save a place for him in one of the tents. He soon found him, listening to a report on his charger from the farrier, while keeping half an eye upon his squire who was chaffering with a stout North-countryman for a basket of rather small and wrinkled apples for which Renier had a fancy, though he was not prepared to pay for them more than a quarter of the ridiculously high price that was being asked. The squire was being scornful and overbearing, and the man, in his slow, deliberate northern speech – which it seemed so strange to Stephen to be hearing once again – was maintaining that there were few enough apples to be found in the whole of England at Eastertide and his were worth their weight in silver, at least – even if not in gold.

Renier, who had been knighted on the same day as Stephen and was still on the best of terms with him although they had so little in common, greeted Stephen cheerfully, assured him that all his baggage and his charger had arrived safely, and told him that they were sharing a tent with Sir Fulke Fitz-Hugh. Stephen was glad of this, since Sir Fulke was one of his uncle's older knights, with many years of military experience – exactly the companion whom two such newcomers to war as he and Renier needed.

Renier was casually pitying over Walter Boncourt's misfortunes, and he looked Walter's successor up and down with interest, receiving in return from Thomas a furious frown which drew from him a laugh and, in a voice loud enough for Thomas to hear, the remark, "Holy saints! Red hair – and a temper to match it, I'll be bound! You'll have fun knocking that temper out of him, Stephen."

EIGHT

Four evenings later, returning to their tent after leaving Sir Fulke with his cousin Peter Boncourt, Stephen found Renier just finishing his supper and about to set off with his squire.

"I'm going into Newcastle to see if there are any good taverns and pretty wenches there. Are you coming with me, Stephen?"

Laughing, Stephen declined and wished Renier good luck. "If the landlords and the girls are all such cheats and skinflints as those pedlars and such who come round here selling their trash, then I shall need good luck if I'm not to be penniless by the time I get back," said Renier light-heartedly; adding as he went, "I'm sorry you'll not come with me. I cannot understand half that these North-country folk say. I'd have been glad of an interpreter."

Thomas set out platter and drinking-cup on the little trestle table, and Stephen told him to fasten back both flaps of the tent-opening to let in the light and the fresh air while he ate his meal. He was not sorry to be alone, or, at least, alone save for Thomas, after four days of close companion-ship with Sir Fulke and Renier and their squires – part of that time having been of necessity spent in the confined space of the tent – and he sat down on his stool at the table in grateful silence.

That evening, for the first time, there appeared to be a very faint and subtle change in Thomas's attitude towards Stephen as he waited on him. Stephen, always perceptive of the unspoken emotions of others around him, noticed it at once, but could not put a name to it. There seemed, some-how, a slight lightening of the atmosphere between them, a fraction less sullenness in Thomas's air; and he displayed a degree more interest in what he was doing. It was so faint that it was hardly noticeable and it was certainly indefin-able, but Stephen, aware of it, hoped that it might be the beginning of a relaxing of the tension between them. As he ate bread and cold meat the feeling persisted, though still almost imperceptibly; but when he reached out his hand for the cup of wine which Thomas had poured for him, the sen-sation suddenly grew stronger – perhaps there had been a momentary catch in Thomas's breath, an expectant stiff-ening of his muscles, of which Stephen had been aware with-out even looking at him – Stephen had no idea of what it was that had warned him, but he was fully alive to something imminent. As his fingers closed around the cup, he gave a quick glance out of the corner of his eye; Thomas, the sullen expression quite vanished from his face, was watching Stephen's hand, unmindful of Stephen's brief scrutiny.

Stephen, now quite convinced that something was afoot, brought the cup very slowly towards his lips. Then he remembered Baron Simon telling him of an occasion, three years or so before, while Thomas had been a page in that neighbouring household from which he had later been sent home – twice – in disgrace, when he had persuaded one of the other pages to help him put tadpoles into the wine-jug for the high table.

Instead of tasting the wine, Stephen looked into the cup. There appeared to be nothing in it but wine – certainly there were no tadpoles. He looked sharply at Thomas, who instantly assumed an expression of indifference, so extreme as to be unbelievable. Stephen took a chance on being mistaken. He put the cup down in front of Thomas. "You will please drink my wine for me," he said.

When the quick look of surprise on Thomas's face was succeeded by one of apprehension, Stephen knew that he had been right.

"Drink it for you, sir?" said Thomas. "But . . . but why?"

"Because I am telling you to do so."

After a long, dismayed look at Stephen, Thomas picked up the cup, hesitated, then drank off half the wine very quickly. He put the cup down on the table and abruptly fled from the tent.

He returned about five minutes later, looking rather green. He said nothing, but Stephen asked pleasantly, "What had you put in the wine?"

As defiantly as was possible under the circumstances, Thomas replied, "Salt."

"I see." Stephen considered this. "It seems to me a really rather childish trick," he said without rancour. This was, he reflected, Thomas's first open rebellion. The truce, it seemed, was over. Most men, he thought, would now simply have sworn at Thomas and thrashed him soundly and that would have been an end of the matter. Stephen found the idea distasteful: it was far too easy for him to imagine himself in Thomas's place – which was foolish of him, since Thomas was of a far less sensitive nature and therefore far less likely to take such treatment as hardly as he himself would have done at Thomas's age. But there must be another way of dealing with the matter. There was; it came to him in a flash.

Almost before he realized what he was going to do, he had gestured towards the cup and said, as sternly as he could manage, "You had better drink it all." Immediately he had spoken, Stephen regretted it. Supposing Thomas dared to disobey him? He would then, he supposed, be obliged to beat him into submission. Heaven forbid! he thought.

Thomas's jaw dropped. He had not expected this. He began a feeble protest, and Stephen, relieved that it was no more vehement, hastily seized his advantage and said sharply, "Do as I tell you."

After only a short delay, Thomas picked up the cup and swallowed another mouthful and was obliged to leave the tent again. This time Stephen waited only a minute or two, then he took the yet unemptied cup and went out after Thomas. He found him still retching slightly and looking even greener than before. When he thought Thomas was sufficiently recovered, he held out the cup to him. "Now finish it."

"I . . . I do not think I can."

"Nonsense. You can and you will. We are both going to stay out here until this cup is empty."

Thomas accepted the cup reluctantly. He looked into it and bit his lip.

"You're getting off very lightly, you know," remarked Stephen.

After a moment, Thomas looked straight at Stephen. "I would rather you beat me," he said.

Very quickly, Stephen replied, "Unfortunately for you, it's not your preference but my convenience which I am considering. Now be quick and do as you're told."

Thomas raised the cup half-way to his lips, then balked, looking with revulsion at its contents.

Stephen, suddenly too sorry for him to carry the punishment to its end, said, "Come on, Thomas. It makes me feel ill even to watch you. Hurry up and empty the cup," and pointedly turned his head away so that he could no longer see what Thomas was doing. When a full minute had passed, he turned round again. "Well, is it gone?"

"No, sir." Thomas was still holding the cup, which contained not a drop less than when Stephen had last looked into it.

"You fool! Why did you not pour it away while my back was turned and you had the chance?"

"I almost did," Thomas admitted; going on to say, "And then I thought that it would, somehow, be cheating. After all, I'd tried to play a trick on you. I failed and you caught me at it; it seems only just that I should take the consequences. But," he added, "it's not very easy." Looking woebegone and still rather green, he raised the cup again.

"Why did you think I turned my back on you?" Stephen put out a hand and took the cup from him. "I said that we should stay out here until this was empty." He tossed the last of the wine out on to the ground and handed the cup back to Thomas. "It's empty now, so we can go in." He made his way back into the tent, saying over his shoulder, "You'd better find me some drinkable wine," and reflecting as he spoke that he had probably behaved with imprudent leniency; but knowing that if he had it to do all over again, he would act no differently.

Thomas said nothing that evening; but the next morning, quite unprompted – since Stephen had, as promised, considered the matter closed – he knelt and asked Stephen's pardon. Stephen, who had expected nothing of the kind, was pleased at this forward step in their relations. He smiled at Thomas. "Tell me, Thomas, what had I done to you bad enough to make you want to play such a stupid and irresponsible trick on me?"

"Nothing, sir." He added frankly, "That was it. Unlike everyone else, you'd done nothing. I wanted to liven things up a little. I wanted to find out what you'd be like when you were angry."

"And now you know?"

"No, sir. You were not angry." Thomas said it almost with disappointment.

Stephen could not prevent himself from laughing. "What a pity! Another time give me warning, and I'll try to do better."

To his surprise, there was a brief flash of a smile in return, and Thomas gave a quick chuckle. It was the first time that Stephen had ever seen his heavy features relieved by amusement, and he was surprised by the difference it made.

NINE

In the intervals between spells of duty, the knights whiled away much of their time in tilting on an open space beyond the camp. Stephen and Renier had been thus engaged one morning, and at one point Stephen had neatly unhorsed Renier by means of a stratagem shown him by Sir Pagan.

Afterwards, as Thomas was helping Stephen dismount and taking his lance from him, he said impulsively and eagerly, and quite unexpectedly, "That was a good feint, sir, by which you unhorsed Sir Renier."

Stephen was astonished – and pleased – by this unprecedented sign of interest on Thomas's part. He smiled. "Did you think so? It was a trick I was taught once, when I was about your age." There seemed no lessening of Thomas's enthusiasm; and after a hesitation, Stephen said diffidently, "If you'd like, I'll show you how to carry it out." Even while speaking he blamed himself for a fool, for having exposed himself to what he presumed would be the inevitable snub.

But Thomas's face lighted up and for a moment his blue eyes sparkled with unusual animation, as he said, "Would you really, sir? Thank you."

After that they spent a fair amount of time together on the tilting-ground; and in the course of giving each other bruises, their good relations developed considerably. Though it was always uphill work trying to manage Thomas at this time, Stephen found himself less cautious and less reluctant, and more competent, to make an effort with the boy; and Thomas, though he was as likely as not to be moody or rebellious ten minutes later, showed himself – and for increasingly long periods – capable of being quite cheerful and willing and lively.

TEN

After Easter, King Edward went with his army to Berwick-upon-Tweed, to assist Edward Balliol and his Scottish supporters in the siege of that town whose unfortunate citizens were only too rarely free from the miseries of war. The town, clinging to its hill-side, looked down on the river and on the huge army which cut it off from all communication with King David's forces, both by land and water. But Berwick was used to being in a state of siege; the town was not unprepared and it was well victualled and ready and able to hold out – so the citizens and the garrison hoped – until it was relieved.

But relief was slow in coming, and the siege went on until well into the summer, with the English army kept idle before the walls of Berwick and the English fleet ready to turn back any help that the Scots might try to send by sea.

It was slow and monotonous, and after a few weeks Stephen and Renier – who were finding it very different from what they had expected of war against the Scots – were beginning to wonder if they would ever see any real fighting. Meanwhile, Stephen devoted much of his time to Thomas.

By June, Thomas's behaviour and disposition had so much improved – and were daily growing even better – that Stephen had begun to find him unexpectedly likeable and worth the trouble taken over him; while Thomas, for his part, had discovered in Stephen the first person for three years who did not treat his faults with untempered severity and who was, moreover, always ready to give his errors the benefit of the doubt, and he was beginning to feel a real affection and admiration for Stephen. So well, indeed, were matters progressing, that by this time Stephen was almost ready to believe that his methods of reforming the unmanageable Thomas were well on their way to succeeding where other, harsher means had failed.

And then one day there was a commotion outside the tent, an angry and upraised voice demanding Stephen, and he came out to find a knight from Kent, one Sir John de Forrest, and two companions, and with them Thomas, sullen and scowling. It took Stephen a few moments to calm Sir John, and then a few more moments to piece together his indignant tale; but in the end it appeared that Thomas was being accused of having struck down Sir John's squire, William Reynolds, and of having battered his head in with a wooden mallet.

"Is he dead?" asked Stephen, appalled.

"Not yet," said Sir John. "Not yet. But he will be at any moment. We left him lying in a pool of blood. He can hardly last much longer."

Sir Fulke, who had come out after Stephen to see what was afoot, and who had met with Sir John de Forrest several times before and had small opinion of him, remarked drily, "If that is so, then it seems strange to me that you have not stayed with him, to comfort his last moments on earth."

This remark temporarily diverted Sir John's attack to him, and Stephen was able to ask Thomas, "Is this true?"

Sir John, hearing the question, turned from Sir Fulke to break in, "Of course it's true. Do you doubt my word?"

Stephen paid no attention to him, but waited for Thomas to reply. Thomas, his eyes smouldering and his mouth set in its old, stubborn lines, said, "Yes, quite true. Except" – he turned and looked insolently at Sir John – "there's less blood than he said."

Stephen, inwardly cursing Thomas for making matters worse by not showing a becoming contrition, hindered a further flow of indignation from Sir John by saying soothingly, "I know that brawling is deplorable, but one cannot prevent spirited youths from disagreeing and settling their quarrels between themselves. You and I have done such things, when we were their age. It's unfortunate when the result is serious, as this appears to be, but – "

Sir John interrupted him furiously to shout, "You are mistaking the matter and attempting to make light of a grave affair, Sir Stephen. This was no youths' quarrel, this was a murderous assault."

"If that is so," persevered Stephen, although his heart was sinking, "I expect it was provoked. Thomas was no doubt defending himself from attack."

"That's not so," said one of the two other men. "I and Bernard here, we saw it all. One moment they were talking

220

together in a friendly manner, and the next moment this young hell-hound was beating out poor William's brains. We could hardly drag him off."

"It's lucky we were not farther away when it happened," put in the other man.

To Stephen all this sounded exaggerated, even for one of Thomas's misdeeds; and he asked him, "Were you defending yourself? Did he draw his dagger on you?"

Thomas, seemingly utterly ungrateful for this attempt to shift some of the blame, said shortly, "No." Adding a moment later, with what he intended for defiant bravado, but which Stephen could only consider, under the circumstances, as deplorable candour, "He had no dagger. He'd been telling me that he'd nicked the blade of his and had left it with the armourer."

Sir John exclaimed, "As I said! It's one thing for two youths, well matched, to settle a quarrel with weapons while their friends stand by to see fair play; but quite a different matter for one of them to break open the head of another who is unarmed."

Stephen, still trying to defend Thomas, asked – hopelessly enough in the face of Thomas's stubbornness – "But why did you do it? You must have been provoked."

Thomas shrugged his shoulders. "He said something which annoyed me, and I lost my temper and hit him with the mallet which was lying there."

"What did he say to you?" demanded Stephen.

For the first time, Thomas was unable to meet his eyes. He looked down at his feet. "Oh, it was nothing. Only some stupid lies which no one could believe."

"If they were so stupid that no one could have believed them," commented Sir Fulke, "it's a pity that you chose to take them so seriously."

At the same moment, Sir John said triumphantly to Stephen, "You see, he admits the attack was unprovoked."

"I see nothing of the sort," persisted Stephen. "He must have had very good cause for it."

And so it went on, for another quarter of an hour or so, with Sir John and his two friends accusing and angry; and Stephen, growing ever more perturbed, trying in vain to shift some, at least, of the blame from Thomas; and Thomas himself giving Stephen no help, but sullenly admitting everything; until Stephen was forced to concede that it must indeed be the incontrovertible truth that Thomas had been talking with William Reynolds close by Sir John's tent, and suddenly, at something William had said to him, had picked up the wooden mallet with which the tent pegs were hammered in, and with it had struck down William – who was half a head shorter than himself – and then had cold-bloodedly struck him again as he lay on the ground, not once, but four times more, and would have gone on had not Robert and Bernard come running to prevent him. To it all Thomas admitted; but he would not repeat the words which William had said to him, thereby depriving himself of his only chance of lessening his guilt in some degree. That William Reynolds was indeed seriously hurt was attested by Sir Fulke, who went to Sir John's tent to see with his own eyes, and returned to report that William's head was badly cut and that he showed no signs of coming to himself.

When at last Sir John de Forrest had been in some measure appeased, and he and his two companions had gone, still angry but no longer so clamorous, Stephen and the others went into their tent.

"Dear saints in heaven!" exclaimed Renier, who had turned up in time for the latter half of the altercation. "What a to-do!"

"I'm glad that I never thought much of that John de Forrest," said Sir Fulke. "I need a drink," he added to his squire.

222

The youth, who together with Renier's squire had been watching and listening with eager enjoyment to all that had been going on, hastily fetched wine.

Stephen, feeling drained of all strength by his efforts on behalf of the unhelpful Thomas, but nevertheless still persevering, said gently, "Thomas, they're gone now and it can surely not matter our knowing. What did he say to you? There are some things which no one is expected to take calmly. If he insulted you, it will give you an excuse, and heaven knows you need one."

Thomas, at the end of his tether, turned on him and shouted, "Let me be! Must you, too, badger me?"

For a moment there was complete silence as everyone stared at Thomas. Stephen, understanding as always, would have been quite ready to pardon such flagrant discourtesy, which he found, under the circumstances, perfectly defensible, and he was just about to pass it off with a very mild rebuke; but Sir Fulke, in the act of taking the cup which his squire was handing him, thrust it away, spilling half the wine, and strode over to Thomas, seized him by the shoulders and shook him violently. "You impudent pup!" he exclaimed. "How dare you speak like that to Sir Stephen? Have you not sense enough to see that at this moment he is the only friend you have?"

Thomas wrenched himself free of Sir Fulke's hands, his blue eyes flashing, and was about to answer him furiously, when Stephen, moved to rare anger, cried out, "Leave him alone, Fulke! What business is it of yours?"

After that, a quarrel between the lot of them was only narrowly averted.

ELEVEN

This unfortunate incident should have given Stephen a quite warranted excuse – that excuse which he had once so much desired – for sending Thomas home; but now that he had an excuse, he found that he no longer wanted one. Instead, he wished to keep Thomas with him and see him through his present misfortune. He defended Thomas tirelessly from all censure – whether coming from Sir Fulke and Renier or from friends of Sir John – and he never ceased to put forward reasons to justify Thomas's conduct. To all Stephen's attempts Thomas appeared completely indifferent and he made not the slightest effort to help him. That Stephen's endeavours were largely successful, owed nothing to Thomas.

For more than a week Sir John's squire remained senseless – lying, it was said, between life and death – while Stephen waited as anxiously for the outcome as did Sir John himself.

During this time, Thomas was barely either civil or respectful to Stephen, and his sullen, disobliging demeanour surpassed his former ungraciousness at its very worst; so that on occasion even Stephen found it hard to make allowances for him. But in spite of all his discourtesy and his unrelieved sulking, Stephen, realizing under what a strain Thomas must be living – continually wondering whether William Reynolds was going to live or to die – was unfailingly considerate and forbearing; though both Sir Fulke and Renier made no secret of their disapproval.

Word of the matter even came to the ears of Peter Boncourt, and he demanded an explanation. "What is all this I hear about your squire, cousin Stephen?" he asked.

Stephen told him, exculpating Thomas as much as he could while doing so.

By the time he had finished, Peter was frowning slightly. "I know that Baron Simon is an old friend of my father, but even so, I'm sure that my father would not wish Simon's son to be making trouble for us. It might be best, cousin, if you sent the boy home now, before he causes more ill-feeling."

But Stephen pleaded for Thomas. "I assure you," he said, "there will be no more trouble. I take full responsibility for his future conduct." It was rash, and he knew it; yet he was determined to stand by Thomas.

Peter Boncourt hesitated, but he finally shrugged his shoulders and said, "Oh, very well, cousin, as you wish. But, remember, I'm relying on you to see that our good name is not injured by a silly, headstrong boy."

Sir Fulke, who had heard this exchange, was ill-pleased and asked Stephen, "Are you sure you are doing wisely?" While Renier said frankly, "What a fool you are, Stephen! There was your chance to be rid of that tiresome boy and blame it on Sir Peter. Now you'll have to be watching him every moment of the day to make sure he does not try to kill anyone else."

"That's nonsense. He'll give us no more trouble, I'm sure," said Stephen with a confidence he did not feel.

When, after nine days, they learnt that William Reynolds had recovered his senses and that there now seemed a fair chance that he was not going to die, their spirits rose considerably. Only Thomas, the cause of all the anxiety, remained apparently unmoved.

Catching Thomas alone shortly afterwards, Sir Fulke said to him irritably, "It's a great pity that Sir Stephen cannot bring himself to harden his heart and send you away. He'd be better off in every respect without you – and I'm not the only one to believe that. Far too many people think he's a fool to protect you."

Thomas brooded over this remark. He had long been ready to admit – to himself – that his presence brought little benefit to Stephen: he had realized that from the beginning. Yet the implication in Sir Fulke's words, that Stephen himself wanted to be rid of him but was prevented by pity, increased to an unbearable extent his already considerable distress. It was not only that the thought rankled, that in championing him so unremittingly Stephen had been prompted only by pity, but that Thomas did not wish his continued presence to damage Stephen's credit. If, because of him, others were thinking Stephen a soft-hearted fool, then he would have to leave Stephen, and soon. Accordingly, without further ado, he packed up all his belongings, informed Stephen that he wished to return home and asked his permission to leave in the morning.

Stephen was completely taken aback. He had presumed, and not entirely incorrectly, that the last thing which Thomas wanted was to go home in disgrace again – and to go home at such a time could amount to nothing else – and he could conceive of no reason for Thomas's decision. What he did not guess was that to return home was only the second to last thing which Thomas wanted; the very last thing of all was to injure Stephen.

For a moment Stephen was too surprised to manage a reply to Thomas's request. Quite apart from not wishing to have failed with Thomas, and not wishing Thomas to have failed his parents, he found the prospect of losing him a very un-pleasing one. At first he had no idea how he should handle this new elaboration of his difficulties; then he decided that perhaps Thomas could best be reached and persuaded through his pride. He feigned an irritation which he would not have been far from feeling had he been less distressed. "I'd have thought that even you would have had more consideration for me. Not content with all the annoyance you've caused me, you now propose to ride off and leave me without a squire. Had I known that you wanted to be sent back to your father in disgrace yet once again, I could have packed you off weeks ago. But I thought that, however little you cared to be with me, you'd have cared even less for that. I put myself to considerable inconvenience for you, and now, the moment you make things too hot for yourself here, you get scared and want to run away home."

"I'm not scared and I'm not running away."

"Do not contradict me – your manners are atrocious. Your manners are indeed atrocious, but if I've borne with them for this long, I can bear with them for a little longer. You have not my permission to go home. Do you expect Sir Peter to spare a couple of men to escort you home to Lincolnshire?"

"I can go alone."

"You'll not go alone. Do you suppose I want your father thinking I'm ready to let you traipse half across England alone? You're staying here with me and facing up to the trouble you've caused, so you had better start unpacking."

Thomas began to protest, but Stephen cut him short. "There's no more to be said. You are staying here with me. I did not go to all the unpleasantness of defending you to Sir John and his friends just to have you run away now and make me a laughing-stock." Stephen stopped. Thomas was glowering at him. His tactics seemed about to fail, Stephen thought ruefully. Perhaps he should have tried another approach. But which?

Successfully deceived by Stephen's attitude, Thomas said with bitter insolence, "My parents should be very grateful to you for all that you have done for their sake, but you must amply have repaid their hospitality by now. There's no need for you to inconvenience yourself further on my behalf. I'm going home."

Stephen looked steadily at Thomas, who stared back at him, by now half-defiant and half-ashamed of what he had said. When Stephen spoke, it was very quietly. "I do not think I need to tell you that that remark is insupportable. I have nothing more to say to you except to repeat: you have not my permission to leave here." Stephen was at that moment very inclined to think that there were times when Sir Fulke and Renier were right and that Thomas was indeed insufferable. He went out of the tent with a gesture to Thomas to stay behind, so that, free of him for a space, he would not find it so hard to hide the distress that he was feeling; consequently, he did not see the look of hopeless misery which Thomas sent after him. But in the entrance to the tent, in spite of himself, he paused a moment without turning, to say, still quietly, "Whatever my reasons for bearing with you in the first place, it happens that I did not defend your latest conduct for your parents' sake, but for your own." He did not wait to see if Thomas would answer, but went.

He had quite expected Thomas to ride off immediately; but when he returned to the tent a half hour later, Thomas was not only still there, but had unpacked his bundle and spoke no more of going home. Stephen thought that it had perhaps been Thomas's last piece of insolence – shocking when judged even by Thomas's recent standard of courtesy – that had shamed him into obedience; but in reality it was Stephen's final remark that had been too much for Thomas to resist. If Stephen really cared whether he stayed or went, then he was staying, as he had all along wanted to do.

TWELVE

Three days later, Renier – who not ten minutes before had gone from the tent with his squire, having announced his intention of hunting out a pretty Scottish girl and whiling away a pleasant hour or two in her company – came back grinning. "Have you heard the good news?"

William Reynolds, it appeared, was well on the way to recovery and even able to walk about a little. "So now our valiant hero is not a murderer any longer," Renier added with a glance at Thomas who was morosely polishing Stephen's helmet.

Stephen, too relieved and pleased by the news even to have heard Renier's last remark, said feelingly, "Heaven be praised! I cannot say how thankful I am." Smiling, he turned to Thomas. "And I know you must be thankful, too. It's all been rather like a nightmare, has it not? But now, thank God, it is over and we can start to be ourselves once again." More seriously, he went on, "Thomas, I think that yon should go and see William Reynolds and ask his pardon. It'll not be an easy thing to do, I know, but it would – "

"No!" Thomas jumped to his feet and stood glaring at Stephen defiantly. "No, never! You cannot make me do it." He threw down Stephen's helmet and the greasy rag with which he had been cleaning it and flung out of the tent, pushing past Renier.

"There's gratitude for you," said Renier. He laughed with less amusement than was usual with him. "If I were you, Stephen, I'd wring his neck for him and feed him to the crows. Well, I must be off. I only came back for a moment to tell you about young William." He beckoned to his squire and they left together.

"Poor Thomas. Now that there's nothing more to worry about, no doubt he'll mend his manners," said Stephen, making for Thomas one of his by now habitual excuses.

Sir Fulke, in no way convinced, murmured doubtfully; and Stephen added, "Whatever William said to him, it must have been something very vile, that he can still feel so strongly about it. I wish we knew what it was, it would make it easier to deal with Thomas."

After a moment's silence, Sir Fulke said casually – far too casually, "If I were you, Stephen, I'd not try too hard to find out."

His tone aroused Stephen's suspicions. "Why not?"

"Well . . . For Thomas's sake. It's all over now. Let bygones be bygones and give the poor lad a chance to forget it."

Since it had been Sir Fulke, even more than Renier, who, for the past two weeks, had not had a single good word to say for Thomas, this confirmed Stephen's suspicions.

"You know what it was that William said, Fulke, do you not?"

Awkwardly, Sir Fulke admitted, "I did hear something yesterday."

"From whom?"

Sir Fulke shrugged his shoulders. "It seems that when William Reynolds came to himself, he talked to Sir John and gave him his tale of what had happened, and Sir John – the devil take him – has been passing it around. With trimmings of his own, no doubt."

"What was it William said?"

"It's all a lot of nonsense. No one in his right mind could believe it," Sir Fulke said quickly.

Stephen said very quietly, "You, for one, believe it, Fulke, or you'd have told me what it was by now. Tell me what he said. I must know."

"It's nothing worth repeating."

"Do you want me to get it from someone else? From Sir John de Forrest, perhaps?"

"Very well, if you must." Sir Fulke gestured his squire outside and when the two of them were alone, he said with embarrassment, not looking at Stephen, "It was only some foolishness about you and a Worcestershire knight named Paine Someone-or-other in Gloucester. How you had been traitors and the other man was executed but you were not because . . . oh, because you'd sold him." His voice tailed off unhappily.

230

Stephen stayed very still. For a moment the past was very close, pressing down upon him in the confined space of the tent, suffocating him and swallowing him up. He clenched his fists at his sides and closed his eyes. Then with a great effort he opened his eyes again and unclenched his fists and said, quite without emotion, "I wonder how they found out."

Sir Fulke, very red in the face, muttered something about having some matter or other to which he ought to be attending, and made his way to the entrance of the tent. As he was moving aside the flaps of leather that covered the opening, Stephen said after him, still in the same expressionless voice, "You may care to know this: I did not betray him."

"I could have told you that," said Sir Fulke gruffly. "And if anyone else tells me that you did, I'll knock his teeth down his throat for him."

Somehow, Stephen managed to give a little laugh and to speak lightly. "So long as you do not use a mallet to do it with . . ."

Sir Fulke, very thankful that Stephen seemed to have taken the slander so well, laughed in reply, let drop the tent flap and went.

Stephen stood staring after him, motionless. Poor Thomas, he was thinking. Poor Thomas.

THIRTEEN

After careful consideration, Stephen came to the conclusion that it would be best that Thomas should be told that he knew what William Reynolds had said about him. Now that there were others who were repeating the story, it was not unlikely that Thomas would hear it again from someone else, and it might well prevent him from future embroilments if he knew that Stephen admitted the truth – or most of the truth – of what was being said. Stephen had no way of knowing whether Thomas's fury with William had been prompted in part by liking or admiration for himself, or whether Thomas had only been avenging the slur on his own honour, which he would naturally consider disparaged by such a defamation of the knight he served. Merely the latter, Stephen suspected; but, one way or the other, he was certain that he must tell Thomas the truth, and that the sooner he did so, the less chance there was of Thomas's getting himself into further trouble. Accordingly, he decided to tell him the following day.

Stephen did not find it possible at any time during the next morning to be alone with Thomas; but in the afternoon he told him to come with him, and led the way to a spot a little beyond the camp, outside the protecting ring of baggage-wagons, to where the trampled ground gave way once more to unspoilt grass. He sat down on the side of a felled tree and motioned Thomas to do likewise; but Thomas, after a momentary hesitation, sat down on the ground a good five feet off from Stephen and a little turned away. Almost as though ignoring Stephen, he sat bent forward and moodily plucking at a tuft of grass.

Above them, and over the river valley, and over the bare, grey Lammermuir Hills in the distance, larks sang in a blue sky; behind them were the noises of the camp: the metallic hammering of smiths and armourers, the neighing of horses, the shouts of men – all the busy bustle of a great army, prepared and waiting and relentless. And still the larks burbled on, indifferent and joyous. Could they hear the larks in Berwick, too? wondered Stephen, for a brief moment forgetting Thomas and himself. They must be growing hungry now in Berwick – growing hungry and losing hope.

Then, glancing at Thomas and reflecting that it was not going to be at all easy, but that it was best to come to the point straight away, Stephen said quietly, "Thomas, I want to tell you that I know what it was that William Reynolds said to you."

It was as though he had struck Thomas. Thomas's head jerked up and he twisted round to face Stephen, his sullenness, his indifference, all gone in a flash to be replaced by appalled incredulity. "No!" he gasped. "No! How could you know?"

"I was told."

"It was a lot of cursed lies," said Thomas quickly. He began, distractedly, to improvise, as though by what he was saying he could alter what Stephen had been told. "He said I was a coward and that it was . . . it was no use your taking me to war with you, as . . . as I would turn tail and run back home at the sight of the first armed enemy and – "

Stephen broke in gently, "Thomas, thank you. But there's no need. I told you: I know what he said – about me."

Thomas's gabbling died away. He blushed to the roots of his red hair, and then, almost as quickly, became very pale. He looked down at the ground beside him. "William is a liar. No one will believe him," he said clumsily. Then abruptly, as though the thought had only just come into his mind that, if Stephen had been told, someone must have done the telling, he turned again to Stephen, his own confusion forgotten now that he was angry. "Who told you? Tell me who it was and I'll kill him for you."

It was then that Stephen knew for whose sake it was that William Reynolds had almost died. He shook his head. "No, Thomas, that's what I want to prevent. I do not know exactly William's words to you, but if he said what I was told he said, then they were true – all save that I betrayed a friend. I could never have done that." When Thomas, now staring at the ground, did not reply, Stephen said, "I'm sorry, Thomas. For your sake I wish I could deny it all."

After a long silence Thomas, still without raising his head, said in what was a poor pretence at a casual manner, "Were you – I mean, was he – involved with the Scots?"

The idea of Sir Pagan's having been involved with the Scots was ridiculous rather than shocking; and in any case, to someone born into a family which had admired Thomas of Lancaster, being involved with the Scots did not seem so very terrible. But Stephen could imagine that to the son of a man who had so often campaigned with that King Edward who had been called the Hammer of the Scots, it must seem an unforgivable crime. For Thomas's sake he answered with a show of indignation, "The Scots! Of course not! He wanted to restore the late King."

Thomas cheered up at once. "If your friend was not a traitor and you did not betray him, then William's tale was as good as a lie." After a moment he said awkwardly, "I've not thanked you for all you did . . . For standing up for me . . . Have I? But I am grateful, you know, even if I've not seemed so."

Stephen smiled. "I've not thanked you, either, for standing up for me. So we're quits."

With even more embarrassment, Thomas mumbled, "I bungled it. I lost my temper. I'll be more careful next time."

"Thomas, it is a next time that I want to prevent."

For a moment Thomas looked rebellious once again. "But why should I – " He checked himself and glanced sideways at Stephen. "Yes, sir. I'm sorry. I'll try and keep out of trouble," he said with surprising meekness; but added with a defiance that belied his former tone, "Yet only for your sake, because you say so."

"Thank you," said Stephen with mock gravity. "I'm very much obliged for your consideration." He glanced sideways at Thomas, as Thomas had glanced at him, and added, smiling, "You incorrigible wretch."

Thomas grinned impertinently at Stephen. "Everyone has been calling me that for the last three years, but you're the only one to make it sound like a compliment."

"I assure you, it was not meant for a compliment," said Stephen. And then they were all of a sudden both laughing with heartfelt relief.

After the laughter, Thomas got up off the ground and came and sat on the tree-trunk, where Stephen had earlier bidden him sit. "This knight, sir," he said after a pause, "your friend, was it he who showed you all those jousting tricks?"

Stephen, who in his tilting instruction with Thomas had never failed to give all the credit for his skill to his teacher, said, "Yes, it was."

"He must have been a fine knight," said Thomas simply.

"He was." After a long moment Stephen added slowly, "The man who did betray him, he's dead. I killed him four years ago. I've never told that to anyone else before."

Thomas turned his head to consider Stephen, who was staring straight ahead of him, back into the past. Thomas's no longer sullen face was alight with satisfaction and approbation and his blue eyes were bright. "I'm very glad," he said with feeling. Then, a little diffidently, "Will you tell me about it, sir?"

Stephen came back from the past and looked at Thomas. "Not now, Thomas. But I will, some day." As he turned away again, he was thinking how strange it was that he had meant what he said, and that he would indeed not find it as impossible to speak of himself to this unruly, moody and unpredictable youth as he found it to speak to everyone else that he knew.

After that, Thomas was more consistently cheerful and talkative than he had ever been. He seemed at last completely to have accepted Stephen as a friend and someone to be trusted. He spoke quite often of himself, and from the things he said – and perhaps even more from those which he did not say because he did not himself realize them – the apparent contradictions of his character explained themselves in part to Stephen and he could understand what Thomas's parents, too close to him, had failed to discern. With his swift perception he could sympathize with the spoilt and adored only son, the centre of his parents' world, too long kept at home, and then, suddenly, when he had grown to look upon admiration and indulgence as his rights, thrust into an alien household where he was no more regarded than any other boy. And though it was not all plain to him, Stephen, sensitive and imaginative as he was, could even begin to visualize Thomas, resenting bitterly the loss of the undivided attention to which he had in the past been accustomed, and being in himself no more than ordinary – neither particularly beautiful nor particularly clever, nor in any way outstanding – trying, without even comprehending his own intentions, to win back his preeminence in the only way he could: by being more troublesome and more ill-behaved than any of the other boys, and thus proving his superiority over all others in that one respect at least.

FOURTEEN

As the days went by and supplies grew short and no Scottish army came to attack the besiegers, the keeper of Berwick, Sir Alexander Seton, hoping to save his town from destruction at the hands of the English, sent to King Edward pledging his word to surrender upon a certain date, if the town had not by then been relieved. To this the King agreed, taking from Sir Alexander, as proof of his good faith, several hostages, amongst them his own son Thomas.

It began to seem as though Berwick would fall without the regent's making any attempt to keep for Scotland that town which was the gateway to the Lowlands, and Stephen and Renier wondered whether, after all, they were not to see battle. Renier acknowledged himself disappointed; but Stephen was unsure of his feelings and did not know whether he was sorry or otherwise.

And then, before the date fixed for the surrender, a small band of Scots, determined at all costs to save Berwick for King David, managed to win its way through the English guard and gain entry to the town. Sir William Keith, its leader, as the hero of the hour, was popularly acclaimed and chosen as the town's new governor. Declaring that the entry of himself and a handful of men into Berwick had been a relief of the beleaguered garrison, when the appointed day came, he refused to surrender the town.

King Edward, with characteristic anger, had a tall gallows set up opposite the gates of Berwick and here he hanged young Thomas Seton within sight of his father in the town.

Later that day, looking at the body which still hung high before the walls as a warning to the enemy, Renier said to Stephen with satisfaction, "That should show them that they cannot trifle with us. I doubt if they'll try to cheat us again."

"God help the rest of the hostages if they do," said Stephen. One Scotsman more or less meant nothing to him – no more than it meant to Renier – and a hostage always had to expect the chance that he might be sacrificed by those who had handed him over; and men were hanged for one reason or another all over England every day – and what did it matter except to those who knew them? But for all that, Stephen could not help thinking of Thomas Seton's father and wondering how he had felt, watching his son die when he might have been saved.

Half to himself, Renier forgotten beside him, he said, "It must be so much worse when one knows that there was something one could have done to prevent it, and did not."

"Whatever are you talking about?"

Stephen came back to the present at the sound of Renier's voice repeating the question for the third time. "Nothing," he said. "Nothing at all. I'm sorry, I was not listening."

"What's the matter with you, Stephen? You're as white as though you'd seen the Devil. Have you got the belly-ache? I'll not be surprised if you have, because I'm always having it myself. It's the filthy food we have to eat. Fulke says it's often like this in camp in the hot weather. There's no way of keeping the meat cool. Oh well" – he gave a chuckle – "I'll wager the food is even worse in Berwick. We have little enough to grumble about. Come on, let's find some wine and drink damnation to the Scots. The wine is still good, thank heaven."

FIFTEEN

One day, by chance and quite unexpectedly, above one of the many groups of tents surrounding Berwick, Stephen had seen the crimson sanglier fluttering in the breeze. For a moment he had been surprised and then, with a smile, had reflected that the astonishing thing would be if there should be a war and the de Beauvilles were not there.

He had thought no more about it, and then one morning a fortnight or so later, one of his cousin's squires came running to say that he was wanted by Sir Peter. As he approached his cousin's tent, followed by Thomas, he knew why he was wanted.

Outside the tent his father – looking, for all the ten years that had passed, not a day older – together with Godfrey and Henry, was sitting, talking to Peter Boncourt about the recent hanging of Thomas Seton, and drinking wine. They all of them fell silent when they saw Stephen, and the three de Beauvilles observed him curiously. Stephen stopped and

stood staring back at them, and in a moment all the inter-
vening years that had gone by since he had seen them last,
slipped away as though they had not been, and for a moment
he was once again the nervous, diffident boy that he had
been at Greavesby, and he was at a complete loss as to what
to do or say. But only for a moment. Still feeling the awk-
wardness of the situation, but covering his discomposure as
well as he could, and his mind no longer a blank as to what
should be done, he stepped forward and courteously knelt
before his father, saying no more than, "My lord."

"It's been a long time since we met, eh, Stephen?" Earl
Robert handed his wine cup to a waiting squire, rose and put
his hands under Stephen's elbows and hauled him to his feet,
slapped him on the back and told him he was looking well.

"And how you have grown! But I suppose it would be
foolish to be surprised at that!" He laughed.

Stephen's half-brothers greeted him affably; Henry with
almost good-tempered amiability, and Godfrey with only
the very faintest trace of condescension.

"Ten years ago, this would have been one of the last
places we should have expected ever to find you, Stephen,"
said Henry.

"We have been hearing from Sir Peter how very skilled
you have become at jousting," said Godfrey. "I must confess that I can hardly credit it." He smiled, with amusement
at his own incredulity rather than with any sign of real
disbelief.

Stephen murmured something polite, but Sir Peter broke
in to say, "Stephen is too modest. He is quite the best of all
my father's younger knights."

Stephen was sure that he must be blushing like any silly
girl, and he was glad to find a squire at his elbow offering
him a cup of wine, so that he could turn away for a moment
to take it and drink.

Earl Robert, accepting a second cup of wine, said, "It's not often that I am mistaken over a foal or a hound pup or a boy, but I acknowledge now that I was mistaken over you, Stephen. Though I doubt if I was the only one." He drained the cup and admitted handsomely, "I was sure that the only life for you would be that of a monk, but I was wrong, quite wrong, it seems. Was I not?" He looked to his two eldest sons for confirmation.

"As you said, sir, you were not the only one. I thought as you did," said Godfrey.

The Earl turned again to Stephen and said with hearty approval, "I'm only glad that you had the pluck to run away from Richley and prove to us that we were wrong. I'd be sorry to think of any son of mine wasting his life in a monastery when he could be doing better things."

"It's as well that there are no churchmen around to hear you say that, Father," remarked Henry; and they all laughed, and Stephen with them.

Earl Robert turned to speak with Sir Peter; and Stephen's brothers, talking as if to an equal, began to tell him the news from Greavesby. Their stepmother had died at last, two years before, and the Earl had lost little time in finding another wife: this Stephen already knew. Joanna was married, with two fine sons: he had heard about the marriage, but not about the sons. Alison had grown into a great beauty and was betrothed: this was news to him. John was to be knighted that year. Thomas and Edmund had been left in charge at Greavesby while the others were at war.

As they talked and he replied to them, easily now, and without any outward trace of embarrassment, Stephen suddenly realized that this was the moment for which he had waited for so long: the fulfilment of the second of his two ambitions. His family had accepted him as worthy of being a de Beauville and admitted to having been at fault. It should have been for him a great moment; and so it might have been, but for the fact that, in that instant, beyond Henry, he caught sight of Thomas – his Thomas – waiting respectfully in the background, watching him. Watching him and not the renowned Earl of Greavesby or his two stalwart warrior sons – watching him, Stephen the weakling, Stephen the misfit, with a look of admiration which he was making no attempt to hide. For that one instant their eyes met, and Thomas immediately grinned at him, impertinently, trustingly and affectionately, in typical Thomas-fashion; so that for a second Stephen almost forgot himself and nearly grinned back. Recollecting himself in time, he turned again to Godfrey, who was speaking, but there was now a warm, comfortable glow in his heart that had not been there before. In that one short glimpse of Thomas he had learnt that the admiration of one person for whom one cares, is worth all the praise, the respect, the flattery, that could possibly be offered one by those for whom one cares nothing. And all at once it no longer seemed particularly important what his family thought of him, so long as Thomas admired him. This strange truth made plain to him, with difficulty he brought his mind back to his brothers and found that it was now Henry who was speaking. He managed to make the right responses and ask a few questions without appearing too abstracted, and then he saw that his father was about to take his leave of Sir Peter.

Before he mounted his horse, Earl Robert said to Stephen, "When Berwick has fallen you must come to Greavesby and pay your respects to your new stepmother. She is younger than you are, you know." He laughed heartily at the oddity of this; and Stephen was about to make some courteous but indeterminate reply, when Sir Peter, who had never approved of Stephen's breach with his father, broke in to support the idea enthusiastically and to give his permission –

for which Stephen had not intended to ask – for Stephen to leave for Yorkshire with the Earl immediately the campaign was over. So Stephen, willy-nilly, found himself committed to accompany his father to Greavesby and remain there for several days at some future date – perhaps not so far in the future, either, for Earl Robert was saying, "They'll not hold out much longer, unless they want to see all their hostages go the way of young Seton. I warrant it will all be well over by Lammastide."

Earl Robert was right: Berwick was to yield before August.

SIXTEEN

At the beginning of July, fearing for the lives of the remaining hostages, Sir William Keith sent again to the King, now offering to surrender if the town were not relieved within the next fifteen days. This time, it was popularly supposed in the English camp, Berwick was as good as theirs; but belatedly the supporters of little King David, led by the regent, Sir Archibald Douglas, made an effort to save the town. A very large Scottish army marched towards Berwick and was encamped a short distance away by the eighteenth of July.

The English, many as they were, were yet outnumbered; but King Edward had time to choose the most advantageous position in which to meet the enemy. On the nineteenth of July, having left just sufficient of his troops to prevent the defenders of Berwick from breaking out of the town, he marched with the remainder of his army to Halidon Hill, a short way north-west. On the hill-side he drew up his men in three battle-lines, with the woods behind them and, before them, the marshy ground at the foot of the hill. Save for a very small reserve of mounted men, the King ordered all his knights and men-at-arms to send their horses to the rear and fight on foot until such time as he should give word for them to mount. Each of the three battle-lines was made up of heavily-armed knights and men-at-arms in the centre, flanked by wings of archers. Edward Balliol commanded the left line, the King's brother, John of Eltham, the right line, and the King himself – on foot like all the rest – led the central line.

To Stephen waiting on the hill, looking down upon the Scottish army as it approached, the sun glinting on its banners and its weapons and armour, it seemed like no more than a tournament, such as he had taken part in so many times before. It was too vast, somehow, too impersonal, to seem out of the ordinarily dangerous. There was always the chance of danger to life or limb in any tournament – that was a risk which the participants took – but the accidents were never deliberate when they occurred; and, against all reason, it seemed no different today. Perhaps it was because the siege had dragged on so long and the war on which they were engaged had become remote, he thought. He remembered a time when he had waited on another hill-side on the slope above the road from Evesham to Tewkesbury. Then, it had seemed real enough; then, he had been nervous and apprehensive and afraid. Was it because he had been younger and with little experience of tournaments; or was it because it made a difference whether one was going into battle for the sake of the King of England – a stranger – or for the sake of one's friend?

He tried to remind himself that it was real and deadly, and that by sunset many men would have died – perhaps even he; but not all his knowledge of its reality could dispel his feeling of its being no more than a sham. It was his first battle and he was taking it as casually as any seasoned warrior – or rather, he was despising it in a way that no seasoned warrior would have dared to despise it. He smiled a little at himself inwardly. By tonight you will know better, he told himself. By then you will have learnt that this is no mock battle. And please God, you will not have learnt it too hardly.

By that night Stephen was indeed to have learnt what war was like; but in not quite the way he had expected.

The Scottish army picked its way across the marsh and drew up at the foot of the hill in three closely packed columns. Then, proudly remembering Bannockburn and Stirling Bridge, Sir Archibald Douglas, the regent, boldly and confidently led his countrymen up the hill-side, to be met by a rain of English arrows. In a vain attempt to reach the English lines and engage their enemies in closer combat, the Scots pressed on in the face of a now ceaseless flood of arrows; but only on the right, where John of Eltham led, did the English give a yard of ground. On the left and in the centre the Scots were flung back down the hill, disorganized and utterly dismayed. Then King Edward gave the command for his knights to mount and attack, and they galloped down the hill after the retreating Scots.

Thomas, eager and excited, brought Stephen's horse from behind the battle-lines and Stephen mounted and joined in the pursuit, down the hill and on to more level ground. It still seemed to him no different from a tournament – a tournament where one side has proved easily the stronger and has put the other to rout. But what followed was outside the rules of any tournament. The English took few prisoners and gave little quarter. Here and there a group of desperate Scots would stand together and turn at bay, only to be charged and scattered by the victors. But most of them fled in any direction, many of them to be ridden down before they had gone half a mile.

Riding eastwards with a group of English knights, Stephen pursued and struck down as the others did, with no thought of what he was doing. It was still unreal to him. And then, as their blood warmed to it, and as the slight Scottish resistance grew even less, it became half a sport to them, like hunting, and their flying quarry less than men.

The day wore on and the slaughter continued; and then suddenly, near the seashore north of Berwick it ended – for Stephen – when he became aware of the Scottish man-at-arms, spitted on the end of his lance, as a human being like himself. He was by no means the first to die that way, on that same lance, but he died a little harder than the others, and so Stephen had time to notice him, writhing on his back on the grass with the lance through his middle, screaming as his legs flailed and kicked and his two hands clutched impotently at the shaft. He was only a cursed Scot, and an enemy; but the Scots, as Christians, were far above the Saracens; and the Saracens, as Stephen had learnt, were human beings and capable of generosity and kindness – so how much more the Christian Scots? Shaken by the reflection, Stephen almost flung himself off his horse that he might with all speed draw his sword and cut off the man's head and so end his agony. But for God's mercy, he thought, it might have been he who had been lain there that day, with a Scottish lance through his belly, screaming out his life on the grass.

He looked about him and saw how many of the Scots driven down over the rocks and pursued even to the edge of the sea, were making a last stand for their lives. Between the sea and the victorious enemy, they had no chance; they either fell, hacked to pieces; or where their wounds were slight, they drowned. Stephen remounted and turned his horse's head and rode back for the camp. All the way, wherever he looked, there were dead and dying and wounded; and the sea-gulls and the crows were already flying low and screeching and croaking overhead.

In that day's battle, the English reckoned their losses at one knight, one squire, and twelve foot-soldiers. Scotland had lost its regent, six earls, and countless knights and men-at-arms.

Berwick opened its gates to the English the next day, and King Edward ordered a general thanksgiving for his victory.

SEVENTEEN

It seemed strange to Stephen to be approaching Greavesby again after so many years. The grey castle still looked the same, poised on its grey rocks, frowning across the green dale. Long before the Earl's army reached the village at the foot of the spur, the horns from the gatehouse had blared out a welcome to their lord and been answered from below; and long before the Earl's horse had set one hoof upon the road which wound up the hill, the drawbridge was down and the gates were open wide to receive him back from war. All was the same as it had always been, thought Stephen. All was the same, save that this time he was amongst those who were returning, and not amongst the women and children within the walls.

His half-brother Thomas and his cousin Edmund rode down the hill to greet the Earl, eager for news from Scotland; and in the gateway of the inner bailey stood the new young Countess with her waiting-women, and just behind her, a nurse holding Stephen's latest and youngest half-brother in swaddling clothes. Earl Robert was pleased by this. His previous Countess, pale and wan, had always waited for him beside the fire-place in the solar; which was no sort of welcome home for a man. He dismounted, kissed his wife heartily and admired the baby, which had not yet been born when he had ridden away.

The rowan-tree still stood in the courtyard, Stephen was glad to find. He recognized a number of the servants, and the jester was there, too, older, but still as lively as ever; yet since he had never had any friends amongst them, it was the rowan-tree's being there which meant more to Stephen.

His half-brother Thomas, and his cousin Edmund, though both surprised to see him, did not appear displeased, and both greeted him affably enough; though Thomas, as usual, jested a little at his expense, and Edmund seemed, as he had ever been, somewhat scornful of him. Edmund had grown into just the young man that Stephen would have expected him to be: of his own height, but broad-shouldered, large-handed and seemingly firm and immovable as a rock.

Sitting at the high table, eating of the feast that had been prepared against the Earl's homecoming, while the musicians played and the jester capered, and everyone ate and drank and talked and laughed too much, Stephen thought how, although they had all accepted him and were all being civil and friendly, he did not really belong amongst them. He belonged now no more than he had done before – he was still too different from them. Here, he felt like a guest: Greavesby was no longer his home. Had it ever been? he wondered.

Suddenly Edmund, his face flushed with wine, and grinning, shouted along the table at him, "Cousin Stephen, what's this I hear about your being a good jouster?"

"What about it?" said Stephen.

"I do not believe it, that's all."

"I never asked you to believe it, Edmund."

"Is it true?"

Stephen shrugged his shoulders and smiled. "How can I answer that? You should ask someone who has watched me."

"But is it true?" persisted Edmund.

"I've been told so." Everyone at the high table was listening to them by now, and Stephen wished that Edmund would grow tired of the subject.

"Well, I do not believe it," said Edmund loudly. "And I'd like to see you attempt to prove it."

Into the silence that followed, Stephen said quietly, "You can, whenever you like, Edmund. I'll not prevent you." He smiled at his cousin and turned away, meaning to try to start speaking with someone else and so end the argument.

But his half-brother Thomas asked, laughing, "Is that a challenge, Stephen?"

The suggestion appealed to the Earl; and before Stephen could answer, he had said, "Of course it's a challenge, is it not, Stephen? We'll match you two against each other on the tilting-ground tomorrow. What about it, Edmund?" He gave Edmund no time to do more than nod an eager agreement and throw a mocking glance in the direction of Stephen, before adding, "Edmund is a pretty good jouster, you know, Stephen."

"I'm quite sure he is, sir," said Stephen, who had no doubt whatever of it: Edmund had always done everything of that sort well. But, thanks be to God – and to Sir Pagan – he was not afraid of disgracing himself. He would be able to hold his own against his cousin, at least for a while; and though Edmund was bound to be the victor in the end, he would not have done so ill himself. All the same, he thought, it was a pity that the situation had arisen.

Helping him to undress that night, Thomas said to him, "Your cousin Edmund dislikes you very much, does he not?"

Stephen smiled. "If he does, that's only fair, since I dislike him, too."

"Well, I hate him," declared Thomas savagely.

Had it been anyone other than a member of his family whom he was to meet, Stephen, with the remembrance of the conclusions of past contests to encourage him, would have been confident enough, and not unhopeful of the issue. But Edmund was a de Beauville, and all the members of his family were superior to him, therefore Stephen was prepared for defeat; it was, he felt, inevitable. Edmund, his own age, had always been his better in every respect that mattered: so it would be Edmund's victory. Stephen did not even feel that, so long as he did his best – and that best was, after all, not so very poor – there would be any reproach in being worsted by someone who had always worsted him in every way. When the time came for the test, he was quite resigned to his defeat; and undoubtedly, without his intending it to do so, this attitude would have had an adverse effect upon his performance on the tilting-ground.

But he had reckoned without Thomas. To Thomas FitzAmory, Stephen was far and away the best of his family and the only one of the de Beauvilles who mattered. Kneeling on the rushes, fastening on Stephen's spurs, without looking up, Thomas said confidently, "I'm glad you are having this chance to show your skill. I hope you break a few of your hateful cousin's bones when you send him to the ground. I'd like it to be his neck, but I'll settle for two arms and two legs instead."

It was like a pail of cold water over Stephen. In his acceptance of the inevitable he had not considered Thomas. For a few moments he could say nothing; then, with a cheerful assurance which he felt must sound as false to Thomas as it did to him, he said, "I'll do my best." Then, thinking it cruel not to give Thomas at least some warning of what was undoubtedly going to happen, he added, "Of course, I'm not certain yet that I shall be able to beat him."

"Of course you will." Thomas was unperturbed.

Stephen tried again. More seriously he said, "I mean it, Thomas. Edmund may very well get the better of me."

This time the words had some effect. Thomas sat back on his heels and looked up, a lock of red hair fallen across one eye, his mouth open in shocked astonishment. "But you must beat him, sir. You cannot let us down!" he exclaimed, appalled.

It was that which changed Stephen's frame of mind. Seeing Thomas's concern, Stephen knew that it was true: he could not let Thomas down – Thomas who believed in him; Thomas who was worth more to him than all his family together. He smiled at Thomas. "I'll not let us down," he said. And by "us" he meant the three of them: Thomas, himself – and Sir Pagan.

When Stephen rode on to the tilting-ground, he was no longer thinking of Edmund as his cousin and a de Beauville. Edmund was now merely another antagonist such as Stephen had met with so many times before: a stranger, his equal or possibly inferior to himself; and the combat would be like any of the scores of others in which Stephen had taken part and acquitted himself well. His family banished from his mind, he levelled his lance at the stranger at the other end of the field and waited for the signal to charge.

The whole castle had turned out to see the combat. Since they were all familiar with Edmund's skill, the onlookers were all presuming he would be the victor. But had there been anyone at Greavesby who had seen Stephen joust before, he would have had no doubt of the outcome, even before the combat began. Edmund had skill but he was slow-thinking, conventional and unimaginative, and he relied too much on the power of his lance-thrusts and the strength of the muscles that guided them. Stephen found him no mean opponent, but he had unhorsed him within the first five minutes of their meeting; and the only one there who was not surprised, was Thomas FitzAmory.

All things considered, Edmund took his defeat remarkably well; and Stephen, who always did, took his victory without vaunting. And so, as a whole, the de Beauvilles were not un-pleased with their newly-accredited kinsman. Stephen's remaining days at Greavesby went well; though he was glad to leave there a week later, with the excuse that he was expected in Lincolnshire by Thomas's father, for Greavesby held too many unhappy memories for him.

EIGHTEEN

Edward Balliol paid for the English help which had won him the crown of Scotland, with half the Lowlands – and with the whole of the love and respect of his fellow-countrymen, who hated and despised him for betraying them to the English. In May 1334, young David Bruce, whose supporters could no longer guard him securely, fled to France; but once he was safely there, they rallied, gathering followers. Edward Balliol's adherents quarrelled among themselves, and the King of England soon found that his Scottish lands were his only in name. He was in Scotland for the greater part of the winter of that year with a vast army, overrunning the Lowlands at enormous expense, and he kept his court at Roxburgh that Christmastide.

Stephen was with the English army for much of that year and he was with it again in the summer of 1335, when the King and Edward Balliol led two great forces through the Lowlands to converge on Perth, which was holding out for King David. All the time, the Scots harried the English and Balliol's men, laid ambushes and made surprise attacks, but refused to give battle. The indecisive situation seemed likely to drag on and on; and then, in November, there was a truce. It was not to last long, but while it lasted it was welcome. Peter Boncourt and his father's men took the opportunity of going home, and set off at once for Berwick and the Border, talking of Christmas at Manningfield.

Stephen was not sorry. The long-drawn-out campaign in Scotland, of which he had seen a good deal, had accustomed him to war, but it had not taught him to enjoy it. He had found it bearable only because of Thomas's companionship and the pleasure he obtained from watching Thomas's youthful enthusiasm, which had stimulated his own. Thomas had thoroughly enjoyed it all, the excitement and the weariness, the adventure and the discomfort alike; and his attitude had done much to reconcile Stephen to happenings he would otherwise have found distressing and actions he would else have found it distasteful to perform.

But now it was over – at least for a time – and Stephen was glad. In the last months he had seen enough of the destruction and misery brought about by war, and the famine and disease which too often followed on the heels of an invading army. It was with quite a light heart that he set off with his companions, telling Thomas that they would leave the others at Nottingham to make their way into Lincolnshire to see Thomas's parents – for the first time in more than two years – before continuing southwards for Christmas at Manningfield Castle. He was looking forward to showing off Thomas to Baron Simon and Lady Alis, and to watching their pleasure and pride at the reformation of their son; for, after the fall of Berwick and their days at Greavesby, Stephen and Thomas had been no more than three nights with them; too short a time in which to prove to two people who had learnt to expect the worst of him, that Thomas was indeed changed for the better.

They made their way southwards from Perth with good speed, and were all in high spirits in spite of the dreary weather and the ravaged countryside through which they passed. But by the time they reached Haddington in East

Lothian, Thomas seemed to Stephen unduly silent, riding listlessly and staring sullenly before him, almost in the manner of his very early days with Stephen. Stephen wondered whether it was because, as far as they were concerned, the campaign was over, and he tried to cheer Thomas out of his mood; but Thomas made little effort to respond. Later in the day Stephen surprised him with his head bent into one hand, pressing and rubbing hard with his fingers on his forehead, as though he would have thrust back something which lay behind his brow.

Stephen thought that he now understood the reason for Thomas's silence. "Have you the headache?" he asked sympathetically.

Thomas instantly took his hand from his brow. "No, no. It's nothing," he lied, touchily.

"It will no doubt be better in the morning," said Stephen.

But by the next day it was worse; so much so that Thomas was obliged to admit that his head ached, though he tried to make light of it. But a few hours later he had to admit, also, to a pain in his back. The next day he was flushed and feverish, and it was obvious that he was sickening for something.

During that morning they passed through a burnt-out and deserted village where the English, subduing the Lowlands a year before, had left no single dwelling standing, and, a little farther on, a small stone manor surrounded by a wall of wooden palings. The house itself seemed untouched, save for the lower storeroom, but most of the wooden outbuildings had been burnt and the gate had been broken down and still lay, with grass growing tall and yellowed about it, at the foot of the palings.

A serving-wench who had been cutting rushes, looking up to see the horsemen approaching, dropped rushes and sickle and ran for the house. On Sir Peter's orders, two of the men-at-arms galloped after her and caught her before she reached the gateway. They brought her, struggling, to him to be questioned as to how far away the nearest religious house might be. It lay, according to the girl, more than twenty miles on. Released, the girl fled, and Sir Peter said, "We should be there before dark." Adding, with a glance at Thomas, "If Thomas can ride that far."

Thomas passed his tongue over his dry lips. "Of course I can ride that far, sir." He added complainingly, "If only my stomach were not so confoundedly queasy!"

They went on, but they were no more than a mile beyond the manor when it became evident to Stephen that Thomas would not be able to go on, and he said so to his cousin. "I'll find some house here to take him in, and then, tomorrow or the day after, we'll join you at that priory of which the girl told us, if you will wait there a day or two."

Sir Peter, watching Thomas, doubled up, retching by the side of the roadway, asked, "And what if, by that time, he's still not fit to travel?"

"Then you must go on to Manningfield without us if you will, and we'll come after you as soon as we can. In any case, cousin, we had only been going together as far as Nottingham. I'd have parted from you there, so that Thomas could see his parents on the way south."

"That's true," agreed Sir Peter. "Very well, cousin, we'll leave you here. I hope we see you in two days' time. But if not, we'll not wait for you."

He left three of the men-at-arms with Stephen and rode off with the rest of the company. Stephen went to Thomas and told him of their plans.

Thomas, whom the fever had made irritable, snapped, "I'm sorry I'm being such an inconvenience to you."

Stephen put an arm around him and helped him to his feet.

254

"Come on. Let's see what Scottish hospitality can do for us. Do you think you can ride a little farther? We'll go back to that house we passed. The girl went in there, so it cannot be deserted."

"Scottish hospitality!" said Thomas. "They'll probably cut all our throats in the night." As two of the men-at-arms were heaving him into the saddle, he said, "They are welcome to cut mine. It would at least cure my headache."

Once back at the manor, Stephen sent one of the men to knock up the folk inside. The door of the storeroom on the ground floor had been broken open and stood against the house wall, unmended. The man glanced inside and called back that there was nothing there save some firewood and a little hay, before going up the outside steps to the hall-floor and hammering on the door with the butt of his lance. Stephen and the other two men helped Thomas from his horse and sat him down on a pile of dry-stone rubble that had once been the wall of a sheep-pen or a pigsty.

There was no move from inside the barred and shuttered house until the man-at-arms began to yell out that unless the door was opened they would set fire to the place. Then, after about five minutes, the door was unbarred and opened a little way by a woman. The man would have thrust his way in past her, but, leaving Thomas, Stephen hastened to prevent him.

He began to speak courteously to the woman, but she interrupted him. "There's nothing left here worth looting. You English took it all, twelve months ago. Can you not leave us even to our sorrow in peace?" She was middle-aged and gaunt and she wore an apron over her faded gown; but the stuff of the gown was good and there were both dignity and courage in the way she stood in the doorway facing her enemies, one hand on the door's edge and the other on the doorpost, her arms a bar to keep them out.

"Madam," said Stephen, "I would like to speak to the master of this house."

"My husband – God rest his soul – has been dead these ten years and more. He was a brave and honourable knight and I thank God that he was spared the knowledge of all this." She flung out a hand towards the broken gate and the blackened outbuildings. "My three sons – may God give them joy in heaven – were killed in battle by the English. I am now the master of this house, and as such, I ask you to go."

"My squire is ill and can ride no farther. He must be under a roof and in a bed with no delay."

"Not in any bed under my roof," she said.

"Madam, he is ill and must have shelter." Stephen gestured towards Thomas. "He is only young, what harm could he have done to you or yours?"

"He is English, that is harm enough." She looked past Stephen towards Thomas, sitting on the pile of stones, his head in his hands, and added bitterly, "My youngest son was little older, yet he died with his brothers."

"We wish you no mischief, madam, and I will pay you well for food and lodging."

"Pay! I would not touch English gold, if it were offered. As for food, we have barely enough for ourselves." She drew herself up even straighter and said, "We are only women here, with no men left to protect us. I cannot prevent you from entering my house, but no Englishman shall ever step over my threshold again with my leave."

Stephen glanced at Thomas and turned back to the woman, hardening his heart. He pitied her and he admired the courage that had brought her to stand there defying them, her body the only barrier between five armed enemies and what remained of her household; but Thomas meant more to him than the widows of a thousand Scottish knights. "Madam, I am determined to enter. My squire must find shelter here. For the love of God do not force me to use violence against you."

For a moment she seemed to waver and her eyes went past him again towards Thomas. Then her hands grasped more firmly at door and door-post and she looked at Stephen. "There are three young serving-girls in the house. Do you swear to me as a Christian that no harm will come to them?"

"No harm will come to anyone in your house from us, I promise you."

There was silence while she considered him, her pale-blue eyes hard and cold as stones, then with a slight shrug of her bony shoulders and a movement as though she were drawing aside from something unclean, she stood back from the door, leaving it open for him.

Stephen smiled at her with sincere relief. "May God reward you, madam." He called to two of the men to bring Thomas and told the other to see the horses stabled as well as was possible, and went into the house.

The great hall was bare and seemed empty, furnished as it was with no more than a trestle table and two benches made from rough-hewn planks laid upon logs; and only a small fire burnt on the wide hearth with a cooking-pot hanging above it. Just inside the house door were two goats tethered, brought in for safekeeping when Stephen and the others had ridden by, half an hour before.

Across the hall, at the foot of the ladderway which led to the upper floor of the house, four women were standing. Three of them were young girls huddled together – one, the girl who had been gathering rushes – but the fourth was old, a short-legged, square-seeming figure with a huge head, standing determinedly in front of the others, holding a pitchfork. As the mistress of the house, followed by Stephen, approached, the four backed farther away, the old woman keeping her pitchfork pointed at Stephen.

With biting irony her mistress said, "These men are my guests, Elspeth."

"Guests! Cursed English dogs!" The old woman spat into the rushes on the floor.

One of the men-at-arms upon whose shoulder Thomas was leaning heavily, called out cheerfully, "You wait until I've got my hands free, you old hag, and out you'll go, on to the midden."

Stephen stopped and turned round. "No one is to offer any sort of violence to anyone in this house, no matter what the provocation. Those are my orders. Do you understand?"

"Yes, sir."

"And see that Jack is told when he has finished with the horses."

"Yes, sir."

Stephen went up the ladderway after the woman, followed by Thomas, stumbling and slow, and the two men, one helping Thomas and the other carrying his gear.

In the upper room, the woman gestured towards the bed. Thomas sat down on its edge with his head in his hands. The woman asked Stephen coldly, "Does he expect me to find him food and drink? There's nothing here to offer a sick lad but well water or a little goats' milk. The English took our cattle and killed our hens and burnt the furniture to cook them by – but they left us two of the goats."

"Thomas? Would you like some goats' milk?"

Thomas raised his head a little. "Goats' milk? No! My stomach is still queasy."

Stephen passed on his refusal to their unwilling hostess in rather more courteous terms; and Thomas, as if reading a rebuke where none had really been intended, made a great effort to be civil. Turning towards the woman, he said, "Thank you. I'm most grateful for your kindness to me." His head sank back on to his hands.

She remained unmoved, but remarked to Stephen, "I do not know where I am expected to find food for the lot of you."

Stephen smiled at her unavailingly. "My men shall go out to see what they can buy for you in the district. I trust we shall not need to be a burden to you for many days."

She left them then; and after reminding the men of his orders to behave themselves, Stephen sent them downstairs. He helped Thomas to undress.

Thomas tried to grin. "Scottish hospitality! What a fearful woman."

"I know. But one cannot blame her. She has little cause to love us. There's hardly a stick of furniture left in the house, and what there is, is broken. She cannot be expected to welcome a second visit from the English." He turned back the coverlet and the bedrugs. "At least the bed looks clean and comfortable enough. In you get."

Looking down at Thomas, lying in the large bed, he asked, "How do you feel now?"

"I've never felt more ill in my life."

"Poor Thomas." Stephen pushed back the thick red hair and laid a cool hand on Thomas's forehead, noticing as he did so, the row of dark spots that had appeared along the hair line. "I've no doubt you'll feel better tomorrow. Try and sleep, if you can."

"You'll not leave me? You'll stay here with me?"

"Of course I'll stay. I'll have to go downstairs every now and then to make sure that the men are not bullying that old spitfire or trying to flirt with the girls, but that will not take long."

Thomas dozed a little on and off during the day; but most of the time he moved and turned restlessly on the bed while

Stephen sat beside him. He refused all Stephen's offers of obtaining food for him, but he drank the cold water which Stephen had one of the men fetch from the well. Spots, like those on his brow, were now also on his face and were spreading rapidly down his neck to his chest.

Their hostess did not come upstairs again that day; but in the evening old Elspeth, the steps of the ladderway creaking under her, brought Stephen a bowl of thin stew and a slice of loaf that was little better than horse-bread, and slapped them down on the bed near him. Before Stephen could thank her, she said, "The Lady Catherine Ramsay bade me bring ye these, or I'd not have done it otherwise. I'd see ye go hungry as we've had to, if I had my way. If our food's not good enough for ye, ye can leave it. There's others would be glad of it." She looked at Thomas. "She also bade me ask ye if the lad was wanting anything." Her whole attitude defied Stephen to dare ask for anything for Thomas. She ignored his thanks and stamped off down the ladderway, her two eyes staring fiercely and balefully at Stephen until her large head had disappeared below the level of the floor.

Lady Catherine Ramsay did not come up to the bedchamber that night; presumably she preferred to remain downstairs in the company of the servants and the men-at-arms to sharing the upper floor with her two guests. But in the morning she came up and asked shortly, "How is he?"

"The fever seems to have left him," said Stephen.

Thomas's fever had certainly abated, but he was very weak and felt little better; and Stephen was disturbed by the red spots.

Lady Catherine came over to the bed and looked at Thomas's face, less flushed now, but thickly covered with spots. Without a word she stretched out her hand and twitched the bedclothes down and stared at Thomas's naked body. There, the red spots were less closely set than on his face, but they were all over him. Her stony expression did not alter a fraction. She flung the bedclothes back to cover him and looked across the bed at Stephen. "Not content with all else they've done to me, the English have to bring the smallpox into my house," she said bitterly.

"The smallpox! Are you sure?" Stephen did not look down at Thomas, but his hand reached out for Thomas's, as Thomas's reached for his.

"Of course I am sure. I've nursed it before."

Even in that moment, Stephen remembered to say, "I am sorry to have been the cause of this further trouble to you." He looked then at Thomas, smiling as cheerfully and confidently as he could. "So we'll not be quit of Scotland for a while yet, it seems. It's ill-fortune for Lady Catherine that we are in her house; but it's good luck for us that she has nursed the smallpox before. She'll be able to tell me what to do for you." He pressed Thomas's hand reassuringly and added, "We'll be home for Candlemas, anyway."

Lady Catherine said, "I'll be sending the girls away. A house full of the smallpox and Englishmen is no place for them. Old Elspeth can stay, she has had the smallpox." Stephen did not need to ask her if she had had it herself, he could see the old pockmarks on the skin that was stretched so tightly over her cheek-bones. She added unexpectedly, "If you wish, you can go. I'll nurse the lad."

"You are very kind, madam, but I want to stay with him." Thomas's grip, which had tightened on his hand at her offer, relaxed, and Stephen smiled down at him. "Never fear, Thomas. Not all the Scots in Scotland will drive me away."

NINETEEN

Stephen told the three men-at-arms that he would be remaining with Thomas, but that if they wished to rejoin Sir

Peter and go straight with him to Berkshire, they might. Two said that they would stay with him, which both pleased and surprised him; though, with his usual modesty, he did not realize how great a compliment he was being paid. The third chose to go home, and Stephen sent a message by him to his cousin, telling him that he would be following after him when Thomas was recovered. He still had hopes that Lady Catherine might be mistaken, and that Thomas had merely caught some feverish rash; but twenty-four hours later it was obvious even to Stephen's unpractised eye that Thomas, whose fever was now quite gone, had smallpox.

Lady Catherine produced some faded red hangings, which she laid over the bed and all about Thomas; the colour red being, she said, possessed of properties most efficacious against the smallpox, as all the greatest physicians knew. She spent a good deal of her time with Stephen and Thomas, and slept on a truckle bed which she set up in the bedchamber. In spite of her dour unfriendliness, Stephen was glad of her calm efficiency and good advice; though Thomas disliked her intensely and preferred to have Stephen do everything for him. Thomas was a fretful, restless patient, alternately grumbling about his bad luck and cursing Scotland and the Scots, and almost tearfully apologizing to Stephen for always having been such a trouble to him. Stephen was unflaggingly kind and gentle, and as cheerful as he could manage to be; though he was naturally worried on Thomas's account.

On old Elspeth, without the three maidservants to help her, fell the work of running the house and cooking for the unwelcome guests. Stephen had told the two men to give her all the help they could; and having nothing better to do with their time, they were not sorry to draw water and go wood-gathering. They also went out foraging in the district; and when they returned with game or poultry and cheeses,

Elspeth did not inquire where or how they had obtained them, but snatched from them everything they brought her without a word of thanks; though Stephen, who had told them to pay for anything they wanted, and Lady Catherine, who had good reason to loathe the looting habits of the English, would both have been shocked had they known how some of the good things were obtained. But they were too busy caring for Thomas to question the source of the ingredients which went into the oatcakes and the chicken-broth which came up to them.

Old Elspeth refused to help with nursing Thomas. At the outset, when she had heard that it was the smallpox which he had, she had come up to the bedchamber and stood looking malevolently at him and said firmly, "Ye need not expect me to lift a finger to help him, mistress, not even if ye bid me to. For all I care, he can die of it, the English whelp." But now that the servingmaids were gone and Lady Catherine slept upstairs again, she, too, came up at nights and lay on the floor at the top of the ladderway, like a snoring bundle of old rags, being unwilling to trust herself to the two men-at-arms. "Those English devils, they'd cut out my heart for the pleasure of it, while I was sleeping," she declared.

On the third evening after their arrival, Stephen, who had not slept for two nights, was preparing to sit up yet again with Thomas, when Lady Catherine came to him. "I'll watch by him tonight," she said shortly. "Go and get some sleep."

Stephen protested, but she said drily, "While you can, you'd best be saving your strength for when you'll be needing it. He'll be a lot worse before it's over, and no doubt you'll not wish to be sleeping then."

Stephen, seeing the sense of this, lay down on the bed beside Thomas and slept quite soundly, knowing that Thomas could wake him in an instant, should he want to. After that,

Stephen and Lady Catherine took it in turn to sit up with Thomas at nights, so long as he was no worse.

About a week later, Thomas became feverish again, as the blisters which covered his body began to harden into pustules. That morning, returning into the house from the yard, after no more than five minutes' absence from Thomas, Stephen heard Thomas's voice raised in a frantic outcry. He ran along the hall and flung himself up the ladderway into the bedchamber to see Thomas sitting up in the bed pointing at old Elspeth – who was standing squarely in the middle of the room, looking at him – and screaming, "Take the witch away! Take her away from me! Take her away before she kills me!" and fighting off Lady Catherine who was trying to calm him.

Stephen was across the room in a moment and on to the bed, with his arms about Thomas. "It's all right, Thomas. No one is going to harm you. There's no witch – for the love of heaven, madam, get the woman out of here! – I'm with you, Thomas. You're quite safe. No one can harm you."

As Elspeth waddled on her short legs towards the ladder-way, she gave a laugh as deep as a man's. "These English dogs, give them a dose of their own poison and they howl for mercy." Stephen heard her chuckling evilly to herself all the way down to the hall below; and he could not refrain from casting an apprehensive glance over his shoulder in the direction of the ladderway and crossing himself.

By that evening, Thomas no longer knew where he was. He tossed on the bed, talking nonsense; referring to people unknown to Stephen; speaking names of which Stephen had never heard; pathetically trying to excuse himself for long-past misdemeanours; repeating over and over again that the Scottish witch had put her curse on him; and calling for his mother and for Stephen. But since he could not recognize him, Stephen's presence was no comfort to him. By the morning his reddened, bloated face might have belonged to a stranger; and had it not been for his copper hair and the intense blue of his wildly staring eyes, Stephen would almost have thought him someone else. By morning, too, he was growing quieter, and the swelling in his throat made breathing difficult. An hour or two later he was in a coma.

Lady Catherine, without saying anything to Stephen, sent one of the men to fetch a priest, with Elspeth, like a squat goblin, riding pillion behind him to show him the way. The first Stephen knew of it was when, sitting on the bed helplessly watching the unconscious Thomas, he heard footsteps behind him and turned to see Lady Catherine and the young priest carrying the chrismatory of holy oil. Then, at last, he realized what she had known, that there was probably no hope for Thomas.

The priest stood as far from the bed as he might and only approached Thomas when he had to; and he hurried through his prayers and his ministrations and left again without a word to Stephen. But who can blame him? thought Stephen. He, too, is a Scot, even if he is a priest. Why should he wait with his prayers for the end? Why should he risk the smallpox for an English youth? And, lacking a priest, Stephen tried to say the prayers for Thomas himself.

At about mid-morning of the next day, Thomas died.

TWENTY

Thomas was buried in a Scottish grave on a fine sunny morning with white clouds flying and a thrush singing. Stephen, standing by dry-eyed and uncomprehending, more conscious of these things – the thrush, the bare boughs of a wind-bitten hawthorn tree against the blue sky, the faded green of Lady Catherine's cloak, the red earth of the open grave – than he was of Thomas's death, surprised old Elspeth wiping away a tear with her apron. She glared at him defiantly and said defensively, "He was a bonny, red-haired lad, and young, even if he was a cursed Englishman." He hardly heard her at the time; but later her words returned to his mind, and he knew from them that she was, after all, no witch, and that it was indeed the smallpox, and not her curse, that had killed Thomas.

The past two weeks had been for Stephen too much like a nightmare for him to be moved immediately by his sorrow for the loss of Thomas. Exhausted almost beyond the point of feeling, once Thomas was buried, only half knowing what he did, he made ready to leave Lady Catherine's house without delay, so that she might be rid of the enemies in her home.

But she said without emotion, "You'll no doubt be taking the smallpox yourself, so you might as well bide here where there's someone to look after you when you're not able to be looking after yourself."

Stephen, who had thought it very likely that he would catch the smallpox – an added reason for leaving her house speedily had been in order to get away before he fell ill – was surprised. "I have caused you enough trouble already, madam. I shall always be grateful for what you did for Thomas and me, but there's no need for me to be yet further in your debt."

"Since you are so far in it already, a little further will make no difference. Besides, why should someone else have the task of caring for you when I am prepared to do so?"

So Stephen stayed – to wait for the smallpox.

The men were a little put out by his decision, but they shrugged their shoulders resignedly after grumbling to each other. For the greater part of two days, Stephen, emotionally and bodily worn out, slept; and he woke strong and mentally alert enough to realize the truth of what had happened and to begin to feel his grief. There were two now, he thought, for whose souls he would always pray.

When he came upon his bored men whiling away the time unprofitably in dicing, he set them to repair Lady Catherine's gate for her and to rebuild her burnt-out stables. They found this better than being idle, and worked quite willingly; and after a day of brooding, Stephen joined them and worked alongside them, sawing logs and beams to mend the gate and setting up the drystone wall of the empty pigsty. The men thought it more than odd of him, but they were not sorry for his help; and for his part, Stephen found that the hard work took his mind off his memories of Thomas and made him sleep at nights; and, besides, he felt that it was somehow more fitting that he should occupy his time usefully and in a way that might in some measure repay his hostess, while he waited for the smallpox and – he was by now presuming – death. He found that he could think quite calmly – and even gratefully about the fact that in no more than two or three weeks' time he, too, would lie in Scottish earth, and that by then everything in this world would be at an end for him.

He had become so used to the idea that he would soon be dead, that it came as a shock to him when, after some eighteen days, Lady Catherine said to him, "If you've not taken the smallpox by this time, you'll not be taking it at all. God has been good to you. I hope you deserve it." For the very first time there was a slight warmth in her voice and the faintest hint of a smile on her lips.

Before he left, he tried to thank her, but she cut him short, saying, "You need feel no gratitude. All that I did, I did unwillingly. But you seem to me a good and honourable young man, and from this time on I shall think with a little less hatred of all Englishmen, for your sake."

Since he might give Lady Catherine nothing, he gave all the money he had to spare to Elspeth. "Perhaps there is something you could buy for your mistress that she needs for the house," he suggested.

"She needs so many things, I'd be hard put to it to know where to start. This'd not begin to buy a thousandth part of it." But, looking at the money, she added with satisfaction, "I'll be buying her a couple of piglets for fattening – they eat anything. And a few hens. It'll be fine to have eggs again. And with what's left I'll be able to buy some corn, even at the shocking price it is these days since you devils came into our poor country."

TWENTY-ONE

On his way south, Stephen went into Lincolnshire to tell Thomas's parents of his death. Had he been less grieved himself, he would have found the task all but impossible; but he was so personally affected by the loss, that he did not find it as hard as it might have been.

Seeing Stephen's sorrow, they both had the extreme courtesy to try and hide their own. Baron Simon said gruffly, "If he had to die, it's a pity that he could not have died fighting against the Scots; but it is as God wills. He was a wild, bad son, and it is better that he should be dead than that he should have lived to disgrace us."

"No, you are wrong," said Stephen. "I wish you could have seen how much he had changed in these two years. I had such great hopes for him, and I know you would have shared them, had you seen him. There was so much good in him." He stopped, unable to go on.

The baron seemed to grow more cheerful at the knowledge that he had lost a promising son rather than a bad one; and Lady Alis, the tears streaming unheeded down her pretty face, took Stephen's hands in hers, saying, "You, too, loved him. I am so glad of it," and smiled at him through her tears.

TWENTY-TWO

In the first days that followed his return to Manningfield, Stephen had no room in his heart for anything but his grief for Thomas. He went about his usual daily round, he spoke to others, he gave orders and received them, he even smiled; but during none of these days was he wholly in the presence of those people in whose company he passed the time. He scarcely noticed what he did and his attention was only half upon those with whom he spoke; a part of him was gone for ever and lay in a Scottish grave with Thomas.

Later, when the cutting edge of sorrow had been worn down by daily use, and the time came that he was once more fully aware of other people around him, he found that he wanted to shun them, to pretend he had not heard them when they spoke to him, to turn aside when he saw them approaching; and he had to struggle with himself to prevent this being apparent to everyone. His daily life as a knight – that life for which he had once so much longed – seemed to him empty and meaningless and he found himself thinking more and more often of those afternoons with Brother Ernulf at Richley.

And then one day, finding a sheet of parchment, an inkhorn and a quill lying on a desk in a room off the gallery, where they had been left by his uncle's secretary, Stephen sat down at the desk and took up the pen. With it poised above the parchment, for a moment he considered his contemplated act of self-indulgence and hesitated, then he dipped the pen into the ink, bent closer over the desk and began to draw. He drew a ship with a little tower like a castle at either end of it – the ship in which he had sailed on pilgrimage – and behind the ship, the city to which it was bound. Half an hour later he had still not been disturbed, and his ship and his city were finished. He suddenly came to himself, looked around guiltily to see if he had been observed, as though the old strips of moth-eaten hangings – banished many years before from the solar – which covered the chamber walls, might conceal a watcher. Hastily he laid down the pen and began to roll up the parchment with the ink still wet on it, so that he might remove all traces of his eccentricity before the clerk returned to see it. But with it half-way rolled up, he opened it out again and took a long, slow look at his work; and then smiled a little to himself. The drawing was stiff and unpractised perhaps, but in his years at war he had not forgotten how to draw. He heard a sound as of someone approaching and hastily concealed the parchment.

Five minutes later, the secretary, returning to his little room, found his parchment gone, and his pen, which he had not used for two hours, still damp with ink. He suspected one of the other clerks of having used his writing-tools and was annoyed; and he never knew the truth.

But Stephen had been nearer peace of mind in that half hour than at any time since Thomas's death; and he realized that the moment had come when he must take stock of his life. He did so, carefully and at length, over many thoughtful hours, and finally reached certain conclusions.

So long as he had had an ambition to be fulfilled, or so long as he had had someone for whom he cared to share that life with him, he had found that his life satisfied him. But, his ambition once achieved, and no one left on whom to spend his affection, satisfaction eluded him. He had once believed it to be the loss of Sir Pagan's companionship that had made him indifferent to the practice of arms; he now knew that this was not so. Just as, later, it had been Thomas's enthusiasm and his own affection for Thomas which had made enjoyable for him the hours he had spent in instructing Thomas in fighting-skill, so it had been Sir Pagan's companionship that had made for him a pleasure and a delight out of something which – he had since learnt – was alien to his nature and for which he cared little.

He was committed by the profession of knighthood to killing. There was enough of death and destruction in the world already; why should he add to it? Had not Sir Pagan died, and Thomas? He wanted to create, not to destroy – the truth could no longer be denied – to create something of beauty that would last to give joy to others like himself when he was dead and gone. His present life was empty and profitless and he knew that it must not continue. Yet, having chosen this way of life, he did not know what else to do.

There was no one at Manningfield to whom he cared to speak of his doubts and his self-searching. His uncle was kindly and in all likelihood ready to be indulgent, but he was a practical man of affairs and would not understand. He tried praying for guidance, but God did not seem to hear him; and there was no one else to whom Stephen could bring himself to uncover his heart.

And then, very early one morning, between sleeping and waking, he suddenly remembered Sir Pagan's words to him in the dungeon at Gloucester Castle – remembered them so vividly that it seemed as though he were hearing them again. "Always be yourself. Do not be afraid to do what you want to do, so long as it hurts no one else. We are each of us as God made us, and if God has seen fit to make you in an uncommon mould, be brave enough to be different."

Stephen sat up in bed, his hands clasped about him against the chill air, and stared before him at the faint line of grey light that showed between the window shutters. He stared before him with his mind fifty miles away in Gloucester, in another, narrower, room, and he knew what it was that he wanted to do – that he had to do.

Half an hour later, when the light beyond the shutters had increased sufficiently for shapes in the room to have taken on an added darkness of their own, Stephen became aware of his surroundings and of the fact that his naked body, where it was unprotected by the bed-rugs and the coverlet, was as cold as marble to the waist. Shivering now, he got out of bed, taking care not to wake the other sleepers who shared the bed with him, groped for his clothes and put them on. With his cloak wrapped closely about him, he left the room silently and made his way up a winding stairway to the battlements. There it was dim and grey, but the east was growing steadily lighter. He bade the sleepy guards good day, and at his coming they roused themselves to seem alert and active; but he passed them by and went to the parapet and leant on the cold stone looking out over a crenel towards the rising sun.

"Do not be afraid to do what you want to do." There was no point in fighting any longer against it; no profit in denying his nature; no virtue in stifling his talent.

"Be brave enough to be different." He, the son of a long line of noble knights, wanted to be an artist; he had it in him, he believed, to be an artist – "Be brave enough to be different" – and an artist he would be.

But there was only one place he knew of where it was possible for him, Stephen de Beauville, to be different, to do what he wanted to do. Very well, he thought, that is where I must go. If I have to confine myself in order to be free, I shall return to Richley. And then, close on his decision, came the surprising thought that, after all, his father had been right all those years before, while he himself had all along been mistaken; and he smiled to himself, wryly.

His decision taken, he felt a great relief, as though some heavy, unseen burden had been lifted from him; and he knew an upspringing of hope for the future, and an eager looking forward to what was to come.

The first rays of the rising sun, appearing now with sudden swiftness, shone full upon Stephen's transfigured face, all its lines of doubt and indecision wiped away in the golden light. He was unaware of the slow tears which dropped gently down his cheeks to grow cold in the freshness of the dawn, for they were tears not of sorrow, but of release. After a while he bent his head on to the hard stone of the parapet and gave thanks to heaven that his problem had been resolved for him. But at the end of his prayer of thanksgiving there was another sentiment of gratitude that was not a prayer. God might have answered his appeals by bringing to his recollection the words which had shown him what to do: yet it was Sir Pagan who had spoken those words in the first place. I owe you so much and so much, Stephen thought. So much in the past, and now this, today. May I always be worthy of you.

TWENTY-THREE

When Stephen told his uncle of his decision, Earl Bartholomew did not try to dissuade him from his purpose. He only said, "I have had it in my mind for some months now – perhaps I should have spoken sooner – to give you my manor at Longbourne. It is not a large estate, but I have fancied it was one of which you were fond, and I would have been glad to see you settled there with a wife and sons."

Stephen was touched with this mark of his uncle's affection; but he said, "No, sir, it would be no use. I know what I want to do, and it is not to marry and live at Longbourne."

After a thoughtful pause, the Earl asked, "Had I spoken four months ago, Stephen, when you returned from Scotland, would you then have said the same? Four months ago, would I already have been too late?"

"No, sir, I think that you'd not have been too late then, therefore I'm glad that you said nothing. For I might have accepted your offer, only to find afterwards, that it was not the life for me. So, you see, I have yet one more thing for which to be grateful to you – that you did not speak sooner."

Another moment, and the Earl said earnestly, "I am not trying to make you alter your mind, Stephen – indeed," his uncle smiled a little sadly, "I think that I could not – but you are still young. You are only twenty-six. Are you sure that you will not postpone your final decision for a year or two?"

Stephen shook his head. "No, sir. My mind is made up. I'd not be likely to change it in a year or two." He added sincerely, "I hope that my decision does not displease you. You have done so much for me and I am deeply grateful. I'd not want you to be disappointed in me."

Earl Bartholomew, very moved, put his hands on Stephen's shoulders and said, "Stephen, you are my very dear nephew, and little Orabel's child, and I shall be very sorry to lose you. But it is your own life that you have to live, and it is your right to decide how you shall live it. It is with my blessing that you will go to Richley Abbey. May God keep you, and may He grant that there in Richley you will find whatever it is that you seek."

And so it was that, some four weeks later, in May, Stephen left Manningfield Castle and rode into Bedfordshire.

TWENTY-FOUR

Stephen had not been sure of what his reception at Richley by Abbot Waldo would be, seeing that, ten years before, he had run away from there. But the abbot was frankly and unfeignedly pleased to see him back and to know that, after all, the convent was to have a de Beauville brother; and he made very light of Stephen's past defection.

"You were too young in those days, my son," he said, "and you could not have known your own mind. Besides, it had been another's choice for you, and not your own. But now you have come to us to serve God of your own free will, and that is of infinitely greater value."

Stephen, who had expected it to be far more difficult, felt almost guilty at this smoothing of his path, and tried to make his way back rather harder by countering the abbot's indulgence with self-reproach; but for all his admitted shortcomings Abbot Waldo had a bland excuse, and to all his doubts a good answer; so that at last Stephen was left with only the one thing which it was hardest to confess. Slowly he said, "I do not think that I have come back to serve God, my lord, but only for peace of mind, to pray for my dead, and to draw."

Abbot Waldo may have been a kindly snob, but he was no fool. He answered a little drily, "My son, since peace of mind is a gift from God, He is as likely to choose to deny it to one in a monastery as anywhere else. You need feel no uncertainty on that score." He paused a moment for Stephen to reflect on this, and then went on, "As for praying for the dead: that is one of the things for which we monks are here in this world. We have time for many prayers, and it is right and good that we should pray for the dead – for those whom we have loved as well as for those whom we have not. And as for your drawing: your talent is also a gift from God, and it is proper that it should be rendered back in some measure to Him. What more fitting than that it should be used to the glory of its Giver – and where more easily could that be done than here? And I think that there would be many – and far more learned and wiser than you – who would agree with me that to use fittingly, and to the glory of God, those gifts which He has given you, is to serve Him fully and well." When Stephen did not answer this, he waited a little, then asked, "And now, my son, have you any more stones to strew in your path? Because if you have, scatter them now, that I may pick them up while I am in practice."

Stephen watched Abbot Waldo's round face crease into smiles that almost hid his eyes, and thought how little – save to grow plumper – the benign, placid man had changed in ten years. He was very willing to let himself believe the abbot; and, after all, he had every reason for so doing, for was not a churchman of some forty years' standing better qualified than he to judge in such matters? He found himself smiling. "No more stones, thank you, my lord."

"I am glad of it." The abbot's smiles became almost complacent. "I am grateful with all my heart that God has seen fit to bring you back to us."

His doubts demolished and none left to trouble him, Stephen asked after the novice master and those others of the obedientiaries whom he remembered best. They were, it seemed, all well and still at Richley, save the chamberlain, who had died three years before.

"And Brother Ernulf, how is he?"

"Brother Ernulf? He has grown older, as indeed we all have – even you, too, my son." Abbot Waldo smiled happily. "Brother Ernulf is a little mellowed by the years, I think; a little less inclined to grumble at us all. But you will soon be seeing him for yourself. He will be glad of your return, I know."

TWENTY-FIVE

When Stephen, once again in a novice's habit, knocked on the door of the last room of the scriptorium, Brother Ernulf's voice from within bade him enter with a decided lack of warmth.

He opened the door. The little room had not changed at all. It was the same as he remembered it, only that now it appeared to him smaller and therefore even more crowded and untidy, with the two cluttered tables and the rows of jars on the shelf, and, under one of the tables, the stool Stephen had left there ten years before – no one, it seemed, had ever taken it away.

Brother Ernulf was bent low over his desk under the window. As Stephen entered he straightened up slowly without turning his head. "Who is it?"

Stephen closed the door and stepped farther into the room. "The new novice."

Brother Ernulf turned himself about on his stool and looked towards Stephen. His head was still craggy and formidable, though the lines had bitten deeper and the ring of hair was no longer grizzled, but white. He narrowed his eyes to peer at the intruder. "The new novice? Which new novice? Can you not answer a simple question, man? I want to know your name, not what you think you are."

Stephen came to stand beside him. "That's not the way it was last time," he said softly. "I remember that then you blamed me for answering with my name."

"And what if I did? I can please myself, surely? And you've still not answered my question. Who are you?" Before Stephen could reply, Brother Ernulf had suddenly bent forward and grasped at his arm, staring into his face with his deep-sunk eyes. "You're not that boy who ran away, are you? Stephen Whatever-his-name-was?"

"Stephen de Beauville. Yes, I am."

An indefinable expression came over the old monk's face; but before Stephen could translate it, Brother Ernulf had turned his head away and was looking down at the piece of vellum that lay on his desk – it had lettering on it, but, as yet, no drawing. He said with apparent indifference, "So they caught you at last and brought you back, eh?"

"No, I came back of my own accord, because I wanted to."

Brother Ernulf snorted. "So you have learnt a little sense at last, have you? It took you long enough." He picked up a paintbrush and his square, stubby fingers moved restlessly up and down the handle. "Can you still draw?" he demanded

"I think so. I am out of practice, though."

"Of course you are out of practice. What do you expect? It is ten years, is it not? You should be flogged for wasting your talent. I hope you're ashamed of yourself."

Stephen found himself smiling – and not entirely ruefully. If Brother Ernulf had indeed mellowed as the abbot had suggested, there was so far little sign of it. But in the old man's discouraging reception and carping manner, he found a kind of welcome. It was, in a way, like coming home – and after not too long an absence. Those ten years of which he spoke so tartly, Brother Ernulf was certainly disregarding, and he was behaving as though Stephen were still the shy, uncertain boy of ten years before.

Stephen said with real amusement, "I have been a knight for five years and I have fought in battle. I have seen Jerusalem and Damascus. I have, like the centurion, told other men to go and to come, to do this, that and the other. And yet you can still make me feel like a child."

"We are all children," retorted Brother Ernulf. "We are all children playing with our own toys. The only difference is that some of our toys are worthwhile and others are not. You have been" – he gave an exclamation of scorn – "playing at soldiers, and I have been playing at making a book. I'll leave you to judge which is the better way to spend the time God's given one." Without a pause he went on, "If you think you can still draw, you'd better prove it quickly. As you've probably noticed, my sight is no better and I need help if my Gospels are to be finished. Find yourself a pen and parchment and show me what you can do."

278

While Stephen was searching on the cluttered tables and selecting a pen, Brother Ernulf asked abruptly, "You've been to the Holy Land, you said?"

"Yes. I was very fortunate. My uncle went on a pilgrimage and I went with him – May I borrow your inkwell, please? I cannot find another – On the Mount of Olives, I thought of you and wished you'd been with me to see it all." Stephen carried the inkwell to one of the tables where he cleared a space.

"Did you now?" Brother Ernulf's voice was oddly different for a moment. Then he snapped in his customary tone, "A lot of good that would have been to me! I'd not have been able to see a thing. Now stop chattering so much and get on with what you've been told to do." He added, almost as though he were making a threat, "I shall want to hear all about the Holy Land some other time."

While Stephen sat drawing at the table, Brother Ernulf rose from his stool and then knelt for a while in prayer beside his desk. He was praying, Stephen supposed, either in gratitude for the possible help that had been sent, or that the help might prove to be adequate; and Stephen felt oddly humble – which was strange, he thought, since being needed should make one feel proud.

"Are you not finished yet?" Brother Ernulf was back on his stool.

"Almost."

"Well, hurry up. How much longer do you expect me to be without my inkwell?"

When Stephen brought him his drawing, Brother Ernulf snatched at the parchment and held it close to his eyes, peering at it in the bright light from the window above him, studying it carefully, line by line: on the left of the drawing a young man in rags, sitting beneath a tree, three pigs rooting at his feet; and on the right, the same tattered figure and a plump man with a beard and a fur-trimmed robe extending his arms in greeting and, a little behind them, two servants killing a young ox.

Brother Ernulf grunted. "The prodigal son. You're an impudent young jackanapes. You need expect no fat calves here. But they might open a new barrel of salt herring for you, if you behave yourself this time." He tossed the drawing aside. "It will do. You'll need weeks of hard practice yet, but at least my Gospels will be finished." He was silent for a moment or two, then he said, impersonally and without emotion, but in a voice far less harsh than usual, "For years my sight has been worsening and I have been working ever more slowly. Now, I can hardly see; and very soon I shall be blind. I have prayed and prayed that God might think fit to spare my sight until my work was finished; but He did not think fit and – may He forgive me for it – I'd almost given up hope. I have completed St. Luke, but there is the whole of St. John yet. God has not spared my sight for St. John, but He has sent me a new pair of eyes. You shall do the drawings for St. John and finish the Gospels for me. I shall tell you what I want you to draw and give you all the advice I can, but you will carry out the work."

For a few moments Stephen was too astounded to say anything. At last he found his voice. "But I could not! I have not skill enough. You must find someone else, or leave them unfinished. I could not do it for you."

"Of course you can do it. And if I say so, you can and you shall. And as for not having skill enough: you must be blinder than I if you cannot see your own talent."

Stephen said slowly, "I can see that I have a certain ability, but it cannot compare with your talent." As if fully realizing for the first time just what the old monk's demand entailed, he said urgently, "You must not put this thing on me. It is too much to ask of me."

"Since you seem to find the task so distasteful," remarked Brother Ernulf drily, "perhaps you could regard it as a penance for your sin of running away." Before Stephen could answer this, he went on impatiently, "You are a fool, of course, not to see it for yourself. Your talent will, one day, not only equal mine, but it may even be, in time, far greater." He stopped Stephen with an abrupt gesture when he would have spoken. "You must allow me to be the better judge. What do you know of the matter?"

Haltingly, Stephen said, "You are trying to give me encouragement; to make me bold enough to undertake the task. You are kind in what you say, but it's not true."

"Kind!" exclaimed Brother Ernulf indignantly. "No one has ever called Ernulf of Peterborough kind before. I have certainly no wish to be kind to you. I'd like – God forgive me – to knock your head against that wall to put some sense in it. And you need not call me a liar, either, because it's the truth I've told you. I am no liar." He was silent for a long moment, and when he spoke again his voice was low and he sounded suddenly weary. "After you had gone, I regretted that I had not told you what I believed, or part of what I believed, about yourself. I might at least have praised you a little, perhaps, or given you some encouragement. Being such a fool, of course you could not see it for yourself, as I well knew. But I've always thought that the young should be kept strictly in their place. I'd no wish to see you growing conceited and complacent and ready to give up striving for perfection, so I kept silent. When you were gone, I blamed myself. But it was too late then."

Stephen said nothing. It was still quite unbelievable that he might have it in him to surpass one of whom he thought as a matchless artist; though he did not for a moment, now, doubt the old monk's words. Brother Ernulf believed what he was saying, and Brother Ernulf, of all men, should be the best judge of the matter.

Suddenly Brother Ernulf asked in a fierce, aggressive manner, "Had you known it then, would you still have run away?" When Stephen hesitated, he shouted, "And I want the truth. None of your kindly tact to spare an old man's feelings." He smashed his fist down on the top of the desk so that the pens shivered and several paintbrushes rattled in their jar, "In God's name give me the truth! Am I to blame for what you did! I want the truth."

And you shall have it, thought Stephen. You shall have it. I'd not insult you with a lie.

He thought the question over carefully before he replied; then he said gently, "It is difficult, ten years later, to be certain what one would have done when one was a boy, but I think that, had I known what you've told me today, I would have stayed with you."

Brother Ernulf sat very silent, one elbow on his desk and his hand over his eyes. Then he asked quietly, "Do you regret having gone? Again, no lies, if you please." He appeared, at that moment, very old and sightless and defeated.

Stephen considered all that had happened to him in the ten years which had passed since he had last seen Richley. That which he had run away to achieve, he had achieved – and it had proved of little worth to him. He had found sorrow, which, had he never gone, he could have avoided. But he had also found – even if only fleetingly – happiness; and two friends to love. He thought of his fulfilled ambition and dismissed it as valueless and to be regretted, when weighed against the truer satisfaction of art. Then he thought of what he had gained and learnt from the world and from others; from Sir Pagan and Thomas, each of whom had given him much – especially Sir Pagan, who, from a diffident, timid boy had made a man who was capable of knowing himself and of taking a decision such as he had taken a few weeks since – and he said firmly and with conviction, "No, I do not regret it."

After a moment Brother Ernulf took his head from his hand. He was no longer a bent, blind old man, but the pride – and the gadfly – of Richley Abbey, the finest artist in southern England. With heavy sarcasm he said, "You've wasted ten years of your life, but if you do not regret it, then why should I?" He sat up straight and glared at Stephen. "You may have wasted ten years of your own life, but that's no reason why you should waste ten minutes of mine. Bring that stool over here and I'll tell you what I have in mind for the first chapter of St. John. And give me the two boards tied with a red cord which you'll find on that table. My rough sketches for St. John are in them."

As Stephen brought the stool to the desk and handed him his sketches, Brother Ernulf remarked irritably, "No doubt the bell will ring for vespers and interrupt us – it always does when one's busy – but we shall at least have made a start."

Five minutes later Stephen had forgotten everything save the question they were discussing; and the world had narrowed for him, convincingly, adequately and satisfyingly, to the confines of a single page of vellum – a blank space to be filled in beautifully above the Evangelist's opening words: *In principio erat Verbum* . . .

HISTORICAL NOTE

All the castles and demesnes belonging to the fictitious characters in this book are imaginary; so is the Golden Lion Inn at Gloucester. There were few inns in England in the early fourteenth century, but Gloucester was an important town and may well have had an inn in 1327. There were certainly two inns in Gloucester at a somewhat later date, but neither was called the Golden Lion.

Sir Pagan's attempt to rescue Edward the Second is, of course, fictitious; but that there were attempts to free him – one of them, at least, being temporarily successful – is a matter of history. Anyone who is interested can find details in *The Captivity and Death of Edward of Carnarvon* by T. F. Tout.

ABOUT THE AUTHOR

Barbara Leonie Picard was born in Surrey, England, and left there at the age of three for Sussex, where she has lived ever since, except during her schooling at St. Katharine's School in Berkshire. She decided, while she was at school, that one day she would write – but it was not until 1943 that she made any serious attempt to do so. Then she started to write imaginative stories of the type she had enjoyed as a child, and in 1947, she had a story broadcast on *Children's Hour*. This was followed by many others, some of which were afterwards published in anthologies and annuals. Her first book was published in 1949 and more than twenty-five have come since.

One Is One originated, Miss Picard says, when, knowing her interest in mediaeval history, "A friend once asked me what I thought happened to the misfits in a mediaeval society. I replied that they entered a monastery: there would have been nowhere else for them." *One Is One* was written to amplify her answer. Besides mediaeval and ancient history, Miss Picard numbers among her wide interests embroidery, collecting Japanese prints and complete recordings of grand opera, archaeology, languages, mythology, comparative religion and folk-culture.

INTRODUCING
The Nautilus Series

1. *One Is One* by Barbara Leonie Picard   1-58988-027-7

2. *Pageants of Despair* by Dennis Hamley   1-58988-028-5

3. *The Chess Set in the Mirror* by Massimo Bontempelli
   1-58988-031-5 (forthcoming)

One Is One and *Pageants of Despair* launch **The Nautilus Series** from Paul Dry Books. We think of these titles for young adults like seashells washed up on the beach. As a beautiful shell picked from the sea's edge can fascinate the beachcomber, so the rightly chosen book delights a reader. Such books please the eye, the ear, and the imagination – they seem to arrive from a great distance, bearing wondrous sights and sounds.

We hope that with *One Is One* and *Pageants of Despair* many readers will begin their collections of young adult titles from Paul Dry Books.

BOOKS TO
AWAKEN,
DELIGHT,
&EDUCATE